"Mix an intrepid dog groomer with a sarcastic cat, add a generous dose of Southern California, sprinkle with murder, and you get a cozy mystery that's bound to please."

—Laurie Cass, author of the Bookmobile Cat Mysteries

"A fun, charming, and totally unique mystery featuring lots of adorable pets (and one particularly snarky cat). Mimi Lee is a winning heroine with a hilarious family, especially her meddling, marriage-obsessed mother."   —Kerry Winfrey, author of *Waiting for Tom Hanks*

"I laughed out loud more than once reading *Mimi Lee Gets a Clue*, the first book in the new Sassy Cat mystery series. Mimi Lee is feisty, determined, and lots of fun—and I love Ma, her matchmaking mother. The story features an intriguing mystery, and Marshmallow, a talking cat that only Mimi, as his owner, can hear. . . . Sharp writing, a main character I'd happily be friends with, and a talking cat. What more could a reader want?"

—Sofie Kelly, *New York Times* bestselling author of the
Magical Cats Mysteries

"Chow's charming debut is an adorable mystery perfect for pet lovers. Mimi's authentic family grounds the story amidst the glitzy and glamorous backdrop of L.A. I devoured it in one sitting."

—Roselle Lim, author of *Natalie Tan's Book of Luck & Fortune*

Mimi Lee

READS BETWEEN
THE LINES

Jennifer J. Chow

Berkley Prime Crime
New York

BERKLEY PRIME CRIME
Published by Berkley
An imprint of Penguin Random House LLC
penguinrandomhouse.com

Library of Congress Cataloging-in-Publication Data

Names: Chow, Jennifer J., author.
Title: Mimi Lee reads between the lines / Jennifer J. Chow.
Description: First edition. | New York: Berkley Prime Crime, 2020. |
Series: A sassy cat mystery
Identifiers: LCCN 2020010981 (print) | LCCN 2020010982 (ebook) |
ISBN 9781984805010 (trade paperback) | ISBN 9781984805027 (ebook)
Subjects: GSAFD: Mystery fiction.
Classification: LCC PS3603.H696 M58 2020 (print) |
LCC PS3603.H696 (ebook) | DDC 813/.6—dc23
LC record available at https://lccn.loc.gov/2020010981
LC ebook record available at https://lccn.loc.gov/2020010982

First Edition: November 2020

Printed in the United States of America
1 3 5 7 9 10 8 6 4 2

Cover art by Carrie May
Cover design by Judith Lagerman
Book design by Alison Cnockaert

To Aunt Cathy, for being a blessing in our lives
(and for introducing us to shiok *dishes).*

CHAPTER

one

TOOK AN UBER to see Alice, because let's face it, the countdown to Valentine's Day sucked for singles. I knew so from experience. Cupid had kept on missing the mark all throughout my last twenty-five birthdays . . . until I'd bumped into Josh at my apartment complex's laundry room last fall. For tomorrow's February fourteenth outing, he'd planned a special surprise for us. And I couldn't wait to cuddle up with my favorite Los Angeles lawyer.

But today would be about my younger, single sister, Alice. I'd had to close up my pet grooming store early, and the Uber driver dropped me off around four at Roosevelt Elementary with its storybook red brick construction. Despite the conservative look, it still had the usual Californian exterior hallways with interconnected classrooms, the better to appreciate the good weather in the area. I saluted both the state flag and the Star-Spangled Banner, which waved at me from their respective steel poles as I marched up the stone steps into the school office.

I didn't see anyone behind the desk piled high with colorful flyers for after-school activities. The receptionist must have already left for the day. Maybe she'd had pre-Valentine's plans.

Alice and I had a tradition of doing a sister date to protest the annual lovers' holiday. However, since I actually had plans this year, I'd moved our usual outing a day ahead. She'd probably been reminded of the occasion after seeing all those paper hearts and sweet candies being exchanged between her students. And in kindergarten, everyone was required to participate, which meant reminders of V-Day multiplied by twenty-five. Maybe Alice had gotten a few misshapen candy hearts and superhero cards, but I bet she wanted treats from someone else besides five- and six-year-olds.

I heard someone clear their throat from the principal's office. The door was open a few inches, and I could see a flash of blue from within. I wondered what the new head of Roosevelt Elementary was like.

Alice seemed to have a much better working relationship with him than his predecessor. The previous principal had suffered from an icy attitude that had matched her cold steel furniture. As prickly as her pet hedgehog, she'd basically bullied Alice and threatened her with a layoff last year. She'd gone so far as to give my sister a pink slip. The principal had even bypassed the newest member of the staff to do so—until I'd stepped in and defended Alice.

Where was my sister? She'd had a good time estimate of when I'd arrive at her workplace. After all, I'd texted her when I left the apartment, where my cat, Marshmallow, had grumbled at me. He'd given me a piece of his mind: "Have fun deserting me tonight."

2

I knew exactly what he'd been thinking because we had some sort of telepathic owner-pet connection. The whole mental communication thing had scared me at first. I thought I'd been experiencing some sort of psychotic break; I'd studied such things in college as a psych major. Despite not understanding the science behind it, I'd come to embrace our connection, snark and all.

My phone dinged.

Alice: Are you here already?

Me: Yep. Waiting in the office.

Alice: Sorry. Writing up a petition to fund the kinder playground. See you in five.

I heard loud steps coming my way and looked up to find a Black man in his sixties wearing a navy blue dress shirt, striped tie, and tailored slacks. He appeared about twice my size, though that wasn't too difficult, given my petite stature.

Gesturing at my phone, he said, "I heard it ring and figured I should introduce myself." He peered at me through thick-framed bifocals. "Are you related to Alice?"

I nodded. "I'm her older sister. Mimi."

He grinned at me. "You two are practically twins."

"We get that a lot." My sister and I did look alike. We both had the same five-foot frame and shared features such as oval faces, elfin ears, and small button noses. However, I tried and failed to tame my shoulder-length hair while Alice managed a sleek bob.

"I'm Principal Lewis," the man said.

I extended my hand to him at the same time as he stepped forward and gave me a half hug.

A surprising gesture from someone I'd just met, but he seemed genuinely happy to see me. "You're definitely friendlier than Principal Hallis was." I'd nicknamed the old administrator "Principal Hellish" in private.

"Well, I do like to put the '*pal*' in 'principal.'" He gave a small chuckle.

"I see that." No wonder he and Alice got along. They both exuded warm vibes.

"I want my staff to feel connected to me." He twisted the gold band on his left ring finger. "As if they were part of my extended family."

What an intense statement. At least he wasn't a horrific boss. I'd rather have a manager landing on the extreme side of nice.

However, I definitely liked being my own boss and running my pet grooming salon, where I made up my own easy work schedule of ten a.m. to six p.m. I had no one else to answer to—except maybe Pixie St. James, who had gifted me the investment money. It'd been a very willing donation on her part, after I'd rescued her poor shih tzu from the churning waves near Catalina Island.

The side door to the school office opened, and Alice rushed in. "Sorry to keep you waiting," she said.

A heavy book bag, no doubt stuffed with student projects, weighed down her left shoulder. Every teacher I knew had homework, just like their kids.

She did a double-take on seeing my company. "Principal Lewis," she said. "Did you meet my sister, Mimi?"

"Yes, and she's wonderful, just like you." He turned to Alice and gave her a brief hug. Alice didn't seem fazed by the quick embrace. Maybe because Dad also loved giving us giant bear hugs, even now, after we'd grown up.

Alice smiled at him. Then she checked her wristwatch. "We'd better get going," she said. "Shouldn't you leave, too, Principal Lewis? Don't you need to get things ready for your Valentine's date with your wife tomorrow?"

He hazarded a glance at the wall clock. "You're right. I need to go over my plan for the all-day extravaganza." Touching his close-cropped salt-and-pepper hair, he said, "We can do that now that our kids are all adults with cute cuddly babies of their own. I'm starting the day with a scavenger hunt on the beach."

Alice gave him a thumbs-up. We said goodbye to the principal and headed to the staff parking lot.

Once there, Alice said, "That's odd. Helen's car is still around."

"Who's Helen?" I didn't remember my sister mentioning her before.

"She's the newest member of the staff . . . and that's her car." Alice pointed to a white Prius C (unfortunately marked with bird droppings) a few paces away. A car woman after my own heart, I thought. Although I'd opted for a larger size of the popular hybrid.

"Wait. Is that the same teacher Principal Hallis kept on, while threatening you with the pink slip last year?"

Alice closed her eyes for a moment. "That's right."

"You're actually *friends* with her?"

"I'm trying, but Helen's really reserved."

No doubt my sister would be able to get chummy with someone aloof. Alice's temperament was pure sunshine.

She frowned. "I thought she already left campus."

I gestured to Alice's heavy bag. "Maybe she's doing some paperwork in her classroom."

As we crossed behind Helen's car, a poof of fluff caught my eye from below the undercarriage of the Prius C. I paused, but Alice kept on walking.

I crouched down to peek underneath the car but couldn't see anything in the shadows. Huh. Had I imagined an animal?

Straightening back up, I noticed something else looked off. The vehicle was occupied, but the figure in the driver's seat was slouched in a weird position.

Alice finally noticed that I wasn't beside her and turned around. "Everything okay?"

"Odd," I said, peering through the window. The driver's head lolled at an uncomfortable angle. My breath left me.

My sister backtracked to my side and said, "What? Is something in there?" She moved around me and took a closer look.

Alice screamed.

Principal Lewis hurtled through the school doors into the parking lot. He goggled at us shocked Lee sisters standing there. Then he noticed the slumped body in the car, and his jaw dropped. Whipping out his phone, he dialed 911.

Minutes later, the first responders came with their sirens blaring. We watched as the paramedics attempted to revive Helen. The glassy stare of her eyes and her unmoving chest, though, told me that they were too late.

After we gave our statements and provided our contact information for the requisite recordkeeping, my sister started shaking. I hugged Alice tight as the sirens continued to flash and officers inspected Helen's car.

Eventually, I said, "Let's go. I think it's better if you didn't watch anymore."

The principal nodded at us, a grim look on his face, as we left the tragic scene.

• • •

Although I still drove us to Tito's Tacos, we didn't stay to sit down and eat together like we'd planned on doing. Instead, I ordered their signature crunchy tacos to go, and we headed back to my complex.

Seaview Apartments didn't live up to its name and had no ocean view. Instead, I got an eyeful of the nearby 405 traffic.

Probably still in shock, Alice didn't compliment the interior courtyard like she usually did. Somehow she always managed to find the rectangular patch of artificial grass with its scattered potted ferns charming.

We trudged over to my ground unit, one of fourteen (unlucky, according to Ma, who'd said, "Number like meaning for *sure die*"). She always spoke to me in her own version of Manglish, Malaysian English, a kind of pidgin she used with close family.

As I unlocked the door, I said, "Feel free to stay the night, Alice."

My one-bedroom unit didn't really have space for visitors, but I continued, "You can take the bed. I'll sleep on the couch."

Alice let out a shaky breath. "I think I just need some time to calm my nerves. I'll be okay."

When we walked inside, Marshmallow pounced at us. "Back early, huh? Must have missed me too much."

I shook my head, and Alice greeted my cat with a half-hearted pat on his head.

Marshmallow swished his tail and looked back and forth between my sister and me. "What happened?"

Plopping down our dinner on my particleboard IKEA dining table, I sighed. I made sure to settle my sister gently in a chair.

"We don't have to talk about what happened at the school," I said, sitting down by her side. "We could just eat."

Marshmallow's blue eyes glimmered, and he made himself comfortable under the table . . . the better to eavesdrop, I suspected.

Alice grabbed a chip. She dipped it into the salsa and tried to eat it, but she couldn't even finish a bite. "Maybe I should talk about it. Get things off my chest."

"I'm really sorry about your loss, Alice—" Here, Marshmallow hissed, but I ignored him.

"I can't believe it," my sister said. "I'd talked to Helen less than an hour before."

"The paramedics did the best they could."

Her mouth flattened into a thin line. "We found her too late."

"I'm glad we were at least together when we saw her. I don't know what I would've done if I were alone." I shivered. "Who would have imagined she'd be slumped over in her car like that?"

"If I hadn't tried to finish up my paperwork, we'd have gotten to the parking lot earlier . . ."

I put my hand on top of hers. "Alice, you couldn't have known."

She started tearing up. "But I did."

"What? How?" I almost knocked over the salsa in my surprise.

"I ran into Helen in the restroom after lunch. She told me her stomach was hurting and she wasn't feeling very well."

I shook my head. "Not your fault. I get stomachaches at times, and they always go away."

Alice fidgeted with her fingers. "I keep some ginger chews in my desk and dropped some off to her after the last bell rang."

I scrunched my nose and stuck out my tongue. The spicy tang made those my least favorite candies in the world.

"Don't give me that look, Mimi. Ma always says they work great on nausea."

I shrugged. To each their own. I often felt nauseated *after* eating them.

I stared at the tastier food before us. "You should eat, Alice. Food helps settle nerves." I snatched up a taco and bit into it. The tender shredded beef made my taste buds dance with joy, and I motioned to the spread on the table.

Alice gave a tiny nod and picked up a taco. She held it in her hand.

"By the way," I said, "Happy early Valentine's Day."

"Don't remind me. What's so happy about being couple-less while everyone else celebrates with cute dates and gifts?"

I thought about something that might lighten her mood. "Well, you'll get extra bonding time with Ma."

"Why's that?"

I gave her a genuine grin. "Valentine's will be sure to inspire her. And now that she's off my case, you'll be the single Lee daughter she'll work her matchmaking magic on."

"Oh no," she said. "Tell me it won't be like that time she created an online dating profile for you on that sketchy site."

"Maybe it'll be more along the lines of when she ordered Chinese takeout to my shop to set up a lunch date with the delivery guy." I hid my smile.

Alice made a mock face of horror, but she started eating her taco.

Thank goodness Alice had cheered up for the time being. I knew she didn't have anything to do with her coworker's death. Maybe Helen had struggled with some hidden fatal medical condition. Tragic because she'd been young like us, but perhaps inevitable.

I shuddered, remembering the last time I'd been around a sudden death. I'd been shocked to find that the police had considered me a murder suspect. It had taken a lot of sleuthing for me to get my life back on track. I felt grateful that Alice wouldn't need to share the same grueling experience of Detective Brown breathing down her neck.

CHAPTER

two

I LIKE TO SLEEP in on Saturdays, but when I received a call early the next morning and checked the ID, I jolted upright in bed. "Alice, what's wrong?"

My sister's voice shook as she said, "Somebody's at my door, but I don't recognize him. I know it's dumb to be scared just because of what happened yesterday, but what do I do? I never get visitors!"

"Maybe the guy's got the wrong unit."

I heard some shuffling from her end. "I snapped a pic of him through the blinds, and I'm sending it to you. If anything happens to me, you'll know who did it. Tell Ma and Dad I love them. And Marshmallow, too."

I rolled my eyes at my younger sister's dramatics, but an anxious pit still formed in my stomach.

Once I received the image, I recognized Detective Brown right away. Grim features, sandy buzzcut, and signature gray suit.

"What should I do? Call the cops?" Alice asked in a tiny voice.

"No," I said. "He *is* the police. It's Detective Brown. Let him in, but stall. I'm heading your way."

I hung up and changed into presentable outside clothes. As I ran around the house searching for my purse, Marshmallow heard the commotion. "This isn't NASCAR, Danica Patrick. What's the hurry?"

"Detective Brown just showed up on Alice's doorstep."

He hissed. "I'm coming with."

Nodding, I snatched a can of cat food and stuck it in my newly found purse. I rushed us over to the car.

• • •

I may have broken some traffic rules on the way there. Perhaps I could make it in the Indy 500 after all because we ended up at Alice's place in record time.

She lived in a sprawling complex of cookie-cutter tall beige buildings, separated by patches of fresh green common lawns. I pulled into a guest parking spot and sprinted to her unit with Marshmallow in my arms.

After banging on her door, Alice's sweet voice called out, "Come on in. It's unlocked."

I found Detective Brown seated at Alice's cozy dining table, its wooden surface draped with a happy sunflower-patterned fabric. The cop and I locked eyes.

He shrugged one shoulder in greeting, as though unsurprised that another death had occurred with me nearby. Not guilty *again*, I thought, squaring my shoulders.

Then Alice bustled over from the kitchen. She stood before the cop and served him a mug of steaming *teh tarik*. I could smell the sweet scent of "pulled tea" from where I stood a few feet away, though I doubted my sister had prepared the drink using the traditional method of pouring black tea and condensed milk between two containers at increasing heights. She'd probably opted for an instant powder package.

In any case, Detective Brown accepted the mug with thanks, then he turned toward me. "Your sister asked that we wait for you to arrive and offered me snacks in the meantime."

I glanced down at the table and noticed a plate of green speckled soda crackers.

Alice smiled at me. "I'll bring you some tea, too." She knew me well. I'd never refuse teh tarik, a common drink in Malaysia. The tea reminded Ma of her home country, and she made it often during my childhood, so I now associated the drink with happy family memories.

Marshmallow wiggled in my arms, and I let him down. "Don't forget about *my* stomach," he said.

I took out the can of cat food and pulled the tab. "Bon appétit," I said, placing his snack on the floor.

While Alice brought me my teh tarik, Detective Brown stared at the plate of crackers on the table. He picked one up. "What are these green things?" he asked.

"Scallion bits," I said.

"Uh, savory." He raised an eyebrow and nibbled on a cracker.

My sister finally sat down with her own mug of steaming tea. The detective placed his cracker onto a napkin and cleared his throat. "Miss Lee—"

We both looked at him. "Which one?" I asked.

"Alice," he said in a sudden brisk tone, and my sister's light brown eyes widened.

He pulled out a notepad and tapped his pen against it. "It seems that it was you who found the body yesterday."

"We both did," I said, sitting straighter in my chair.

He scratched the bridge of his nose. "Let me start with Alice's account first."

I put my hand up. "You know, Detective Brown, they already took our statements at the scene."

"Well, I wasn't there to do the questioning and to make sure all the details were recorded correctly. I'm in charge, and I insist on doing a thorough job." He cleared his throat and turned to Alice. "When did you find the deceased?"

My sister's eyes dimmed. "Her name's Helen. And I guess we stumbled onto the scene in the late afternoon. Mimi and I had planned to meet up for a girls' night out."

Detective Brown gave a slight nod at the mention of my name but continued to train his sharp gaze on my sister. "Tell me more."

"I didn't know why Helen was still there. When I looked in her car, she was slumped over . . ." Alice shivered and cupped her hands around her warm mug of tea.

The detective scribbled some notes in his pad and glanced at Alice. Maybe realizing he was pushing too hard by her trembling, Detective Brown turned his attention to me. "What was your recollection?"

"I noticed Helen in the car by accident. Thought I spotted some kind of animal lurking under her Prius."

Detective Brown bit the cap of his ballpoint pen. "Hmm, that would explain . . ."

His words trailed off even while I leaned in to listen.

"What else?" he asked me.

I sipped at my milk tea and thought back to yesterday. "Helen's head seemed slanted at an odd angle, one not comfortable for resting." I rubbed my suddenly sweaty palms against my jeans.

A deep line creased Detective Brown's forehead. "Interesting." He took a few swallows of tea and faced Alice again. "Do you have more to add to your statement? Anything you remember could help crack the case."

Case? I tugged at my ear. Had I heard wrong?

Alice had stopped trembling by now. "Helen did complain of a stomachache yesterday."

"Mm-hmm." Detective Brown wrote in his notepad. "When was this?"

"After lunch."

The detective waited a few moments, but Alice didn't seem to have anything else to add, so he slid his chair back and stood up. "Thank you, ladies."

Marshmallow meowed from his place on the dining floor. "Why is nobody getting a strange vibe about this besides me? What is Detective Brown doing here in the first place asking all these questions?"

I hadn't really wanted to think about that, but now Marshmallow had made me confront the facts. Swigging the sweet tea as a soothing mechanism, I instead felt the sugar grains lodge in my throat. The cop had definitely referred to the situation with Helen as a case. "Detective Brown," I said, "is this officially a homicide investigation?"

Alice turned pale, while Detective Brown's ice blue eyes gazed at me, unblinking. "It is an unusual scenario. When a previously healthy young woman dies inside her own car, my department has to investigate."

Alice whispered, "Will you be shutting down the school?"

"No, Miss Lee. We've already scoured Roosevelt Elementary. Feel free to go back to work come Monday."

"Thanks, Officer."

He brushed a hand against his formal gray suit. "It's Detective, actually." Pulling out a business card from his pocket, he placed it on the table. "In case you remember any extra details."

Using a somber tone to say goodbye, he also gave me a brisk handshake. "Mimi," he added, "try not to get in the middle of the investigation this time around."

My back stiffened. It wasn't my fault that Detective Brown had homed in on me as a prime suspect before. I, along with Marshmallow, had needed to investigate to clear my name.

After he left, I watched Alice drink her cooled-down tea in one continuous gulp.

She shook her head. "My Valentine's Days are usually bad, but not at the level of a cop showing up at my door."

I nudged her shoulder. "Well, it can only get better from here, right?"

"Easy for you to say, Mimi. I'm sure Josh is planning something great for you this evening."

I felt my face warm up. How could I respond to that? Perhaps it'd be wise to even cancel tonight's outing. Was I heartless to go out on a date when Alice had discovered a dead body only yesterday?

While these thoughts swirled in my head, I saw Marshmallow jump onto Alice's lap. My sister stroked the puffy white fur on my Persian cat with satisfaction. "At least I get a few more minutes with you, handsome," she said.

He purred. "That's right, gorgeous. And I'm way better than a thousand of those two-leggers."

Even though she couldn't hear him, Alice smiled. Marshmallow had never failed to cheer her up whenever she felt down, ever since the moment she'd spotted him at the rescue shelter and decided to give him to me.

"You know, I could leave Marshmallow here for the night," I said.

Alice shook her head. "You know the rules at this complex. We can't own pets here, and I don't want to get caught. The landlord is testy enough as it is."

She continued, "Besides, I'm feeling better now. Go and enjoy your time with Josh."

With my sister in a healthier emotional space, I breathed a sigh of relief. Perhaps I could focus on my upcoming romantic date without feeling guilty after all.

• • •

Josh and I had been dating for a few months now, but this was our first Valentine's together.

"Should I dress up?" I'd asked him when he'd told me he was planning something. I possessed only one formal thing in my closet: my go-to little black dress.

"No." Josh had shaken his head, his cute floppy bangs swishing across his rich brown eyes. "And actually, you might want to go for a casual look."

What kind of activity would we be doing? I hoped it wasn't something like paintball. The last time I'd gone, I'd ruined my favorite shirt and had sustained bruises that lasted weeks.

When Josh picked me up that evening, I scrutinized his outfit. He'd donned a bomber jacket over a black T-shirt and slim jeans. On his feet, he wore a pair of Keen sneakers.

I looked at his footwear. "Did you want to change into dress shoes?" He shrugged.

"You're so close by. Feel free to go back if you need to." His apartment, unit number one, wasn't very far from my own.

"Nah. These are comfortable. A good break from the usual polished shoes I have to wear for work." He put his arm around my waist and waved goodbye to Marshmallow.

My cat flicked his tail in the air at us from the couch. He stared at the television screen in front of him. I'd left the National Geographic channel on at a low volume to keep him company while we'd be gone.

I kept begging Josh for a clue about where we were headed as he drove south on the 405. After a solid five minutes of begging, he relented. "One hint," he said. "We're doing something international."

"Should've brought my passport then," I said and winked at him.

We shared a laugh, but then he quieted down and fixed his gaze at the moving traffic up ahead. He was pretty good at keeping me in suspense. When we got off the exit in Long Beach almost an hour later, I finally understood our destination.

He'd arranged for us to travel to the Naples of Los Angeles. The neighborhood featured restaurants serving Italian fare and even a series of waterways for boats to glide along.

We ended up at a quaint Italian café where he'd already made reservations for two. We sat in the back at a small square table with a flickering tealight between us. The checkered tablecloth and paper napkins lent an informal atmosphere, but I was still glad I'd changed from my "When Life Gets Ruff, Hug a Dog" T-shirt into a simple top.

According to an advertisement in the window, the restaurant was famous for its handmade pasta dishes. We both salivated at the menu. He ordered penne, and I got the spaghetti.

After the waitress left, Josh flashed me a wide smile. "Happy Valentine's Day!"

I grinned back. "I'm really excited about finally getting to celebrate this day as part of a couple." Oh, wait. How much more of a loser could I sound like? I felt my insides shriveling up in embarrassment.

I switched topics. "Er, how has this past week been for you?"

Josh raked a hand through his hair. "Ugh. It's been so busy at the firm."

True. We'd barely texted over the last few days.

He continued, "Ever since you referred me to PetTwin, my bosses have insisted that I take on more patent law cases."

At the end of last year, I had connected Josh with a pet matchmaking company that used advanced virtual reality capabilities. They'd needed patent protection to secure their cutting-edge ideas. Ever since then, he'd been swamped with work.

Josh took hold of my hand across the table and traced circles with his thumb on my skin. "How's Hollywoof?"

I loved the name and the play on words that I'd given my pet grooming salon. "Business is steady. I'm really glad I hired Nicola. She even handles basic grooming tasks, in between her sporadic acting auditions."

He selected his next words with care. "That all sounds good, but you seem a little on edge tonight."

"Why would you say that?"

Josh pointed to the paper napkin in my hand.

Or what was left of one. I'd picked up a napkin without even noticing and had shredded it to bits while we'd been talking.

"Oops." I pushed the tattered pieces into a pile. "I think I'm still tense with something that happened at Alice's school yesterday."

Josh's jaw tightened. "Is it school budget cuts again?"

I shook my head. "After I met my sister at work and we walked to the parking lot, we found a teacher . . . slumped over in her car."

He raised his eyebrows at me. "Unconscious?"

"No, dead." I gazed at the checkered tablecloth and frowned. "The paramedics came, but it was already too late."

"I'm so sorry. That must've been really hard." His dark brown eyes gazed at me with concern. "Are you and Alice okay?"

I gritted my teeth. "So, Detective Brown showed up at my sister's apartment this morning."

He scowled. "The nerve of that man." Josh and Detective Brown didn't get along, particularly not after the cop's deep suspicion of me last year.

"He ruined Alice's day," I said. "A double whammy since Valentine's isn't the best holiday for singles anyway. He has no consideration, given that it's both a weekend and a special occasion."

"The detective probably didn't even realize it was February fourteenth," Josh said. "The man's a workaholic."

I'd never seen Detective Brown relax in all the time I'd known him.

"I bet he's single . . . by default," Josh said.

I smirked. "No doubt about that."

Our trash talking the detective had lightened the situation and made me feel better. When our food arrived, I could savor the handmade pasta. I loved the chewy texture of the noodles, a consistency that far beat the store-bought packages I always used in my cooking.

Josh gestured to my plate of spaghetti with his fork. "We could eat it together, *Lady and the Tramp* style?"

"I think that kind of thing only works in cartoons. In real life, there's major sauce splashing involved. Besides"—I pulled the dish closer to me—"this is way too good to share."

He gave me a puppy dog pout, and I caved. While we didn't eat both sides of the same noodle, we spooned a little of our pasta onto each other's plate.

When we finally finished eating, I felt like I'd feasted. "This is the kind of traveling I enjoy," I said. "A food-cation."

Josh laughed and checked his watch. "Okay, and now it's about time to move on to our next reservation."

"I hope this isn't going to be a progressive dinner date," I said, patting my full stomach.

"Not exactly."

We ended up walking down the quiet side streets and burning off those pasta calories before stopping at the waterfront. Josh pulled out his phone to make a discreet call as I admired the floating boats nearby.

Five minutes later, a tall blond man strolled over to us with a clipboard in his hand. "Reservations for Josh Akana and Mimi Lee?"

Josh nodded.

"It'll take a minute or two for your guide to show up." The man ticked off some boxes on his papers and then turned to me. In a confident manner, he said, "Asian last name. Is it Chinese, Korean? Maybe Thai?"

"None of the above," I said. "It's from my dad. And he's white."

The young man's face grew red as he looked down at his papers. "Oh."

At that moment, the guide turned up and saved the other man from further embarrassment. The newcomer carried both a picnic basket and a scarlet carnation in his hands. He gave the flower to me and said, "For you, *bellissima*."

Turning to Josh, he passed over the basket. "Are you ready?"

Between the super fake accent and the striped shirt, I figured out Josh's romantic plans. This gondolier would take us out on the water.

We walked the short distance to the docks, Josh holding my hand all the while. A slim black gondola waited for us in the canal. So that's why Josh had wanted to wear water-resistant shoes—in case his feet got wet.

After situating ourselves in the gondola, Josh opened the picnic basket to reveal a small baguette with slices of salami. Though still stuffed, I managed a few bites as the gondolier perched at the stern and maneuvered us through the waterways with his oar.

I relaxed into the romance of the scenario. Even the gondolier's cheesy rendition of "That's Amore" didn't dampen my mood. Gliding down the canals crisscrossing Long Beach, we passed by the elegant homes at the water's edge, dressed up and sparkling in the serene evening.

Soon the gondolier paused underneath an arc. Josh's eyes twinkled at me as he said, "Legend has it that kissing under a bridge means a couple will enjoy never-ending happiness together."

He leaned in, and I could smell the faint whiff of pine. Anticipating his tender kiss, I closed my eyes and tilted my head up.

Smack. His mouth crashed into my nose.

A kiss-astrophe. He'd bumped into my button nose. I rubbed it, hyperaware of the one feature I'd always felt sensitive about.

He leaned in again and brushed his soft lips against the tip of my nose. "You're beautiful," he whispered.

Then he kissed me full on the lips, and somehow his reassurance of my self-conscious flaw made the new kiss seem that much sweeter.

CHAPTER

three

ONDAY BROUGHT A trickle of customers. Matching the slow
pace, Marshmallow napped away in his usual spot of sunshine
near the plate glass window. Or maybe he only pretended to sleep. He
seemed to be giving me the silent treatment after leaving him alone for
most of the weekend because of my Valentine's date.

The wash-and-dry clients (as I called them) came in a lazy wave.
The dogs needed a typical shampoo and blow-dry. I'd already taught
Nicola the skills to do the task, and if any of the customers bringing in
their pets seemed startled by the beautiful groomer, they hid it well.

Nicola possessed a gazelle-like stature coupled with a gorgeous
symmetrical face. Maybe people didn't blink at her good looks because
the Los Angeles area was filled with a number of celebrities and plastic
surgery–enhanced model wannabes. Or maybe the slightly bulbous
nose that she worried about gave her a more approachable beauty.

With the sluggish business, I used the downtime to clean the front of the store. I swept the floor with its Bark of Fame and accompanying doggie stars, dusted the flat-screen TV showing classic canine films, and wiped down the pleather benches in the waiting area. Afterward, I repositioned the searchlight to shine down just so on the cash register.

I'd started refilling the glass jar on the front counter with my fresh homemade dog biscuits when my sister texted me in the late afternoon: School's out. Please come over. Urgent animal dilemma.

I left Nicola to handle the rest of the workday and close up shop. Meanwhile, Marshmallow and I crossed the palm tree–lined plaza to get to the parking lot. In my Prius, we zoomed onto the highway. Due to an unusual lack of traffic, we soon arrived at Roosevelt Elementary.

At the school, I carried Marshmallow in my arms across the zig-zag of outside hallways to reach my sister's kindergarten classroom. When I let him down on the threshold, he paused and sniffed the air in confusion.

What did he smell? I couldn't detect anything in the air. "What is it, Marshmallow?" I asked.

I hoped Alice would write off my question as an adorable pet owner mannerism, but I really had to ask him out loud because Marshmallow's mind connection only worked one way. He could talk to me in my head, but I couldn't speak to him without actually voicing my words. Nobody knew about my telepathic cat—not my boyfriend or any of my family, and I intended to keep it that way. They'd never believe me if I tried telling the truth.

Marshmallow didn't respond to my question. Strange. I usually couldn't shut him up. He sniffed again and shook his head a few times.

I looked around to see if I could spot anything unusual. My gaze slid past the walls filled with life-size crayon-colored versions of each student in the class and over to the whiteboard with the printed alphabet banner hanging above it. In another corner, I spotted the cozy reading area with its rocking chair and comfy shag rug. Nothing seemed off. And Alice herself sat at the teacher's desk on one side of the room.

When she finally noticed me, she bustled over to the doorway and gave me a big hug. "Thanks for coming, Mimi. I didn't know who else to call."

"What exactly is the matter?" I asked, stepping inside more and peering around again.

"I found something," she said.

Marshmallow padded over to the reading nook.

"Yes, over there," Alice said, traveling the same path as my cat. I followed, and Alice pointed to the rocking chair.

Half hidden by a knit pillow, I discovered a matted ball of fur the size of a cantaloupe. A kitten had curled up in the chair. It blinked at me with forest green eyes.

Could it be the same animal I'd seen before underneath Helen's car? I let the little cat sniff my hand. The kitten mewled at me.

"She says hi," Marshmallow said in my head. He understood animals and could translate their sounds to English. That talent had been invaluable during the previous murder I'd been implicated in.

"Why, hello there." My hand hovered near the kitten's head, and she leaned into it.

"It likes you," Alice said.

"She's a girl."

"How'd you know so easily?" Alice tried lifting the cat's tail and peering underneath.

Oops. How could I tell without seeing any features revealing the cat's gender? "It's from constantly working around animals. You kind of get a sixth sense."

Alice nodded at me and made a wistful face. "I think the kitten's a stray, but she seems really young."

I glanced back at the open classroom door. "Did the cat just wander in here?"

"Nope. I found her crying out in the hallway, right in front of Helen's"—her voice cracked—"old room. I picked the kitty up before the substitute teacher could alert Richard, our janitor, about the noise."

I studied the kitten's matted fur and tsked. "This cat needs a bath."

Alice clapped her hands. "Yes, Mimi, could you give her a makeover? Clean her up and make her pretty. Then maybe one of your clients will adopt her."

"You could keep her, Alice."

My sister wrung her hands. "I wish, but you know the rule at my complex. No pets."

"But a quiet cat . . ."

Alice frowned at me. "My landlord would go ballistic. I can't handle any more of his Hulk episodes."

"Fine, I get it." I held up my hands in surrender. "I'll take the kitty and spruce her up."

I picked up the kitten, while Marshmallow gave the little cat a strange look. Why?

"I'll see you later, Alice," I said.

"Thanks again. You're the best sis ever."

I walked down the school hallway, clutching the kitten to my chest. Marshmallow followed a few paces behind. I wondered why he kept his distance from us and stayed so silent. He usually talked up a storm.

As I passed by one classroom, I saw a cart outside the door piled high with stuff. A sign made from construction paper read, "Freebies."

I stopped. Dad would be proud of my salvaging radar. Due to his accounting background, he'd drilled into me the importance of securing bargains. I looked over the items with my arms full of kitten: old workbooks, cans of sardines, and a calendar marked "Property of Helen Reed."

I gasped. The nearby door was labeled with the number 6.

The kitten shivered in my arms. "You must be cold," I said. "A bath will help warm you up. Let's get you home."

· · ·

The chipped kitchen sink in my apartment didn't begin to compare with the industrial-size steel model at my job, but it would suffice. Besides, maybe the poor kitty would prefer being in the cozy confines of a smaller tub.

Making sure to speak in soothing tones to the cat, I turned on the water and let it heat up. I switched the handle to spray mode, figuring a gushing faucet might alarm her even more. Although I'd asked Marshmallow to comfort the kitty, he complained about the cat's smell and insisted on watching us from a short distance.

I started washing the cat with a gentle shampoo, but she shrank away from my touch. Holding her still, I used the lightest of touches to lather her. She shuddered during the whole bathing process. After getting all the dirt off, I rinsed and dried her with a soft towel.

She looked fresh and perky now. "What's your name, beautiful?" I asked.

Her dark green eyes locked on to my face.

I walked over to Marshmallow and tapped him on the head. "Can you translate for me?"

He approached the kitten and gave a brief meow.

She answered with a terse and unhappy sound.

Marshmallow narrowed his eyes at the kitten, and his fur bristled.

"What's going on?" I asked him.

"Nothing," he said. "She didn't say a thing."

But I'd heard her respond myself. Why would Marshmallow lie to me?

He backed away from us. Okay, if Marshmallow wouldn't tell me her name, I'd have to make one up.

Mesmerized by her cloudlike gray fur, I said, "Nimbus. It's nice to meet you."

I stroked her clean fur and smiled. In the middle of her shoulder blades, though, I encountered a small bump. I traced its contours. Could it be a chip? Maybe this kitty wasn't a stray after all.

I'd need a scanner to access her information. Then I could reconnect the tiny cat with her rightful owner. I'd have to call my vet, Dr. Exi, and schedule an appointment.

CHAPTER

≡ *four* ≡

I COULD ALWAYS COUNT on Dr. Exi to have some immediate spots available at his office. His appearance might account for his atypical open schedule. I'd grown used to his uncanny features, all sallow skin and dark inky hair, but his likeness to Dracula might have scared off other customers.

Marshmallow, Nimbus, and I didn't have to stay long in the jungle-themed waiting area before being ushered into an examination room. Unlike the outer reception area, with its curved desk lined with stuffed animals, the room seemed clinical by contrast. The compact, sterile space housed a sink, a computer station, and a centralized table.

When Dr. Exi walked in, he greeted me with a grin, which showed off his Hollywood-straight teeth. "Who's the adorable new guest today?"

"This is Nimbus," I said, lifting the kitten and placing her on the examination table.

Marshmallow let out a small chuckle, the only sign of mirth he'd displayed after getting stuck with a new housemate. "That's what you named her?"

I turned my back on him and faced Dr. Exi. "Of course, you already know the charming Marshmallow."

Dr. Exi nodded but focused his attention on the kitten, checking her vitals and jotting down notes. Then he touched the place where I'd located the ridge, between the shoulder blades of Nimbus. "Mm-hmm. There's definitely something there."

The vet rummaged around the room and pulled out a device that looked oddly similar to a walkie-talkie. He aimed the scanner at Nimbus. Nothing.

Dr. Exi frowned. He angled the device a different way and tried again. "Weird. I'm not getting a readout."

I peered at Nimbus's back. "It's definitely a chip, though, right? Not some sort of medical problem?"

"It's not organic, like a growth or anything. This cat's as fit as a fiddle with her bright eyes and beautiful fur."

The vet darted a glance at Marshmallow and continued, "And it's not like this little kitty has *layers* that might muffle the chip's signal, which makes it all the more puzzling."

"Humph," Marshmallow said, twitching his nose.

"Do you have another scanner?" I asked. "Maybe that one's busted."

"Good idea. Wait right here." Dr. Exi popped out of the room. He returned in a few minutes with the same model of scanner. He tried again but still no luck.

In my head, Marshmallow cleared his throat. "I think I know the problem. It's not set to the right frequency."

"Dr. Exi?" I motioned to the scanner in his hand. "Could the chip be giving off a wavelength that the device can't detect?"

The vet stroked his chin. "Possible. Older chips do use different frequencies."

"Is there somewhere else I can go to get it scanned?"

He nodded. "A rescue shelter could help you. Maybe try the same one where you got Marshmallow."

"Thanks so much for making the time to see us."

"My pleasure, Mimi." He fiddled with the stethoscope around his neck. "While you're here, though, I have a question for you."

"Yes?"

"Do you groom other animals besides dogs?"

I did the usual baths for pups (and one precious kitty) but . . . "I'd consider it," I said.

"Good. I know a bird that needs his feathers trimmed. Can I send the owner to you?"

I hesitated. "I'd need some training first."

"It's a cinch. I'll show you right now. People can even do it at home themselves if they're confident enough." He pulled out a dusty stuffed bird from a nearby cupboard. "I'd schedule in more feather trimmings, but I'd rather concentrate on diagnosing actual medical issues."

Dr. Exi proceeded to explain the difference between various feathers, particularly the primary and secondary ones. I followed along with his lecture and even mock-clipped the correct areas by using my fingers as pretend scissors.

Meanwhile, Marshmallow darted into the shadow of the long examination table, where he proceeded to convulse with laughter.

"You're a natural," Dr. Exi said with a pat on my shoulder.

Clipping feathers couldn't be too difficult, right? "Okay, I'll agree to help out, but let the owner know that I'm new. You might say I'll be stretching my wings to do it." I shot him a grin.

Nobody even snorted at my joke. Then to add to my embarrassment, "Chapel of Love" came blaring from my cell phone. Ma's special ringtone. I'd reserved the tune just for her since marriage seemed to be her primary goal for me in life.

"Thanks again, Dr. Exi, but I've got to take this call." I silenced the ringing. "See you at Marshmallow's next shots."

Marshmallow yowled while Dr. Exi waved goodbye, and I backed out of the exam room with the cats.

In the waiting room, I picked a spot near the back and answered the call. "How are you, Ma?"

"Ah, Mimi. Why you no ring?"

We'd spoken just two days ago. "It hasn't been that long, Ma."

"You and Josh date much time. No propose?"

Oh. That kind of ring. "Things are different nowadays, Ma. It's not like it was with your generation. Love at first sight, engagement within the week."

She let out a small sigh. "You *makan* yet?"

My pent-up irritation flooded out with my next words. "Do you plan your entire day around meals, Ma? I'm not even hungry. Ate a big breakfast actually."

"We lunch today. You and me at Roti Palace. Noon."

I thought about postponing the meal, but at least I still had a few hours to digest my breakfast. Plus, I'd never hear the end of it from her if I bailed. Though born in Malaysia, Ma often showed her Chinese-influenced roots, especially in regards to filial piety.

Anyway, I didn't have many scheduled appointments at Hollywoof today. I could probably dash out during the shop's typical hour-long midday closure.

The remaining time before lunch passed by with the prearranged beauty treatments. While Nicola took care of the cash register, ringing up purchases of homemade biscuits, doggie pouches, and collars, I offered grooming services to the clients. Owners came in wanting a quick nail trim. Or the more glamour-conscious ones asked for pedicures with puppy polish, embellished with stick-on rhinestones or dipped in glitter.

At noon, I left Marshmallow and Nimbus in the trusty care of Nicola. As I drove toward my lunch date with Ma, I started feeling more enthusiastic. I actually had been looking forward to trying out this new local restaurant, Roti Palace.

Like the name suggested, the restaurant served *roti canai*, an India-inspired flatbread, often eaten in Malaysia for breakfast or as a snack. I salivated in anticipation of the layered dough.

Inside, the restaurant took on the atmosphere of a large open-air food court. It even had an immense glass ceiling that let in rays of lazy sunshine. The sun shone down on the dining room full of colorful plastic chairs and tables.

I spotted Ma at a neon green round table. She wore her lucky gold sweater symbolizing fortune and waved me over. "Good you come, Mimi. Talk in person."

"Sure, Ma." I hoped she wouldn't grill me on potential wedding venues right away. To delay her, I examined the menu. "Look at all these choices of roti and dipping sauces. They even have an Americanized version with ham and cheese stuffed inside."

Ma closed the menu. "Everyone know plain *roti canai* is best, *satu*."

"That's my number one pick, too. With curry sauce."

She leaned back in her chair, looking satisfied that she'd raised me right.

I signaled to the waiter, and we placed our identical orders.

"It'll take a few minutes to cook," he said. "If you like, you can watch them making it around the corner."

Ma and I looked at each other and pushed our chairs back at the same time. We skirted around a potted sago plant buffering a sharp corner and came across the large window that let us peek into the kitchen area. Through the glass, we could see workers rolling the dough balls and then stretching them into discs.

"In KL, I eat roti for breakfast every day," Ma said.

Though I'd never set foot in Malaysia, I knew "KL" stood for Kuala Lumpur, the country's capital. "Yum," I said, licking my lips. "How much did it cost?"

"Cheap. Less than one ringgit."

"That's, like, a quarter in American money." I bet Roti Palace charged at least a few bucks for each flatbread.

In the kitchen, one of the workers stretched the dough out farther. He spun the disk in the air and then smacked it onto the table multiple times, creating a rhythmic drumming.

Ma got a faraway look. "I take your daddy eat at best stall. Roti there *shiok*."

"You must have won him over with food," I said.

"*Sup sup sui*. Very easy." Ma smoothed down her golden sweater. "Happy stomach make happy heart."

The worker shaped the dough into a spiral, creating splendid layers. A few minutes later, he rolled it into a disk again. After adding clarified butter, he placed it on the griddle to cook.

We decided to return to our seats at just the right time because soon after we'd settled back at the table, our orders arrived. I tore a piece of the thin flaky bread and dipped it in the accompanying curry.

Too busy devouring the roti, I didn't notice the silence at our table until I'd eaten half the disk. I looked up at Ma and wrinkled my nose.

She'd taken only a few bites and seemed lost in thought.

"Ma, is everything okay?"

She pasted on a smile. "Fine. How your Val-en-tine?" She enunciated each syllable.

I proceeded to tell her about my trip to Naples, Long Beach, and the gondola ride. When she didn't fish for more details, particularly about any velvet boxes, I grew concerned.

I studied her face, which looked quite sad. Her mouth even drooped. "Ma?"

She sniffed and blew her nose on a napkin. "Way should be. Romance for young people."

I shook my head. "Did Dad forget about Valentine's again? He never remembers, Ma. Don't take it personally."

She waved away my comment. "He stuck at golf. Whole day."

"His going golfing all the time isn't about avoiding you. It's just that retired life really agrees with him."

She pursed her lips.

"Or maybe he'll make it up to you on your anniversary," I said. My folks had married on Leap Day. Dad joked that the date of February twenty-ninth had saved him so much money over the past few decades. "That's a big deal. It only comes every four years after all."

Ma dunked a piece of roti in her curry. Chewing it, her eyes misted up. "Probably no."

Maybe Alice or I could sneakily give Dad a hint to do something. But Ma would reprimand us if she got wind of us attempting to influence him. She insisted that Dad take the reins on initiating anniversary celebrations. For her, it didn't really count as special if we kids—or worse, she—had to remind him of the anniversary in order for him to remember.

For the rest of lunch, I steered the conversation to safer topics. And under no circumstance would I divulge how Alice and I had discovered a dead body at the school.

Instead, I shared about a few mishaps from Hollywoof, including the time a customer had accidentally purchased a dog biscuit—and ate it, thinking it was a traditional cookie. She giggled at my story, but I still wondered about her well-being when we left. I'd have to check in with Alice to get her take on things.

CHAPTER

five

'D INTENDED TO contact Alice when I returned to Hollywoof, but a customer showed up earlier than scheduled for her appointment. Instead of a typical grooming procedure, the customer had requested that her French poodle be colored purple. Not just any hue, but a specific lavender shade.

I hadn't wanted to spring for the very expensive puppy-coloring set I'd seen online, so I researched nontoxic dyes. I ended up purchasing a few bottles of blue and purple from a specialty store and had spent last night creating the perfect hue.

The bottle was ready to go in the back room, but the customer changed her mind at the last minute. "You know," she said. "I think periwinkle would suit him better."

I smiled at the client through clenched teeth. "Of course." Unfortunately, in sales, the customer is always right.

After bringing the poodle to the back area, I donned gloves and an apron to prevent any potential staining. The last thing I needed was to turn into Smurfette. To get the new color, I depleted a few bottles of dark blue dye and some light purple as well. Maybe it would've been better if I'd invested in the professional doggie dye. At least it would've saved me on time and effort.

I placed the now periwinkle solution into a sink full of water and proceeded to give the dog a normal bath. However, I let him soak in the solution for a while. Then I blow-dried his newly colored fur. I eventually delivered the very blue (but totally happy) poodle back to his beaming owner.

In the late afternoon, I called my sister from the privacy of the back room while I cleaned up. The steel sink still had an obvious coating of blue on it. "Guess what? I had lunch with Ma today at Roti Palace."

"What? No fair!" she said in a pouting tone.

"She looked worried about something, though." I wandered over to the supply closet. "Ma didn't even pressure me about getting married ASAP."

"Hmm. She hasn't interrogated me about my dating prospects lately, either."

"Not very Ma-like behavior. She seemed unhappy about Valentine's and sounded dejected about their upcoming anniversary." I picked up a box of baking soda and sprinkled the powder in the sink. "Was she like this during the last Leap Day?"

"I don't think they made a big deal out of celebrating their anniversary."

"Really? They did when I was in middle school." Then I'd left for college and missed the next special occasion.

She sighed. "Well, that might have been the last time."

"But that was over a decade ago!" I scrubbed the sink with a sponge.

"Are you worried about it, Mimi?" she asked.

I put away the sponge and swapped it for steel wool. "I don't know."

"They're so much older now," Alice said. "People get less mushy as they age."

"Maybe you're right . . ." I'd managed to get rid of the blue with some hard scrubbing and rinsed the sink.

"Oh, Mimi, I meant to ask. How is the little kitty?"

"I'm calling her Nimbus," I said. "She looked like a cloud after I dried her off from her bath, so that was my inspiration."

"Nice name," she said. "You find a home for her?"

"Uh, no."

She paused then and let out a little gasp of delight. "Ooh, I bet if you make her an Instagram account, she'd get all sorts of followers, and word would spread about her needing—"

"Actually, I found a microchip after I bathed her . . ."

"She has an owner?"

"My vet couldn't scan the chip. I'm going to try the local pet rescue next. Can you give me the info of the shelter where you found Marshmallow?"

"Sure. I'll send it to you right now. I gotta go prep for tomorrow's class, but keep me posted."

I thanked her and hung up. Within a few seconds, she'd texted me the shelter's address. I mapped out the directions so I could visit after I closed up shop.

• • •

Standing outside the local rescue shelter with Nimbus in my arms and Marshmallow at my feet, I admired its canary yellow exterior. A doggie silhouette was painted right above the entrance.

I liked its feel, but Marshmallow shuddered.

"Thank heavens I'm not in there anymore," he said.

And I realized that despite its cheerful outside, the shelter would hopefully be a short pit stop for all the animals stuck inside.

I pushed open the heavy glass door. Marshmallow dragged his paws. I had to promise him a special treat before I could coax him inside.

Finally, we entered a room painted cotton candy pink. The side aisles were lined with wire cages filled with smaller pets. I heard hamsters scrambling in their wheels and noticed bunnies twitching their noses at us.

As we moved toward a massive reception desk in the rear of the room, we passed by an entryway labeled "Cats." Marshmallow arched his back before he hurried past it.

We approached the worker behind the desk. She had a halo of curly brown hair, and freckles dotted her nose. Smiling at me, she asked, "How can I help you?"

"I found this kitty"—I lifted Nimbus up—"and tried to get her microchip scanned at my vet's. He didn't seem to have the right scanner, though. Could you guys possibly help?"

"Sure. Please place the kitten here." She patted the countertop.

I put Nimbus on the scratched-up wooden surface. To soothe her, I rested a gentle hand on the kitten's back. From behind the counter, the worker pulled out a different kind of scanner than the one Dr. Exi had used. This tool appeared wider and flatter than the kind he'd owned. If I hadn't known better, I'd have mistaken it for somebody's modified iPad.

The worker aimed the scanner at the space between Nimbus's shoulder blades and pressed a button. *Eep.*

"Did you get a reading?" I asked.

She blinked at the screen. "Yes, but it's not what I expected."

I leaned over and read, "'Frequency out of range.'"

Stroking Nimbus's soft fur, I said, "Oh. Is there somewhere else I can take her that would have the correct type of scanner?"

She frowned. "I don't think so. This scanner's equipped to read all the common frequencies that are used in the pet registries—for both older and newer microchips."

"So what does the 'out of range' message mean?" I asked.

"I'm not sure." She pressed a few more buttons.

"It's probably too high of a value," Marshmallow said.

Confused, I blinked at him, but then Marshmallow gave a loud purr, making the worker peer over the counter.

Her eyes widened. "Sinatra?" she said.

I picked up Marshmallow and placed him next to Nimbus. "You know my cat?"

"I'd recognize those handsome blues anywhere."

Marshmallow gave me a long look. "I even had a better name back at the shelter."

I patted my cat's head. "I call him Marshmallow."

"I can, er, see where the inspiration came from."

"She's talking about my color," Marshmallow said, "not my width."

"That reminds me," I said to the woman. "Does Marshmallow have a microchip?"

She looked puzzled. "We wouldn't have let him get adopted if he had."

"Actually, I meant if he had a microchip inserted here at the shelter. I've heard that some places will insert them in the animals. Then I can add my info to the registry."

"Ah. We don't do that at our shelter. Only up-to-date vaccinations."

A noise came from behind me, and I turned my head to look. A customer with three young kids had walked in, and one of her children was rattling a bunny's cage.

"Please be gentle," the worker said, hurrying toward the family to intervene.

The recent scan had produced an error readout. What did that mean?

Almost subconsciously, I ran my fingers across Marshmallow's back as I reflected. How often did they miss a microchip? Could Marshmallow have one that the shelter hadn't discovered because of his extra "layers"? I didn't want to give up my furry friend, but I had to know.

I glanced back at the worker, who seemed occupied with stopping the little kids from grabbing the bunny's whiskers. Taking the scanner from the counter, I aimed it at Marshmallow and pressed the scan button.

Nothing. I exhaled in relief and dropped the device back on the counter.

Again I remembered that the digital display for Nimbus had read, "Out of range." How had Marshmallow known it had been too *high* a frequency?

Scooping up the cats, I scurried out of the building. In the open air, I stared Marshmallow down. "You've got some explaining to do when we get back, mister."

CHAPTER

six

A T HOME, WE settled in the living room. Nimbus lay like a little gray cloud on my lime green IKEA sofa, where I sat beside her. Marshmallow paced back and forth before me.

"Spill it," I said to him. "You knew the frequency was too high. How?"

He sighed. "We were kept by the same 'master'—as he referred to himself. He also went by Edgar, a self-given nickname inspired by his favorite author."

My heart sank a little. "You have an owner?"

"If that's what you call someone who found me on the streets and then locked me up tight."

"Where is he now?"

Marshmallow twitched his nose. "Probably living in the same stinky cigar-smelling house."

I pivoted toward Nimbus and admired her sleek fur. When I'd first spotted her, she'd been dirty and had a lingering scent Marshmallow had picked up on. "Was it smoke that you smelled on her that first day?"

Marshmallow dipped his head. "Yeah. Cheap cigars. I thought it might be a coincidence, but when I asked for her name, I figured it out."

"You never told it to me. What did he call her?"

"EFV2." He paused. "I was EFV1. Enhanced Feline Version One."

I pointed to Nimbus's back. "What kind of chip did Edgar put in her?"

"I think it's a high-frequency emitter. Meant to enhance mental capabilities. He wanted to get rich off his invention and was making a prototype of it right before I escaped."

I pointed to Nimbus. "Are you saying she can talk, too?"

Marshmallow trained his gaze on me. "Can you hear anything from her?"

I concentrated for a few seconds but shook my head. "Then again, I'm not her owner. Isn't that how it works?"

"Who knows?" Marshmallow said. "Even without a loving connection, I could project a few words to my old *captor* just by sheer talent. But it might take more compatibility between pet and owner to really make a conversation happen."

I smiled wide at him. "You mean, we can communicate to one another because we have a strong loving bond."

Marshmallow gave me a sideways glance. "Eh. You're all right for a two-legger."

That was about as much of a compliment as I was going to get. I turned my attention to Nimbus, stroking her head. "Well, I'm glad the both of you got away from that mad scientist. I wonder how Nimbus ended up at Roosevelt Elementary. Can you ask her?"

"Sure." He purred at the kitten on the couch, and she whimpered back.

"Nimbus walked for a very, very long time," Marshmallow told me.

"The poor girl." I stroked her some more. "How long had she been hiding on school grounds?"

Marshmallow relayed my question and then translated. "For five sunsets."

"And why was she under Helen's car the other day?"

Marshmallow and Nimbus exchanged meows. Swishing his tail in the air, Marshmallow said, "She was worried about the nice lady who'd fed her before. Wanted to keep an eye on her."

I raised my eyebrows at Marshmallow. "How come?"

"Nimbus thought Helen smelled funny that afternoon."

I gripped the arm of my sofa. "Did she see something suspicious?"

My cat purred to Nimbus, and the kitten hid behind a throw pillow.

Marshmallow sighed. "She doesn't seem to want to talk about it."

I could see her shaking behind the pillow, so I started singing "Somewhere Over the Rainbow" in a gentle voice. Succumbing to the lullaby, she soon fell asleep on the couch.

• • •

I heard the knock at my door around nine in the evening. At first, my heart leapt with joy. Maybe Josh was visiting me. Then I remembered he'd mentioned needing to work late over the next couple of days.

After looking through the peephole, I groaned but swung open the door. "Detective Brown, what are you doing here?"

The cop held a black take-out box with the Cheesecake Factory logo stamped on it. "Happened to be in the neighborhood and thought I'd check in on you."

"I doubt this is a social visit." I pursed my lips. "The last time you came to my apartment, you had a search warrant."

He shrugged his shoulders. "Bygones."

Narrowing my eyes, I said, "I've never known you to stop working."

"Okay, you're right. This visit is related to the case." He glanced at the inner courtyard of my apartment complex. "It's probably better if you invited me inside to discuss things in private."

Not many people used the courtyard, especially with the nippy February weather, but it was better not to chance it. Other residents might walk by to go to the laundry room and hear our conversation. I let the detective in and brought him to the dining area.

"Have a seat." I motioned to the particleboard dining table. "I'm not the hostess with the mostest like my sister. I don't have any drinks or snacks to offer, sorry." I knew I didn't sound very sorry.

"But I do." Detective Brown placed the box in front of me.

I shook my head.

"You're not hungry?" he said.

He flipped open the lid, and I had to tamp down my delight upon seeing velvety cheesecake topped with glazed strawberries and a fluffy mound of whipped cream.

I crossed my arms over my chest. "I don't take bribes."

"Fine." Detective Brown steepled his fingers together. "But I need to get some facts from you to make sure I can close this case. Let's retrace your steps the day you saw your sister. How long were you at the school?"

I gave him the approximate time range.

"And did you meet up with your sister right away?"

I closed the lid on the take-out container to block the temptation. "Pretty much. I met her in the school office."

"I see. Was anybody else around?"

I nodded. "Principal Lewis came out of his office and chatted with me while I was waiting."

Detective Brown's thin lips flattened. "Then there was a period of time when you weren't with Alice."

"I don't understand. Helen died of natural causes. She had stomach issues."

Detective Brown rubbed his buzz cut hair. "We haven't fully determined anything yet. Still waiting for the autopsy."

"What exactly are you trying to get out of me?"

His cold blue eyes assessed me. "I have respect for the work you did on the pet breeder case, Mimi, but I have to level with you. Your sister was the last person to have seen the victim alive."

Which meant Alice was now on the detective's radar. After all, who else had been around that afternoon? I remembered spotting only three cars in the lot: Alice's, Helen's, and the principal's—and I'd just vouched for part of his time.

I slammed my hand down on the table. Startled mewls came from the living room.

Detective Brown didn't flinch at my violence, but he did turn his head to peek at the couch. "Did you get another cat?"

"I'm temporarily taking care of a kitten."

He plodded over to the living room and examined Nimbus. "You found this cat at the school."

How had he known?

"When we searched Helen Reed's classroom, gray cat hairs were found," he said. "I need to take this kitten into custody."

"Sorry, Detective. I already gave her a bath, so there won't be any evidence on her."

His gaze locked on the kitty. "I need to get this cat's health checked to make sure it's not harboring anything contagious."

"Sudden death by cat?" I gave an exasperated sigh. "I've never heard of anything so ridiculous. Plus, she's already been seen by my vet."

"I need to use proper police contacts in this investigation. You know, animals can carry all kinds of diseases." He put on some forensic gloves and scooped up Nimbus. She startled in his arms.

I reached for the kitten but stopped myself short. Detective Brown might call it obstruction of justice if I prevented him from taking the cat.

Meanwhile, Marshmallow purred at Nimbus to calm her down.

I bit my lip. "How long will you need her?"

"I'll have her back ASAP if she's not sick."

After I said a reluctant goodbye to Nimbus and an enthusiastic good riddance to the detective, I stared at the closed front door.

"Do you think Detective Brown will take good care of Nimbus?" I said. "He doesn't own any pets and might not know what to do."

Marshmallow preened himself. "Cats are extremely independent. I'm only worried about one thing."

"What's that?"

"You want to clear Alice's name, right?" He looked at me with his intelligent eyes.

"Of course I do."

"Well, you just let that cop walk off with an eyewitness to the crime."

I gulped and felt sick looking at the cheesecake the detective had left. I'd definitely lost my appetite.

CHAPTER

≈ seven ≈

'D LOST OUR eyewitness, but I could still scrounge up more information. On the pretense of bringing Alice the strawberry cheesecake, I paid Roosevelt Elementary a visit in the early morning before their official start of the school day. The principal would know the happenings around the campus and hopefully give me some clues so I could figure out what happened.

I snuck into the main office when I didn't see anyone stationed at the front desk. Either the receptionist hadn't arrived yet or she'd stepped out for the moment. The perfect opportunity to speak with the principal.

As before, Principal Lewis had left his door open a crack. I knocked on it.

"Come on in," he said. "I'd love some company." He was wearing his usual dress shirt and tie combo.

When I walked through the door, he stood up from his interesting-looking geometric desk. "Mimi," he said, his arms held wide open.

I ignored them, staring transfixed at the room around me. "It looks amazing in here." So different than before.

When the previous principal had ruled the roost, she'd opted for all steel furniture that matched her frigid personality. Principal Lewis appeared to believe in creating a different type of setting for his office. His trapezoid desk, painted forest green, took up the back part of the room while a tufted armchair with a multipatched rainbow design and slouchy beanbag occupied the rest of the space.

"Thank you." Principal Lewis lowered his arms and gestured at the sitting area. "Make yourself comfortable, Mimi."

I selected the armchair and sat on top of some blue, pink, and purple fabric patches.

Meanwhile the principal rolled his forest green computer chair from behind his desk and faced me.

"I wanted to say a quick hello to you and get permission to drop this off in the staff fridge." I held up the take-out container. "Strawberry cheesecake. A surprise for my sister."

"How thoughtful of you."

I shrugged. "The least I can do to cheer her up after the alarming discovery the other day . . ."

Principal Lewis shook his head. "Utterly tragic. We have a counselor available on campus for all our students' and staff members' emotional needs."

I shuddered. "Helen looked around Alice's age. It really makes you face mortality."

"You're too young to worry about all that." He pointed to some of the white hair on his head. "Death is for old-timers like me to ponder."

"Still . . ." I bit the inside of my cheek. "If only I could make sense of her death. Did Helen have some sort of medical condition?"

Principal Lewis jiggled his knee. "Not that she told me about."

"You were here that afternoon. Did she act any differently then?"

"Huh?" He straightened his paisley tie, clearly perturbed by my words, but too polite to shut down my line of questioning.

"My sister mentioned that Helen had complained of a stomachache."

"She seemed fine in the morning. Could it have been something she ate?" He jerked his thumb toward the left. "Helen often ate in the staff room down the hall."

I leaned in. "Did she usually eat with others?" Maybe one of her fellow teachers could shed light on Helen's stomachache.

He swiveled his head in the direction of the lunchroom. "The usual trio of teachers eat there daily: Jessie, Amy, and Donna."

"Who?" I had a hard time keeping track of Alice's colleagues. A brilliant idea then blossomed in my head. "You know, Principal Lewis, it would be great to meet my sister's coworkers one day soon."

He wheeled his chair closer. "I'm listening."

"Wouldn't it be wonderful if you scheduled a social gathering, especially after such a sad event?"

Principal Lewis's brows furrowed in thought before relaxing again. Then he smiled. "I like it. A mixer to bring us together during this time and to celebrate Helen's life."

"A lovely gesture."

Principal Lewis moved his chair back behind the desk. "Now if you'll excuse me, I should get working on the logistics."

"Thanks for your time, Principal Lewis."

As I headed out of the office, I crashed right into the receptionist in the hallway. She stumbled, letting a piece of paper flutter to the floor.

"Sorry," I said as I picked up the folded paper. I saw that it was signed by Helen Reed.

The receptionist plucked the note out of my hand, leaving me in the hallway, and entered the principal's office. "I found this in your mail slot. It looked like it might be important."

I left them to talk in private. Moving down the narrow corridor, I passed the staff restrooms and made my way into the lunchroom. The empty area held three circular tables with chairs.

It also had a small sink on the side, with a metal dispenser filled with flimsy brown paper towels tacked onto the wall above it. A rolling cart sat next to the sink and held a microwave with a spaghetti-sauce-splattered handle. Despite being plugged into the electrical socket, a pumpkin orange Post-it Note stuck on the unit read "Out of Order."

I also spied an old refrigerator with a pebbled surface coated in an obnoxious pea green. It whirred and clanked. The noises grew louder as I approached it. After opening the creaky door, I scanned its rusted shelves. They housed a few labeled lunch containers. I added the cheese-cake next to Alice's bag.

On top of the cheesecake box, I placed a note wishing Alice a great day. Besides serving as justification for my snooping, I really did hope the surprise would bring a smile to my sister.

I retraced my steps back through the corridor and heard the principal saying something in an anxious tone. Did he need my help?

Peeking in, I noticed him hunched over a small piece of paper. It looked like the note the receptionist had dropped earlier. He glared at the paper and mumbled, "Pursuant to CFR . . ."

A trail of numbers followed. I made out the phrase "Title 29." Knowing I couldn't assist, I decided not to bother him.

As I walked down the stone steps of the school's entrance, I noticed a figure on the front lawn. An elderly man with a stooped back, wearing a down jacket with a Dodgers cap seemed to be messing with the flags on the poles.

On second glance, I realized he was pulling the ropes to raise the banners into the sky. He completed his actions in slow motion. Finally, they flew high and proud above the school grounds.

I watched the Stars and Stripes flutter in the wind and remembered that the kids at Roosevelt Elementary still recited the Pledge of Allegiance every morning. The flags also reminded me of my visit on Friday because I remembered admiring them flying in the air back then as well.

Wait a minute. He was putting up the flags in the morning, which meant that the school took the flags down at the end of the day. So if the banners had been flying the afternoon of the death, that meant Helen, Alice, and Principal Lewis hadn't been the only people who'd remained on campus.

I approached the man. Assuming he was the janitor and remembering Alice mentioning his name, I said, "Richard?"

He turned to me with a glacial swivel. In a voice that sounded like gravel, he asked, "Who's there?"

I walked closer and noticed that besides the baseball cap, he also wore huge black wraparound sunglasses. The man must really be scared of UV rays—well, he did already have quite a few age spots on his skin.

He shuffled toward me. "Alice?" he said.

He'd confused me with my sister, but a lot of people did the same thing. Maybe I could even use the mistake to help me in my questioning. He'd be less on guard if he thought I was a teacher at Roosevelt.

I made a noncommittal murmur and said, "You were here Friday after school."

He pulled at his earlobe. "Eh?"

"The flags weren't taken down yet that afternoon." I took a deep breath. "Do you know about Helen?"

"Uh-huh. Poor girl."

"You see her at all that day?"

He tugged the brim of his baseball cap lower. "During last recess. Had to clean something for her."

"Did she look like she was feeling okay?"

He grunted. "I don't notice those sorts of things."

Gesturing at the flags, I said, "I'm surprised they're not at half-mast in remembrance."

"I don't make the rules around here." He shuffled his feet. "If there's nothing else, have a good day."

"Thanks, Richard." I watched him amble off and tried to guess his age. Even under the shade of the cap and behind the huge sunglasses, I'd noticed his very wrinkled skin.

Had the man been around when the ambulance had arrived? The flags had still been up at school, but perhaps he'd forgotten to take them down. I didn't recall him being anywhere near the flashing lights. Or had he stayed away from the paramedics on purpose?

CHAPTER

≈ *eight* ≈

W HEN I TRIED to open up shop, I dropped the keys twice in my occupied mental state with Helen's death. Had the janitor already left before she died, or had he hidden away when the paramedics arrived on the scene?

Nicola showed up a few minutes after opening time and found me fumbling with my keys. "You all right, Mimi?"

I rubbed my eyes. "Up early, that's all." I didn't tell her I'd gotten out of bed to go investigating at my sister's elementary school.

Finally, I unlocked the door, and we entered. Nicola flipped on the lights while I turned the sign over to "OPEN." Marshmallow staked out his usual sunny spot while we readied the place for upcoming customers.

Before long, a Lady Godiva lookalike came in with a covered cage. "Dr. Exi told me about this store."

I could hear a few chirps from the cage and did a double-take at the fabric draped over it.

"I covered the cage because the harsh sunlight hurts Pavarotti's eyes."

"Of course," I said, giving her a polite nod.

Nicola gave me a panicked look and whispered, "I don't do feathers."

Addressing the woman, I said, "You want his wings trimmed, right?"

"Exactly." She uncovered his cage with care and revealed a gray cockatiel with a lemon-colored head. "Can't have Pavarotti hurting himself when he soars around the house."

I flashed the woman a brilliant smile. Hopefully, my time with Dr. Exi and my additional YouTube research would translate to actual physical skill.

"I'll wait right here," the woman said as she sat on the pleather bench and took out a thick novel.

In the back room with Pavarotti, I placed the cage down on the grooming table and brought out my scissors. Better be conservative with the cutting, I thought. First, though, I needed to capture the bird to hold him still.

I lifted the cage door open and snuck several fingers in. He almost nipped them off. Then Pavarotti hopped to the other side of his perch.

Perhaps I hadn't thought this through when I'd agreed to Dr. Exi's request. Just then, I felt some soft fur brush against my legs.

Pavarotti started flapping his wings and moving around the cage. I looked down to find Marshmallow at my feet, his blue eyes riveted on the feathered creature.

"This is a *pet* bird," I said. "Quit scaring it."

"Why? Cat got its tongue?" He meowed out a chuckle, and Pavarotti cocked his head at Marshmallow.

Marshmallow froze. "I think little Tweety understood me."

"You can speak to birds, too?"

Marshmallow twitched his nose. "I've never tried to before . . . because it would have been bad manners to talk with my mouth full."

I cleared my throat. "Can you help me out right now?"

Marshmallow focused on the cockatiel and let out a low warning rumble.

The bird stiffened and stayed still.

"What'd you tell Pavarotti?" I asked.

"I let him know that he should stay put when a human holds sharp scissors near his body and that he should let you do your work."

"Er, thanks. I would have described it in gentler terms." My hand crept toward the cockatiel. "So he won't mind if I bring him out? I don't want him to be scared of you, either."

"That's all right," Marshmallow said. "I told him I'm vegetarian."

"You're not—"

"He doesn't need to know that."

With a now obedient bird, I took Pavarotti out of the cage and extended his wings with care. Making sure not to clip too high, I murmured, "This is like cutting hair. It won't hurt a bit."

Marshmallow translated my words to the bird with a soft purr.

I snipped a few feathers, making sure to trim only the primary ones, those giving the bird extra boost during flight. After all, I wanted Pavarotti to still be able to glide for safety's sake.

After making sure I'd done the best job I could, I placed him back in his cage. Then I brought Pavarotti back out to his owner, who remained invested in her heavy tome. I had to tap her shoulder to get her attention.

She looked up and admired her bird. "His plumage looks stunning. I know it's a simple task, but I just couldn't make myself do it. Best to leave the trimming to a professional, I thought."

"Thanks for coming in. Nicola will ring you up at the register."

"I'll be sure to tell all my avian owner friends about Hollywoof," she said.

"Wonderful." I handed her a stack of business cards. The more animals at my shop, the better.

The rest of the morning involved a few pooch baths, which Nicola and I split between us. Then we closed up shop for lunch. I took out my brown bag while Nicola hurried to make it to a voiceover audition.

I wondered if Alice was enjoying her surprise strawberry cheesecake this very minute. As if through some mystical sister connection, my cell phone rang, and her caller ID flashed on the display.

"What a treat," Alice said when I picked up. "I can't believe you made a special trip to the Cheesecake Factory for me."

"You can thank Detective Brown," I said, pulling my own chicken salad sandwich out of my bag.

"I don't understand." Her voice held a hint of worry.

"He came to see me." I played with the plastic wrap on top of my sandwich, not having the appetite to open it yet. "Told me you were the last person to see Helen alive."

"What?" My sister's voice quavered. "Does he think . . ."

"Were you really the last one to see her? I talked to the janitor, Richard, and I know he went into Helen's classroom. Do you know anything about that?"

Alice sucked in her breath. "The broken glass."

"Excuse me?"

"When I dropped off the ginger chews, Helen had just finished sweeping up some glass. Said she'd broken a bulb earlier while changing it, and there were still some missed shards."

"Isn't that something the janitor should've fully taken care of?" I paused, remembering the man's slow hauling of the flags and his stumbling steps. "How old is he anyway?"

"Almost seventy," Alice said. "But he's not ready to retire yet. Loves feeling purposeful."

I unwrapped my sandwich and took a bite. "One last thing. I didn't see his car late Friday afternoon, but I did notice the flags were still up. Richard—"

"Always remembers to put up and take them down," Alice finished in a hushed voice. "And he doesn't have a car. He uses the bus for transportation."

So Richard could've been on campus at that hour. But then why hadn't he gone to see what the fuss was about when the paramedics arrived? I wondered if Detective Brown knew about Richard's strange behavior . . .

CHAPTER

nine

SHOWED UP AT the police station unannounced. I'd been there before, so I made my way over to the battered desk that belonged to Detective Brown. Like on my last visit, I wondered why the station wasn't dealing with any exciting arrests, complete with yelling and fistfights.

However, I did notice a flurry of activity around the detective's desk. A dozen officers gathered there and let out *oohs* and *aahs*. I stood outside their circle and soon spied the reason for their adoration: Nimbus.

Like a storybook kitten, she'd gotten herself tangled up in a ball of purple yarn. She lay caught inside the soft cage near a seated Detective Brown. The more the cat tried to bat at the yarn, the more she wound the strands around herself. She gave a plaintive meow.

Detective Brown peeked over and grunted at her antics, but stood up. I noticed how he extracted Nimbus from the yarn web with tenderness. Looked like the cat wasn't the only one ensnared.

I tried to make my way toward his chair, but with my petite five-foot frame I couldn't barge through the group. "Excuse me, Detective Brown?"

At the sound of my voice, the detective asked his colleagues to give him some privacy to speak to me. They trickled away.

Detective Brown wound up the ball of yarn before he paid attention to me. "Miss Lee," he then said, "have a seat."

The chair squeaked when I pulled it out and sat down. "You've got your hands full with that one, Detective." I gave a pointed look at Nimbus.

He let out a hint of a smile. "That kitten sure is one furry troublemaker."

"Nimbus gathered quite a crowd."

"Oh, the entire station loves her. They practically want to make her our mascot."

I beckoned to the cat. "Come here, Nimbus."

She came to me, letting out a long purr.

"Traitor," Detective Brown said, shaking his head at the kitten. "After I fed you all those tuna flakes."

"Did you end up taking her to the vet for a checkup?" I asked while stroking Nimbus.

"Yes." He swiped some gray fur off his lap. "A clean bill of health. No diseases."

The words sprang out of my mouth. "Told you so."

He shrugged. "Needed to dot all the i's."

"Great. Now I can take Nimbus back." I took a deep breath and said, "Also, did you realize the janitor was on campus at the time of Helen Reed's death?"

"Yes." Detective Brown took out a worn notepad. "But how did you find out?"

"I remembered that the flags weren't taken down yet when I met up with my sister—I'm pretty sure he does that every evening after school. I also know that he wasn't around when the ambulance showed up. Doesn't that seem suspicious?"

The detective flipped through his notepad. "We got his statement. He was in the bungalows mopping and didn't hear a thing."

Really? Detective Brown had let the man off easy. Where was that kind of leniency when I was under suspicion? "What about the broken glass in Helen's classroom?"

Detective Brown took out a pen and tapped it against his coffee-ringed desk. "We noticed that as well. From a table lamp."

"How much glass was there? Maybe Helen cut herself and got an infection."

"Only a single bulb." Detective Brown closed his notepad. "She couldn't have sustained severe injuries from that. Or gotten sepsis that quickly."

He didn't say it, but I knew that meant he still had his sights on Alice as a suspect. Oh, why had my sister hung around Helen in the first place? But I knew she had a heart for the lonely. Hadn't Alice told me herself that her fellow teacher had been aloof and distant with people?

Hmm, maybe nobody had been involved with Helen's death. I hated to think about it, but it was something to seriously consider. "Detective Brown," I said, "you've worked at the homicide division a long time. Do you think maybe you've ruled out a very plausible alternate reason from force of habit?"

He rolled the pen back and forth between his palms. "And what would that be, Miss Lee?"

"An emotionally detached young woman is found dead in a parking lot. She'd been suffering from a stomachache. Couldn't she have taken something deadly?"

Detective Brown dropped the pen on his desk with a clatter, and it rolled onto the floor.

"Maybe she decided to end it all," I said.

"That scenario doesn't feel right to me."

My cheeks heated up. "You're suspecting murder based on intuition?"

He clenched his jaw. "I'm going to wait for the autopsy report before I make my final verdict. But, Miss Lee, I didn't find a note."

I gave him a blank stare.

"A suicide note."

"Maybe you just haven't located it yet."

A vein started throbbing in his forehead, and I excused myself. I'd better get going. Besides, his mention of a note reminded me of something else.

The message to the principal from Helen Reed. It hadn't looked like a suicide note but had involved some legalese with letters and numbers. Maybe a critical turn of phrase. And I knew someone reliable who could translate that for me.

• • •

Marshmallow followed me as I strolled over to Josh's apartment, holding a grocery bag in one hand and cradling Nimbus with my other arm.

At his unit, I said, "Marshmallow, a little help, please."

My cat scratched on the bottom part of the door with his sharp claws.

Josh opened the door with a wide grin on his face. "At last, I've been looking forward to some quality time with you . . . Marshmallow."

Marshmallow preened while I snorted at Josh's joke.

Josh took the groceries from me but did a double-take at the gray fur in my arms. "Did you get another cat?"

"Just temporarily. Until I find the right owner for her." I placed the kitten down inside the apartment. "Her name is Nimbus."

Josh peeked into the grocery bag. "Are you cooking for me?" His dark brown eyes shone.

"In a manner of speaking. You know, I'm more of a microwave gal, but I'll feed you. Besides, cold food is a tradition with us, right?" The first time Josh had made me dinner, he'd served me spam musubi and poke.

As I walked farther into his apartment, I noticed Nimbus scampering toward Josh's distinctive dining table.

Fsh. A sound like the wind rushed in my ears. I turned back to the open door, but the outside showed me a balmy evening.

"Are you cold?" Josh rushed to close the door. Then he wrapped a comforting warm arm around my shoulder.

I leaned against him.

Fsh. My eyes widened as I finally registered the noise as coming from near Nimbus. Right where she stood admiring Josh's table carved into the shape of a—

"Fish," I said, pointing.

"Right," Josh said. "It's the humuhumunukunukuapua`a, remember? Hawaii's state fish." His parents had bought the special table for him to remind Josh of his roots.

"You seem warm enough now," Josh said. He moved his arm away and headed toward the kitchen with the grocery bag.

While Josh had his back turned to us, I tapped Marshmallow on his head. I pointed to Nimbus and made a sock puppet talking motion with my hand.

Marshmallow blinked at me. "You heard Nimbus speak?"

A little. I held my index finger and thumb a centimeter apart.

Marshmallow cocked his head at Nimbus. "Must be the fancy transmitter with its high frequency. As an animal lover, you might pick up an echo. Besides, Josh didn't hear anything. Speaking of—"

Josh cleared his throat, and I turned around to see him looking at us through the cut-out window of the kitchen. "Everything okay with Marshmallow?"

"He's fine."

"You seemed to be staring at him for a long time."

"He had a piece of lint stuck in his fur."

I pinched away an invisible speck from his body.

Marshmallow bristled. "What? I'm immaculate. Josh won't believe you."

"Glad he's now up to your professional standards," Josh said, unloading the groceries. He placed a loaf of bread, a metal can, and various produce on his kitchen counter. "Need a helping hand?"

"That would defeat the purpose of my cooking for you," I said, my hands on my hips in mock anger.

Josh didn't listen. Instead, when I went into the kitchen, he remained there. I began prepping the ingredients.

Finally, realizing he wouldn't leave, I kept him busy toasting slices of bread. Plus, those would make up half the meal: kaya toast.

When the food in my own pantry got scarce, I usually opted for a quick peanut butter and banana sandwich. Sometimes, though, I craved a more tropical taste.

I fiddled with the can of *kaya* on Josh's countertop.

"What is that?" he asked. Admittedly, the tin looked like it held tuna more than anything else.

"It's *kaya*. From the Malay word meaning 'rich.'"

Once I peeled back the cover, Josh inhaled the scent. "Smells like coconut."

"It's sort of like jam." *Kaya*, made from creamy coconut milk, tasted heart-wrenchingly sweet and brought back childhood memories of Ma spreading thick layers of it on my toast for breakfast.

While we waited for the toaster to heat the bread, I pulled out the salad fixings. I'd bought pineapple, jicama, bean sprouts, and deep-fried tofu.

"Where's the lettuce?" Josh asked.

I shrugged. "It's not a green salad. More like a fruit and vegetable mix."

"Let's make it together."

Using two cutting boards, Josh and I sliced and chopped in a happy rhythm. Despite not wanting his help in the first place, I liked standing side by side focused on the same task. And when we mixed our ingredients together, it felt like we'd been united by food.

Josh smiled at the bright colors greeting us from the bowl: brilliant yellow, earthy brown, and snow-white. "Perfect."

"Not yet," I said, reaching for a nearby jar. I dumped in a few tablespoons of belacan shrimp paste, stirred it in, and sprinkled crushed peanuts on top of the salad. "Voilà."

We sat down next to each other to enjoy our humble dinner. Josh seemed less than enamored with the fruit *rojak*, though. I guess the sweet, sour, and spicy salad required a certain palate.

As I watched Josh down a glass of water to get rid of the belacan taste, I figured I might as well distract him with a question. "Can you translate some legalese for me?" I struggled to remember the exact code. "CF . . . A? Um, something about a Title 29."

He scrunched his eyebrows. "Don't know those terms offhand, and I'm not going to ruin our date by looking right now. But maybe I can check my reference books when I get back to the office."

"Thanks. Let me know what you find out."

Josh picked at his salad. "Where'd you hear that phrase anyway?"

"At Roosevelt Elementary. I went there to ask a few questions."

"Uh-oh. This sounds familiar." Josh had already gone through one investigation with me. (We'd even pretended to be mock renters together on the case to narrow down the culprit.)

At his piercing look, I sighed. "Might as well tell you." I described the recent chat I'd had with Detective Brown.

Josh frowned at the cop's dogged pursuit of Alice. I bet he remembered swooping in on his legal wings to stop the detective from questioning *me* before.

Josh placed his plate of uneaten rojak to the side and bit into the kaya toast. "Super sweet," he said, before hurrying to refill his empty water glass.

When he returned, I heard his stomach grumbling. He'd be too polite to complain, so I made a snap decision. Pulling out my phone, I dialed and ordered a pizza for the poor guy.

He gave me a grateful grin and said, "Well, I admit that was definitely a culinary experience."

With a soft chuckle, I said, "I try to keep our dates interesting."

"Everything's an adventure with you." He touched my face with his gentle fingers. "Just stay safe while doing it."

I knew he was referring to my snooping. "Don't worry. I've got my bodyguard, Marshmallow here." I jerked my thumb at my cat, who lounged on the floor nearby.

Marshmallow blinked at me. "You should be protecting *moi*. As a talking cat, I'm extremely valuable. One in a million, or rather a gazillion."

I glanced at Nimbus, resting underneath the table.

He followed my gaze. "That kitty? She's still in training."

Josh and I said goodbye, and I lingered in his embrace for a few precious moments. Then I headed out the door with the cats in tow.

While crossing the empty courtyard, I thought back to Marshmallow's joke. "What you said back there is actually true. You're both valuable cats. So how come Nimbus didn't have some type of tracker? Especially since you'd already succeeded in your great escape from the same fellow."

"You give humans more credit than they deserve," Marshmallow said. "Right, Nimbus?"

He proceeded to let Nimbus in on the conversation. The kitten stopped short before the threshold of my apartment and gave a plaintive cry.

Marshmallow's jaw dropped.

"What is it?" I asked, looking back and forth between the two cats.

In the dim evening light, Marshmallow turned his glowing eyes toward me. "Nimbus did have a tracker. On a break-away collar. She got it off by rubbing her neck against some bushes near the school."

Nimbus started shivering.

I scooped her up. "Then it might only be a matter of time before Edgar finds her." Rushing them indoors, I made sure to lock up tight. The deadbolt slid closed with a satisfying solid *thunk*.

CHAPTER

≈ ten ≈

TOOK THE CATS to work with me the next day. At Hollywoof, I couldn't help but feel nervous whenever the bell jingled. No Edgar, though. Everybody who came walked in with a pet. I settled into my normal routine while keeping an eye on the lounging cats by the plate glass window.

The third client of the day distracted me from my troubles entirely. His owner requested that I groom the dog into another animal. It required all of my creativity and concentration to transform the white poodle into a zebra.

First, I shaved off most of his fur, sculpting a mane that flowed from the top of his head to his upper body. I also left the fuzz near the bottoms of his legs to create pompoms around his paws. I tried out my new special-ordered nontoxic pet dye and sprayed black onto him in a striped pattern.

The spray paint dried quickly, and when I brought the zebra-oodle back out, I realized his owner hadn't returned yet. Both Marshmallow and Nimbus stared at the transformed animal.

Marshmallow sniffed. "I don't blame the owner for wanting a change. Imagine looking at a dog all day long."

Nimbus yowled, and Marshmallow cocked his head toward her. "I can't believe it. Nimbus wants to go near the dog and take a closer look."

Marshmallow and the poodle exchanged a few words—well, barks or whatever. Nimbus crept over to the poodle, but the docile dog didn't seem to mind her intense scrutiny.

Then Nimbus came over to me and did figure-eight turns around my legs.

"I'll take that as a compliment," I said to her.

The owner returned, but he'd thrown on a trench coat over his clothes and carried an umbrella. I noticed Nimbus dash under the front desk, and I wrinkled my nose at the sight.

However, I had to focus on the customer. "Is it raining?" I asked.

"Drizzling, and I don't want my baby to get wet." He took off his coat. "In fact, I might wrap him in this."

Nimbus crept back out from under the desk and studied the pet owner as he paid for the grooming. The man left me a generous tip.

After the owner left, I turned to Marshmallow. "Nimbus acted oddly. What was with the hiding?"

Marshmallow turned to the kitten and questioned her using some staccato meows.

As the conversation continued, Nimbus seemed to shrink into herself and grow smaller.

Finally, Marshmallow translated for me. "She's got a bad association with large coats."

"How so?" I asked.

"Seems like she saw a dark figure draped in a huge coat very recently."

"When and where was this?"

"Outside Roosevelt Elementary." Marshmallow's blue eyes looked deep into mine. "And get this. Nimbus saw this eerie man the day Helen Reed died."

I gasped. "Did she say anything else?"

"Yeah." Marshmallow bared his teeth. "Even through the chain-link fence, she could smell smoke on the guy. Bet you he stank of cheap cigars."

"Sounds like your mad scientist master. Could he have been involved in Helen's death somehow?"

Marshmallow growled. "I wouldn't put it past the guy."

Right then, the door to my shop opened, and Alice walked in.

What was my sister doing here? I hurried over to her. "Is everything okay?"

"Yes," she said. "I wanted to check on Nimbus." She strode over to the kitten and stroked the top of her head.

Marshmallow approached my sister and grunted.

Alice also gave Marshmallow a love pat on his head.

"About time." He purred for a long stretch.

"No takers yet for Nimbus?" Alice asked.

"I'm still vetting candidates." I needed to delay the inevitable. Not only because Nimbus was so cute and deserved the best, but since she might also be a key witness to a crime.

"Actually, I do have another reason for stopping in," Alice said. She handed me a flyer printed on cotton candy pink paper.

"'Family and Friends Day,'" I read.

"Principal Lewis told me you gave him the idea."

I laughed. "Only because I couldn't put faces to your coworkers' names. He mentioned a lunch group trio . . ."

"Jessie, Amy, and Donna?"

"Uh, right."

"I'm sure you'll get their names straight once you meet them in person."

A loud *ding* erupted from my phone and drew me away from the conversation. Josh's name came up, and I hurried to reply.

Josh: Can't find CFA. Could it be CFR you saw?

Me: It's very possible.

Josh: Code of Federal Regulations. Title 29. Well, section 1604.1 covers work discrimination against those who are pregnant. Is this any help?

From the corner of my eye, I saw Alice glance at her watch.

Me: Thanks, Josh. Got to go now. Doing some sister bonding. XO.

I put my phone back in my purse, feeling caught off guard. Pregnancy? Perhaps there had been a reason behind Helen's upset stomach.

Crinkling the pink flyer, I asked, "Do you think Helen could have been pregnant?"

"Excuse me?" Alice backed up a step.

"I thought it might explain her nausea."

"I see." Alice picked at her cuticle. "She never said anything to me about being pregnant, but she was dating someone."

Hmm. If Helen had been in a relationship (and maybe pregnant), she probably wouldn't have chosen suicide. Then Detective Brown might be on the right track. Homicide.

Alice tapped the flyer in my hand. "Why are you asking all these questions anyway?"

I sighed. "When I went to drop off your cheesecake, I happened to see a note addressed to Principal Lewis from Helen."

"She said something about being pregnant?" Alice's brow furrowed.

"Not exactly." I described the glimpse of a note I'd read and Josh's translation of the legal code I'd remembered. "He was the one texting me just now."

Alice gave me a side glance. "Are you bringing Josh to the Family and Friends Day?"

"No, he's way too busy." Also, the truth was I didn't think he'd appreciate seeing me snooping around again, my entire goal for the social event. "But I'll definitely bring the cats."

Marshmallow began purring, and Nimbus joined the chorus.

"I'm thinking about extending an invite, too," Alice said.

"Ooh. Who's the lucky guy? Have you been holding out on me?"

She shook her head. "I'm talking about our parents. We should tag team and convince them to attend."

"Huh?" Although truth be told, it had been a long time since they'd done something together. Dad had his golf, while Ma joined the gossiping aunties at the mah jong table. "Well, maybe. What's your plan for getting them to say yes?"

She jingled her keys at me. "Boba run."

CHAPTER
⚌ *eleven* ⚌

A T THE TAPIOCA café, Alice and I stocked up on our parents'
favorite drinks. (We also added our own faves to the mix.) My
sister chose the peach kiwi green tea with aiyu jelly, and I opted for
hazelnut milk tea with golden boba. For Ma, we got taro milk tea with
boba, a bright purple drink that didn't match the color of the root vegetable in real life.

Dad, on the other hand, couldn't stand boba. The chewy black balls
made from tapioca starch made him gag. We'd tried to initiate him into
the beverage, but he insisted that "chewing and drinking something at
the same time is nuts—pick one or the other." He also disliked the tapioca texture; the glossy coat felt too slimy, and the chewiness seemed
indecisive, unable to boldly go to either extreme of crispy or soft.

When we showed up at my parents' place, I smiled upon seeing the
familiar ranch house. I'd grown up in the one-story cookie-cutter building. With its load of cozy memories, it felt like visiting an old friend.

Alice rang the doorbell, and Dad answered.

"Surprise!" I said.

He beamed. "And what a wonderful one at that. Both of my princesses on my doorstep."

Dad started in on the hugging. First, he scooped Alice into his embrace. We'd long passed the stage where he could hug both of us at the same time.

When it got to my turn, I relaxed in his arms. Everything felt all right when he held me in his big six-foot frame.

I looked into his warm brown eyes. "Thanks, Dad. I needed that."

Dad wore his typical golfing attire: belted shorts and a polo with its imitation unicorn logo.

"We brought you and Ma drinks," Alice said, lifting up the cardboard cup holder so he could see.

"Boba?" he said, making a face as he waved us inside.

"Don't worry. We ordered something else for you," Alice said.

Walking into the interior of the home, I was reminded how much I loved the mishmash of the house I grew up in. Two cultures crisscrossed in an odd fusion that somehow worked. For example, I delighted in the lucky goldfish sketches which hung on the Benjamin Moore muted color walls.

Dad sat down at our dining table, and Alice placed our family's drinks on the lazy Susan. While Dad grabbed the iced coffee (without boba), Alice and I peered around the common living area.

"Where's Ma?" I asked.

"In the bedroom," Dad said. "She told me she had a headache."

I gave Alice a nod, indicating that I'd check on Ma. She started chatting with Dad about his latest golf game while I moved toward the master bedroom.

After knocking on the closed door, I heard, "Greg, I very sick. Feel like died-ed."

"It's me, Ma."

"Mimi?"

I opened the door to find Ma in the California king bed with its bamboo headboard. She seemed to be browsing through a thick photo album.

Walking over to her side, I placed my palm against her forehead. No fever. "Are you okay?"

"Need quiet—nobody *kacau* me here."

"So you can look at these pictures?" I saw younger versions of Ma and Dad wearing unfashionable clothes peering back at me.

She pointed at the photo of them smiling. "We at Malaysia."

"Was this taken during the bus tour?"

She nodded.

My parents had fallen in love while Dad was visiting the country for business. After the required conference, he'd taken extra vacation days to extend his trip. One of the tour guides on the extended bus ride happened to have been Ma.

Ma flipped the page. "Look, wedding," she said.

I peered over Ma's shoulder at the sepia photo. Ma wore a lacy white gown, and Dad had donned a tuxedo. I wouldn't have known it was taken in another country if she hadn't told me. Though Ma did wear a hibiscus in her hair, the national flower of Malaysia. "You look so beautiful, Ma. You and Dad make a great couple."

Ma squeezed the bridge of her nose and blinked.

I continued, "Alice and I brought you some taro milk tea. Want to join us at the dining table?"

She caressed the edge of the gilded photo album. "Put fridge can ah?"

"Ma, there's boba in the drink." When refrigerated, tapioca balls grew rock hard and inedible over time.

She waved me away. "You go lah. I stay."

I gave her a worried look, but she ignored me. She concentrated on the old photographs before her. It was a lost cause to change Ma's mind once she'd decided something. Biting my tongue, I backed out of the master bedroom.

When I returned to the common area, I found Dad and Alice still chatting away. Alice raised her eyebrows at me. As sisters, we didn't need to exchange words in order to understand each other. I shook my head. *No, Ma doesn't want to come out of her room.*

"So, do you think you two can make it to this?" Alice asked Dad, tapping the pink flyer on the table.

He squinted at it and harrumphed. "Need my reading glasses to see a darn thing."

"I'll tell you the details." Alice summarized the Family and Friends Day at the school.

"Such short notice," Dad said. "What day is it again?"

Alice repeated the date.

His face fell. "I can't. I already set up a game with Walt."

I pointed at the word "Family" on the paper. "Maybe you and Ma *should* go," I said. "She seems down and perhaps getting out—"

A blaring sound came from the kitchen. "My phone," Dad said, rushing to the counter and grabbing it. "Sorry, Princesses One and Two. I need to take this call."

Dad moved away from us into another room, but I heard him say "Walt" before he went out of range.

Alice and I looked at each other across the dining table.

"What's going on with Ma?" my sister asked.

"I'm not sure, but she's really sad. And Dad doesn't get it." I shook my head. Why would he be spending his time talking to Walt instead of to her?

But those were minor puzzles compared to the main mystery I needed to solve. I gazed at my sweet little sister. First things first. I needed to clear Alice's name from the murder case. I knew just the place—and event—to do some extra sleuthing.

* * *

It took time to wrangle the cats, and I arrived late to Family and Friends Day at Roosevelt Elementary. Already after the lunch hour, the sun shone down its fierce golden rays.

On the school's lawn, I spied half a dozen people. I thought there'd be higher attendance. Maybe the short notice had thrown off the numbers.

Alice waved to me from the shade of a jacaranda tree at the back of the field. Its brilliant lavender flowers had blossomed earlier than usual this year and added a nice touch of color to the lawn.

I spread my checkered picnic blanket half in the shade and half in the sunshine. The cats, of course, took over the sunbathing area.

"Oh, Mimi," Alice said. "You just missed the most beautiful poem that the principal shared on behalf of Helen."

"Sorry, I had a hard time getting out the door."

"I recorded it, so I can send it to you."

Thank goodness my sister didn't hold a grudge. To ensure her continued goodwill, though, I gave her some curry puffs. They were akin to spicy Asian empanadas. I'd purchased them at the local bakery since I knew Ma would be in no mood to bake them for the event.

"Thanks," Alice said. "Don't take too long eating, though. The ravens around here love swooping down and snatching food."

I bit into my curry puff, savoring the spiced meat and potato mixture inside. While eating, I spied the principal. He sat closer to the blacktop area and waved at me from his low-slung camping chair.

At first, he made a move to get up, but then stopped himself. He plopped back down in his chair.

"Too much effort to get up and say hello?" I asked.

"He's been in a funk lately," Alice said and chewed on her curry puff.

I wondered if it had anything to do with the note he'd received from Helen Reed.

"What's under the canopy over there?" I asked, motioning to what looked like a tent in the middle of the clover-strewn field.

Alice used her half-eaten puff to point toward that direction. Some of the filling spilled onto the picnic blanket. She scooped it back up and stuffed it into her mouth—my sister lived by the five-second rule, while it made me cringe.

"Those would be the Gemini twins," she said, ignoring my look of disgust. "Jessie and Amy share the same sign and always sit together at lunch. They teach similar ages to the class that Helen did, but Amy has a combo class."

"I thought it was a group who ate together, more like the Three Musketeers?" I said. "A trio in the lunchroom."

"Yes, the two of them . . . and Donna. She sits in the staff room, but she's decades older than the other two. And here she is." Alice waved her arms around to attract the attention of a newcomer. An older lady dressed in a flowery homespun dress that might have been a hit in the seventies wandered over, a grocery bag in her hand. Bushy white hair crowned her wrinkled face. She walked with wavering steps toward us in a pair of orthopedic shoes.

I whispered to Alice. "She's not retired yet?"

"No, she's only in her early sixties." Alice stood up when the older lady reached us. "Hi, Donna! Would you like to sit with us?"

Donna lowered herself down with Alice's help and kneeled. She looked mighty uncomfortable. Before I could say anything, Alice spoke up. "I'll ask Richard for a folding chair."

My sister left to find the janitor, and I introduced myself to Donna. "Alice loves her kindergarten kids. What grade do you teach?"

She scowled. "The new principal switched me to fifth grade this year."

"Oh, really?" I finished my curry puff and brushed the crumbs away. "Is it common to change grades?"

"Not for me." Her veined hands fluttered in the air. "The nerve of him. I've taught second grade for decades. I'm comfortable with that age."

She must have been around Roosevelt Elementary for a while and could serve as a fount of information. "Did you know Helen Reed?"

Donna fluffed her white hair. "It sure is a shame when young people die. But life is often like that."

"Was she pretty healthy?"

She shrugged. "I've known folks to get headaches. The next thing I hear, they've gone and died from an aneurysm."

I shuddered. "That sounds terrible. Did you happen to see Helen on that last day? She look any different than usual?"

Donna opened her sack lunch and pulled out a saltine cracker. She nibbled at it. "She seemed fine to me, but she did eat her lunch with a dreamy look on her face."

"Lost in thought?"

Donna finished her cracker. "I find that young folks have a hard time concentrating. An experienced teacher knows how to focus." I could sense the iciness creeping into her words.

Thankfully, at that time, Alice arrived with Richard in tow. He still wore his baseball cap pulled down low. While opening the folding chair and positioning it on the grass, he stepped on Marshmallow's tail by accident.

Yeow. "Watch where you're going." Marshmallow gave the janitor a hard stare.

"Sorry, didn't see the cat there," Richard said.

Marshmallow turned his back on the janitor.

"Thanks for setting up the chair, Richard," Alice said.

He nodded at her before wandering away.

Meanwhile, Donna settled into the seat and smoothed out her dress. She dug into her grocery bag again, pulling out more crackers, along with a pouch of tuna.

I heard a faint whisper . . . *fish.* Nimbus started mewling.

Donna pointed her finger with a long, almost curved, nail at Nimbus and Marshmallow. "Who do those cats belong to?"

"They're mine," I said. "I'm sorry. Are you allergic?"

She shook her head. "I wanted to make sure those cats aren't feral. There was a pesky stray hanging around school recently."

I made a noncommittal murmur.

Donna narrowed her eyes at Nimbus. "Almost like that kitten, in fact—but with dirty brown fur."

"So," Alice said, "how are your kids this year, Donna? I can't imagine teaching subjects beyond the basics."

"It's a lot of work, dear." Donna droned on about the preparation needed to train fifth graders to enter middle school. She talked about the extra studying she'd undertaken to teach those topics to her students. As she did, she opened the pouch of tuna.

Nimbus leaped over to land next to Donna. "Fish, fish."

"You've got a one-track mind," Marshmallow said.

Donna held the pouch out of reach, above the kitten's head. At the same time, I heard a slight rattle.

I located the noise coming from the chain-link fence a few yards away. It separated the field from the public sidewalk. A lean man in a Victorian frock coat gripped the fence. Nimbus froze beside Donna.

Then I heard the swishing of wings. A large raven circled the sky above us. Donna hid the tuna in the grocery bag.

When I looked back at the fence, the stranger had fled. I had no doubt it had been Nimbus's old master.

My heart thumped. Had he seen the cats? Could he recognize Marshmallow from that distance? I wondered if he'd return soon.

On the pretense of cuddling Marshmallow, I whispered in his ear, "You'd better take a walk and hide behind the tent."

Marshmallow crept away without a single snarky comment.

I held Nimbus awhile until she calmed down. Keeping an eye on the street and the entrance to the school, I couldn't find any signs of the man. But I didn't think he was gone for good.

After a few more minutes of checking, I placed Nimbus in Alice's lap. "Could you watch her? Marshmallow seems to have wandered off."

I excused myself and approached the canopy. Two voices floated toward me, one emitting a bullfrog-like croaking and the other sounding like a chattering squirrel.

"It's karma. She was supposed to get laid off last year but . . ." the deeper voice croaked.

"She cheated the system," the chipper lady replied.

"Or had some sort of sway."

"What are you saying?"

"I saw a private note addressed to the principal from Hel—" The bullfrog lady cried out in alarm, "A cat! Get it away from me."

I darted to the front of the tent, where I spied two women lounging. One had her hair up in a high ponytail and wore a fluorescent green outfit. She shrugged and said, "It's just a cat."

The other, with her hair pulled tight into a bun, was wearing a Mr. Rogers–esque knit sweater. She fanned herself and muttered, "Thank goodness it's not a *black* cat. Scared me half to death."

Then they blinked at me as if I were a ghost who had appeared in front of them out of thin air. Perhaps I had. Their tent did act as a canvas barrier between them and the outside world.

"Hi, I'm Mimi Lee," I said and pointed to Marshmallow. "I'm his owner."

The bun lady croaked at me. "I didn't see a collar on that thing."

Marshmallow yowled. "*Thing?* And I don't do collars, lady. They choke me."

"Lee. That last name sounds so familiar," Miss Ponytail said. "My name's Jessie, and this is my friend Amy."

I shook hands with Jessie and kept Marshmallow away from Amy, who'd pulled out an economy-size hand sanitizer. She squirted and rubbed her hands with vigor.

"Don't worry. I keep Marshmallow meticulous," I said, smoothing his fur. "I'm a pet groomer by profession."

"Oh, please." Marshmallow would probably have rolled his eyes if he could have. "Cats can bathe themselves just fine."

"My sister's Alice Lee," I said, pointing to underneath the jacaranda tree, where my sister still sat. "She teaches kindergarten."

"I don't really mingle with instructors of *babies*," Amy said. "The upper grades have separate recesses."

"Well, you must know Donna then," I said, gesturing to the older lady as she chatted with my sister. "She teaches fifth grade."

Amy sniffed. "We three used to all teach second grade and be peers, but Donna got bumped up."

"The principal actually made Donna move up, so her old spot could be given to Helen." Jessie's voice wobbled on the dead woman's name.

I sighed. "It's so sad about Helen. The paramedics tried everything."

Amy gasped while Jessie leaned forward. She looked ready to pounce on my next words. "You were there when it happened? It was all so hush-hush on campus, though we heard an ambulance showed up."

Maybe her morbid curiosity could help me make a connection. "Helen was already gone when I discovered her. However, the police talked to me as a witness."

Amy shivered.

Jessie oohed. "Did the cops say what happened?"

I gave her a Mona Lisa smile. "What do you believe occurred?"

Jessie struck a thinking pose, her chin propped on her hand. "I know that it's not suicide. Her dad's loaded."

He was? So Helen wasn't the usual low-salaried teacher working on love for kids.

Amy piped up. "That doesn't mean a thing. Rich people get depressed—maybe even more than others—and money isn't everything."

"Having more in my bank account would make me happier, not sadder," Jessie said.

"It was probably an accident," Amy said. She rubbed her back and rummaged in the tent to find a soft cushion and placed it behind her.

Jessie tugged at the end of her ponytail and tossed out more conjectures. "What about an overdose? Or murder?"

Amy clucked her tongue. "This is real life, Jessie. Not some murder mystery show." She wagged a finger my way. "Please put her mind at ease. Tell her what the police actually said."

"It's inconclusive," I said.

"We can still make guesses then," Jessie said. "This is the most exciting thing that's happened to me since getting voted prom queen." She gave a million-watt smile to an imaginary crowd.

Amy mumbled, "Even after so many years."

All of a sudden, a loud string of curses came from outside the tent, so salty they made my ears burn.

"Yes," Jessie said. "More drama happening."

I peeked beyond the side of the tent shelter. Was it Edgar come back to catnap Marshmallow and Nimbus?

Nope.

On the blacktop, a man stood towering over the seated principal. The stranger wore conservative dark business attire, but he'd looped a bright patterned scarf around his neck.

I bet everyone around the grassy field could hear him. He continued yelling. "Where did you put her things?"

Principal Lewis stood from his chair and rose up to his full height. His voice also carried across the lawn. "Please calm down, Mr. Reed. We can go into my office to talk."

Mr. Reed stomped his polished shoe on the blacktop. "After what I donated to this school last year, you should know to treat me better."

What? I snuck a glance at Alice. Had that been how Helen Reed had escaped the pink slip last year while my sister had been threatened? I bet with the old principal that money had spoken loudly and swayed her decision.

Principal Lewis shook his head. "Sorry, I had a hard time reaching you overseas. To answer your question, I sent her possessions back to her roommate—"

"Take me right now to Helen's classroom. I want to see it." Mr. Reed marched toward the principal, who backed up a few inches.

I decided to get some distance from the argument and returned to Alice's side, Marshmallow trailing behind me. "He's being so mean to Principal Lewis," I said to my sister.

Her eyebrows drew together. "It could be the sudden news. Death makes people act weird."

I nodded. I'd read all about the Kübler-Ross stages of grief in my undergrad textbooks. Helen's father seemed very stuck in the anger stage.

I jerked my thumb at Mr. Reed, who had lowered his voice now. No longer could I distinguish every word he spoke to the principal.

"Strange," Alice said. "The way Helen avoided talking about her parents, I almost thought they were both dead."

"Her father looks very much alive at least," I said. "And extremely mad about not being able to see his daughter's things."

Alice slapped her palm against her forehead. "Poor Marina. She must feel devastated."

"Who?"

"Helen's roommate. I've met her once before. Helen's car was in the shop, and I ended up dropping her off at her place."

Really? My mind worked double-time. Seeing Helen's home and her belongings might yield some valuable information.

Nimbus purred from near my feet.

"We should visit Marina," I said.

"Of course, to give her our condolences." Alice paused. "If you don't think it'll be too intrusive . . ."

I shook off the picnic blanket and folded it up. "I think it'll be fine. Plus, she is missing one more thing that belonged to Helen—a very adorable kitten."

CHAPTER

twelve

HELEN AND MARINA lived in a gorgeous sandstone townhouse. It didn't share any walls with its neighbors, and a small patch of blossoming petunias greeted our group of four near the front steps.

Nimbus purred in my arms. "Do you like the place?" I asked, stroking her ears.

Marshmallow scratched at the door. "Nimbus said she recognizes it here."

Before I could ponder his statement further, Alice had rung the bell. Pattering footsteps sounded behind the white wooden door. "Coming," a female voice sang out.

Marina turned out to be a young woman with wild wavy brown hair. She clasped her hands together at the sight of us, jangling the bamboo bracelets on her bronze skin. "Alice, it's so great to see you again. And I can tell this is your sister."

I nodded. "I'm Mimi. Sorry, I brought these cats along. Hope you don't mind."

She didn't give them a second glance as she said, "The more the merrier. I could use the company. The place feels so empty now that—" Her voice broke, and Alice gave her a hug.

Once Marina had recovered, she welcomed us into the clean, bright home. Everything was done in a crisp white, from the fluffy carpet to the furniture to even the light fixtures. The kitchen cabinets were coated in white paint, too, and sported chrome handles. The only "splash of color" came from the beige curtains at the windows.

A lone staircase crept up to the second floor, where the bedrooms must have been located since I could already spy the rest of the space on the bottom level. When I passed by the stairs, I noticed a small door embedded underneath them. "What's that?"

Marina giggled. "Our Harry Potter space." A bedroom under the stairs.

Alice, Marina, and I settled on the downy white sofa, while I made sure to place Nimbus on the carpet. The better to keep her gray fur off the plump cushions.

Marshmallow, though, curled up on the arm of the couch.

I narrowed my eyes at him.

"What?" he said. "My fur is snow-white."

Marina didn't complain about his lounging, though. Instead, she focused her attention on my sister, who'd started speaking.

"Do you need any help?" Alice asked. "Meals or something?"

"No, I've got a stash of frozen food, and there's a bunch of easy meal delivery options. Plus, I stay late anyway working hard at Déjà Vu."

I cocked my head, and Marina registered my confusion. "Oh, that's the name of the antique store I work at. I've been putting extra hours in. Even working tomorrow, though I usually take Sundays off."

"Totally understandable. It's good to stay busy so you're not dwelling on, um, the situation constantly," Alice said with soulful eyes.

"Or is she working more to pay the rent?" Marshmallow whispered. "This place must cost a lot of greenbacks. I spotted both an Olympic-size pool and a high-tech gym outside."

Marina started tearing up as she said, "It's lonely here without Helen. I can't even bear to look at her stuff, much less touch her things. Haven't moved a single item."

Really? Everything was in the same state as before her death? My eyes flicked toward the upstairs bedrooms, and Marshmallow caught my glance. He gave me a nod and slipped off the couch. Nobody else noticed him leave.

Gazing around the modern minimalist space, I said to Marina, "You have a beautiful place."

She rubbed her forehead. "Thank you. I've lived here for three years, and it keeps getting better. Not only do we have a spacious unit, everything's well maintained. And we get high-speed Internet plus cable."

I fluffed the cushion behind my back. "Hopefully, you won't have to move out. Would you need to find a new roommate to stay in the complex?"

Alice frowned at me. Oops. Was I being tactless mentioning this so close after Helen's death? Or being practical? I blamed it on the Older Sibling Mentality.

"It might be complicated," Marina said as her brow furrowed.

My sister patted her arm while shooting me a look that said, *Really?*

"Shouldn't be very hard with the two master bedrooms. That's a huge perk."

"Well . . ." Marina rubbed at her temples. "Helen actually bought the place, and I rented from her under the table."

"Oh," Alice said, "she didn't tell me that."

No wonder Marina had claimed it'd be complicated. What would happen now? Especially with Helen's father on a rampage and reclaiming her things?

I leaned toward Marina. "Um, I should let you know. We saw Mr. Reed at Roosevelt Elementary. He seemed really upset, and he may be paying you a visit soon."

"Helen detested him." Marina rubbed at her forehead with force and bent over Nimbus. "Why does this kitten look familiar?"

"She was a stray hanging around school . . . I think Helen was looking after her."

Marina leaned away from Nimbus. "I never quite know what triggers my migraines, but my head hurt before when this cat was around."

"Helen brought the kitten here?" I asked.

"Yes." Marina closed her eyes and sat back on the couch. "She wanted to keep the kitten, but I couldn't handle it."

"Oh, I'm sorry," I said.

Alice's eyes grew wide. "We'd better get going then."

I nodded and made a pretense of looking around the living room. "Only I can't find Marshmallow." I cupped my hands around my mouth and bellowed for him.

A fierce meow came from upstairs.

"Let me grab him. I'll be real quick," I said.

I left the others in the sitting room and sprinted up the stairs. Two doors remained wide open on the second level, but I focused on the one with a purring cat in it. A wooden sign made into the letter "H" hung on the white door.

"What did you find, Marshmallow?" I asked as I entered Helen's bedroom.

The area displayed the same color scheme as downstairs. The furniture all looked the color of bleached dental enamel, except for the beige bedspread and curtains in the room.

Helen had kept a tidy bedroom. No piles of junk lying around. I even peeked into the bathroom, where I found items organized in various caddies.

In the sleeping area, nothing looked out of place. The gleaming mirrored doors of the closet were pulled shut. The bed was made with neat precision, the corners of the comforter tucked in. A nightstand held just a picture frame and a charging cord. I looked for the accompanying phone, but no such luck.

"What did I miss, Marshmallow?"

He jumped onto the taut bed and gestured with his paw at the nightstand. "Who's in the photo?"

I shrugged. "Marina and Helen?" The roommates seemed to be good friends.

Up close, I realized my mistake. It was decidedly not a roommate photo. A dazzling blond hunk stood a few inches away from Helen. Her eyes sparkled in her round face, and her light brown hair seemed to have extra shine as though also glowing from her inner excitement.

My sister called up to me from downstairs. "Mimi, did you find him?"

"Yep, coming down right now."

Marshmallow and I hurried back to my sister and Marina.

"Sorry," I said. "Got distracted by this glamorous shot of Helen and a handsome guy."

Marina, now flung across the back of the couch, opened one eye. "That's her fiancé, Brandon."

"She was *engaged*?" my sister and I said at the same time.

"Yeah," Marina said.

"Where did they meet?" I asked.

"At the beach. He works as a surf instructor at All Tide Up." Marina's voice grew distant. "Oof, I think I need to sleep this headache off."

When we left the townhouse, Marshmallow butted my leg with his head. "What was wrong with Marina?"

I did a slight rub of my head along with a pained expression.

"All of a sudden?" Marshmallow gave a soft hiss.

I held Nimbus in my arms and stroked her fur, tapping on the emitter's location. It made sense to me that the high frequency might mess with Marina's head. Thank goodness I seemed to be immune to the waves. Then again, Dad always said I had a hard head.

I turned to my sister and said, "Engaged. Imagine that. They really did look like a picture-perfect couple."

Probably not suicide then. Unless things had soured between the pair. And that reminded me of an imperative relationship I needed to fix . . .

• • •

After leaving the cats at home, I headed to the local country club. A sprawl of sun-soaked Mediterranean buildings clustered around the emerald green hills. Since the club was located on a cliff that flanked the Pacific Ocean, golf balls often flew into the glittering waters. My dad played there because of his tight connection to Walt, a client he'd worked as a financial consultant for over the past decade.

I looked for Dad on the huge vastness of lush green. It'd be hard to spot him from a distance, but I hoped to recognize his familiar huge frame or lumbering gait.

I stood there burning in the hot sun in my T-shirt—why had I worn black again? As I shielded my eyes with my hand to peer at the flagged holes in the distance, a golf cart zoomed up to me.

Pixie St. James, beloved sponsor of Hollywoof, waved at me from the driver's seat. Though she didn't wear her usual pantsuit and sported reflective aviator sunglasses that covered up half her face, I still recognized her signature cropped hair and slim stature.

She blew a kiss at me. "Mimi, what are you doing at the links?"

"My dad plays here regularly. Have you seen a bear of a man about six feet tall?" I described his typical golf attire, right down to his unicorn knockoff polo shirt.

Pixie pursed her elegant lips. "Can't say I have, but I just got here."

"I didn't even know you played golf."

She patted the bag next to her, full of shiny clubs. "Only when I need to. I rarely use these, but sometimes clients want to talk business while golfing. I've probably seen all the courses here in the L.A. area at least once."

As CEO of her tech business, she would need to schmooze with people who invested in the costly sport of golf. "If you see my dad," I said, "tell him to go to the juice bar."

"Will do," Pixie said as she restarted her cart. "And don't be a stranger, Mimi. Let's get together at my place one of these evenings."

After watching Pixie cut across the lawn, I ambled over to the juicery. If he wasn't fixated on getting below par on his scorecard, I'd find Dad in the snack area for sure. A cheaper alternative to the fancy restaurant next door, it boasted wheatgrass drinks, fruit-flavored sparkling waters, and an extensive array of quinoa snacks. The juice bar was a refuge on boiling days, and my dad often confessed that some-times he thought he spent more time there than on the green.

Predictably, I found him at a cozy table at the rear of the shop. He and his buddy Walt sat there with their heads bent together. Dad seemed to be scribbling furiously on a yellow legal pad.

Sneaking close to their table, I said, "Hi, Dad." A pause. "Uncle Walt." Ma had drilled in my head that all older family friends should be called Uncles or Aunties. When I was younger, I thought we had a very large extended family. Not that Uncle Walt looked anything like us, with his bald egg-shaped head and squinty gray eyes.

They both looked up. Dad's face turned a splotchy red while Walt averted his gaze.

"Princess One, what a surprise," Dad said while sliding his large palm over the notepad.

"Dad, I wanted to talk with you about something"—I glanced at Walt—"in private."

"This isn't the best time," Dad said. "We're really busy."

I jutted my chin. "I thought you were golfing today."

Dad coughed a little and pointed at the organic juice menu. "Tak-ing a break from the heat."

Walt lifted up his glass of sparkling water with slices of lemon bob-bing in it. "We needed to reenergize."

I steeled my voice. "It's really important, Dad. Has to do with *fam-ily*." Would he take the hint?

Dad scratched the back of his neck. "I'm sorry I missed Alice's work event. I'll be sure to apologize to her."

I couldn't stop from rolling my eyes at him. He'd identified the wrong family member to make amends to. But I couldn't bring up Ma's sour feelings with his friend present. A double dose of needing to save face and not airing dirty laundry kept me silent.

My dad raked his hand through his thinning hair. As he did so, my eyes honed in on his recognizable square handwriting. I could immediately read the uncovered words. It started out with, *We need time apart . . .*

Dad said something, but I missed it because I was too busy reading the rest of the sentence.

He cleared his throat. "I said, 'Don't worry.' Alice won't stay mad for long. It's not in her nature."

I blinked at him, and he seemed to think the matter was resolved. He returned to his writing, and their heads bent close together once more.

Dismissed, I stumbled toward the exit. Gooseflesh crawled up my arms, and it wasn't because of the frigid air conditioning.

I recalled the full sentence on the legal notepad. Dad had written in his neat penmanship: *We need time apart because I've fallen in love with someone else.*

CHAPTER

thirteen

ASKED ALICE TO come to my apartment for an emergency meeting. Before my sister arrived, the cats had just decided to take refuge under the covers of my bed. And they had no intention of leaving.

"You're an awful influence," I told Marshmallow.

"Nimbus is suffering from PTSD. Have a heart," he said.

Poor Nimbus did seem to be shivering. I stroked her. "It's okay. Your old master won't find you." I wasn't sure how I would keep my promise, but I had to try.

The doorbell rang, and I hustled to answer it and welcomed in my sister.

After hugging Alice hello, I asked, "Do you mind if we bake while chatting?" I thought it'd be better to keep our hands busy while we talked. It might also take the sting of discovery away. I knew I'd had a hard time, my hands shaking on my steering wheel, when I'd driven back from the country club.

"Sure. What are we making here?" she said.

"Doggie biscuits. We're running low at the shop. I'll stick the extra batches in the mini fridge at Hollywoof."

Alice agreed, so I placed the printed recipe on my kitchen countertop and preheated the oven. Then I laid the dry ingredients out on the counter's cracked tiles: whole wheat flour, oats, and baking powder.

I pulled out a mixing bowl and handed the egg carton to Alice.

"So, why the sudden meeting?" Alice cracked a few eggs into the bowl.

I handed her the whisk with a grumble. "I tried to track down Dad at his important golf game, the one he couldn't pull himself away from."

"It's like *Where's Waldo?* on that course. How did you ever find him?"

I added creamy peanut butter and nonfat milk to the beaten eggs. "He wasn't anywhere near his putter. I found him and Walt in the juice bar."

"It *was* pretty sunny today. Maybe we should've held the Family and Friends Day indoors." Alice dumped in the flour and baking powder.

After mixing the oats into the batter, I added my special flavoring of chopped bacon bits into the bowl. "Found him scribbling a note at one of the tables."

She stirred the ingredients together. "That's so old-fashioned. What was it for?"

My fingers clenched into fists at my side. "I can only make an educated guess. He wrote, *I've fallen in love with somebody else.*"

Alice dropped the whisk. The batter sprayed across the counter. "That can't be right. You must have misread it."

I bit my lip. "When I had lunch with Ma the other day, she complained about feeling distant from Dad. No Valentine's activity, remember? And you yourself remarked how there haven't been any anniversary celebrations recently."

My sister snatched up the whisk and whipped with fury. The bowl wobbled and half of the mix spilled out. Oh well. I didn't need that many dog biscuits anyway.

I poured the batter into bone-shaped silicon molds and slid the tray into the oven. "We need to make a plan to fix this."

Alice trudged to the sink and scrubbed her hands with soap and water. "But I know Ma and Dad love each other."

"Maybe Dad's lost some of the fire along the way."

My sister dried up and twisted the damp dish towel in her hands. "Then we need to remind him."

"Perhaps we could offer them a night out," I said as I plopped the dirty bowl into the sink.

"We can re-create how they fell in love."

"By renting a tour bus?" I soaped up the bowl, making the suds overflow and letting the hot water run over my fingers until it almost scalded me.

"We need something to help him remember their good times in Malaysia."

I rinsed out the bowl, making it sparkling clean. "Knowing Dad, he'd love anything involving food."

Alice whipped the towel up like a victory flag. "I've got it. Roti Palace."

Ma had talked about taking Dad to an eatery specializing in flatbread back in Malaysia. "Wouldn't want a more intimate setting?"

"We could do a pre-anniversary Ultimate Date Night at home, but with catered roti."

"Now you're talking." I gave my sister a high-five.

"I'll be in charge of this." She tucked a strand of hair behind her ear. "Besides, I've got some sudden extra time on my hands."

I raised my eyebrows at her.

"After you left, Principal Lewis asked to speak to me in private. Guess Detective Brown phoned him and mentioned something about the case."

My eyes narrowed. "What did the cop say?"

"Whatever it was must have been negative." A hint of pink crept up my sister's cheeks. "The principal asked me to take a few days off until things settled down."

Detective Brown. Always jumping the gun. I was glad Alice could keep her mind distracted by creating the Ultimate Date Night, but I'd need to hurry on chasing down a new lead.

There was one person who was still missing from the puzzle. I decided to take a quick jaunt to the beach and meet Helen's fiancé.

• • •

When I checked into the All Tide Up office, I marveled at the display of waxed surfboards mounted on their walls. At the info desk, though, they redirected me to find Brandon on a stretch of beach about a block away. They assured me he would have finished his lesson by the time I showed up.

At the shore, I saw Brandon waving goodbye to a client in a polka dot bikini when I arrived. Slogging through the hot sand toward him, I assessed Helen's fiancé. Artificially good-looking, but not the genuine handsomeness of Josh.

Brandon looked like the surfer model I'd found framed in her room—but in 3-D and dripping wet. Instead of using a towel to dry off, he'd slung it over his shoulders just so. The sea drops on his body glimmered.

The bottled blond hair combined with sea storm eyes warned me away from his exterior charm. His physical appearance screamed a perfection honed by the gym, waves, and a full-length mirror. I bet he had an equally sculpted ego to match.

"Hi, sugar," he said when I approached. "You looking for me?"

"Brandon?"

He flashed me a radiant smile achieved with thousands of dollars' worth of orthodontics. "The one and only. If you want a teaching session, weekdays at dawn are generally open. Or I can do a special pre-dawn time slot for you."

I put my hands on my hips. "You're Helen's fiancé."

His shiny grin vanished.

"I'm one of Marina's friends, and I . . . just wanted to see how you were doing." I'd decided to keep the degrees of separation fewer. "I'm really sorry for your loss."

He froze and cast his eyes down. "I can't believe she's gone."

I dug into the sand with the tip of my shoe. "It must have been such a shock." He looked like a man who still needed to process things. Maybe empathy would open him up and provide me more clues. People often shared without filtering their words while in the throes of grief.

He sank down in the sand with his knees up. "I just don't understand how this could've happened."

I blew out a breath. "I know the paramedics tried hard, but it was already too late."

He stared out at the sea. I, too, glanced at the water, noticing the surfers riding the crests in the last rays of the sun. "So sudden. It doesn't make any sense. She was super fit. I mean, we rode the waves together all the time."

A small smile lit up his face as he continued, "That's how we met, you know. I taught her over the summer. A natural, she absolutely shredded those waves."

I calculated in my head. "So, you've been together for over six months. You two must have really hit it off for wedding bells to start chiming."

He nodded. "Sometimes you just know, right?"

I thought about Josh and me. Could I imagine marrying him? Yes, but that milestone seemed far down the road. I loved the pure journey of being together in this moment, of having a stable relationship we could build on.

Brandon thumped a fist against his forehead. "I knew I should have checked in when I didn't get a text from her. But I thought it was my phone. It's been on the fritz ever since I got sand in it. But then the police called me with the horrible news . . ."

I thought about the date of Helen's death. February thirteenth. I softened my voice. "Did you two have a Valentine's outing planned?"

"We were definitely going to be busy . . . talking about wedding details."

I bent down and drew a heart in the wet sand near the water. "Oh. When was the big day going to be?"

"Within the next month or two, when our schedules aligned. We'd intended to do a Vegas run."

"No huge dream wedding?"

Brandon brushed some sand off his legs. "Helen didn't want anything fancy. We only needed each other, not some crazy expensive ceremony."

"I see."

Brandon readjusted the drape of the towel around his neck. "Now it'll never be. We ended up waiting too long."

I offered my condolences again, but watching Brandon walk back to the surf shop, I felt the whisperings of doubt. The way he'd honeyed me with his words at first. And how he'd returned to his regular schedule so soon. Was it a way for him to cope with the fact that he was fiancée-less . . . or something else?

CHAPTER
≈ fourteen ≈

MARINA HAD ADMITTED to putting in extra work hours to deal with her grief, so I figured I could catch her early Sunday morning at Déjà Vu. Hopefully, it'd be a slow time for antiques shopping.

The store's sign was done in a stylized Olde English font. When I entered, the interior seemed dim, but the sunlight caught the myriad panels of stained glass windows hanging suspended from the ceiling. Rainbows scattered across the walls.

Everywhere I looked, I found strange items I didn't know the use of. From the front counter, Marina must have noticed my goggle-eyed look. She hurried to greet me. "Want a quick tour?"

"Of course," I said, following her past aisles of noisy grandfather clocks, rusted tools, and fragile pottery.

"Everything here has a history that runs decades or centuries old."

"Wow. How long have you worked here?"

She picked up a sleek hourglass and shifted the sparkling sand inside. "Three years, give or take. Helen was actually one of my first customers."

"Were you pretty close?"

"I was her only friend outside of work. She didn't really socialize."

Marina led me back to the front counter, where a glass case displayed different types of jewelry: rings, bracelets, and earrings. I could also see valuable coins from around the world slipped underneath the clear surface. On top of the counter perched a bronze cash resister with push buttons. "Let me grab you a seat so we can talk," she said.

She brought an overstuffed fringed armchair for me while she sat behind the counter on a black barstool.

"Are you sure I'm allowed to sit on this?" I asked her, gesturing at the ornate floral upholstery on the chair.

She waved her hand around. "It's lasted this long already, hasn't it?"

I settled on the cushy seat, ignoring the burst of dust motes that suddenly rose up in the air. "You were one of Helen's best friends. Tell me, what do you truly think about Brandon?"

"Honestly?" She tossed her wild mane of wavy hair. "They seemed almost golden together."

"True love?" I asked.

"Or lust at first sight."

I tugged my earlobe. "Did I hear you right?"

"Uh-huh. But unlike her usual one-nights, Helen saw Brandon regularly. On her own schedule, of course." Marina's eyes blazed. "Can't blame Helen's distrust of men after I met her dad the other day."

I didn't have to be a Freudian psychologist to know that Helen probably had issues with Mr. Reed as a father. I mean, the man had practically jumped down the principal's throat at the school gathering. "He seems to have some problems with anger."

Marina jutted her chin. "That's putting it mildly. He stormed into the townhouse and claimed rights to everything in sight. Sure, he's biologically her father and there might be some legal tie, but they'd had no emotional connection for *ages*."

"The two didn't keep in touch?"

"Only when necessary. Like last year, when her job had been on the line."

I played with the tassels on the upholstered chair. "Helen didn't invite him to the upcoming wedding then?"

"Please." Marina snorted. "But she might have told him about her plans just to annoy him. He always hated the thought of his little girl getting hitched without his approval."

The shop door opened, and Marina turned toward the new customer, an old lady wearing a silk bonnet. I decided to move my cushy chair back to its previous spot.

I left Déjà Vu feeling bothered. What had the relationship really been like between Helen and her father?

•   •   •

I was looking forward to a humble dinner and a night spent cuddling the cats when my sister called. Alice begged me to come hang out with her colleagues. Though she connected with people fine one-on-one, she sometimes acted like a wallflower when in a group setting unless she had some sort of emotional support. My sister seemed excited to get the sudden invitation, but I wondered about the motive behind the spontaneous event.

We met up early at the restaurant—Do You Fondue?—to get in on the Happy Hour action. Apparently, if we ordered drinks, the preset entrées and desserts came at reduced prices. The Three Musketeers, as I still thought of them, arrived in style: Jessie with pigtails in a fuchsia halter top; Amy wearing a bland cardigan and pearls; and Donna with another homespun dress and her signature orthopedic shoes.

Jessie, the leader of the pack, stepped forward in her brightly colored top. She clasped my sister's hands. "Thanks for coming on such short notice."

Alice beamed at each of them in turn. "We never get to see each other outside of work. This is lovely."

Amy flattened her lips, looking uptight in her Mr. Rogers outfit. Why had they invited my sister if they were acting so dour about it?

To be polite, I expressed my gratitude to them for letting me tag along. Donna nodded while Jessie flashed me a beauty contestant smile. Amy glowered—perhaps remembering Marshmallow's invasion of her cozy tent and his disruption of her juicy gossip session.

Could this be another arrangement for gabbing about Helen? But then why bring Alice along?

We beelined into the restaurant and had an open choice of seating. Amy selected a table in a dark corner for "extra privacy." After we'd placed our drink orders, Jessie started the conversation. In the dim setting, the shadows thrown over her face made her expression turn sinister as she said to my sister, "I hear you're taking a few days off."

Alice gulped.

I looked around for the waiter, who was nowhere to be found. My sister needed her drink pronto.

"It's a, um, personal leave," Alice whispered.

Donna patted my sister's hand, her bushy white hair looking exactly like a fuzzy halo right then. But she spoiled the kindly effect by saying, "It's okay, dear. We all heard how you have to step back because of some hullaboo with the police."

I inched closer to my sister and said, "It's just a tiny break."

Amy piped up. "The police. Does it have to do with Helen Reed's death?"

Alice gave a small nod, while Donna tsked and Jessie twirled the end of her pigtail with her finger. Amy offered a satisfied smirk and leaned back in her chair.

Our drinks finally came. The waiter assured us that the food would be coming soon. He also let us know we could stay as long as we wanted, the better to enjoy the fondue experience.

No wonder the other teachers had selected this eatery. They could gang up on Alice for hours on end.

My sister sipped at the fruity concoction in front of her—a drink decorated with a pineapple wedge. "They think maybe it was something Helen ate . . ."

Amy tilted her half-full wineglass at Jessie. Hmm, she'd downed that pretty fast. "Ha," Amy said, "maybe it was one of those underbaked chocolate chip cookies you made and had her try."

"Not funny." Jessie twirled the swizzle stick in her own frothy drink. It looked full to the brim. She turned to my sister. "How does what Helen ate have anything to do with you?"

Alice frowned and slid the pineapple wedge along the rim of her glass. "I did give her some ginger chews that day."

Donna's mouth dropped open, and she clutched her beverage, something that looked suspiciously like prune juice. "Why, I eat ginger all the time to improve my digestive system. What's wrong with that?"

My sister's cheeks flushed pink—though that could have been from the alcohol. "Helen complained to me of a stomachache—"

"And the cops think you poisoned her," Amy said.

Jessie cocked her head at my sister. "So that's why Principal Lewis gave you a spontaneous vacation."

I used my straw to churn the Arnold Palmer in front of me. Mixing at such a high speed, the lemonade and tea created a mini whirlpool in my glass. "That's ridiculous. Detective Brown will realize he's got it all wrong once he gets the autopsy report."

Amy toyed with the pearls around her neck.

Then the waiter came with the main dishes. He settled a pot of bubbling white cheese in the center of the table. We each got a plate of bread cubes and veggies to coat in the mixture.

Donna dipped an asparagus spear into the melted Gruyère. "Whatever happened, it's a shame. She was on track for the Teacher of the Year Award."

Jessie, whose hand had hovered over the pot, dropped her fork into the container by accident.

Alice fished it out with her own utensil and called the waiter over for a replacement.

I racked my brain but couldn't remember Alice ever talking about this award. "Teacher of the Year? How does that work?"

Donna cleared her throat. "I can tell you, Mimi, having won it several times already." She proceeded to describe the process, which involved the principal shadowing classrooms for the first part of the year and nominating the top three candidates after the winter holiday break. Then the remaining staff and students got to vote for their choices until the beginning of March. A running tally of the ballots was posted weekly in the cafeteria for all to see.

"Who got nominated?" I asked.

"Jessie, Helen, and Alice."

I nudged my sister. "You didn't say a word."

She played with her glass. "I ended up declining the nomination. Too much attention." My sister hated being in the spotlight, even for positive things.

Donna swallowed a cube of bread slathered with cheese. "Helen was in the lead. Probably because I passed on my teaching tips to her. I even gave her some of my darling classroom supplies to win over her students."

Amy placed her arm around Jessie's shoulders. "Helen was only winning because Principal Lewis is biased. He has influence."

So, there had been a rivalry between Helen and Jessie. I popped a cheese-covered bell pepper in my mouth and realized that I much preferred only one type of cheese-dipped food: nachos.

Amy ate a few bites of broccoli dipped in cheese and then downed the rest of her wine. "There was something going on between the principal and Helen, mark my words. I even heard from a reliable source that she passed him a note right before Valentine's Day."

If it was the same slip of paper I'd seen, I was pretty sure Amy had misinterpreted the meaning of it. However, I didn't think she'd want to be corrected in public. Besides which, the dessert platter had arrived.

Our pot of cheese was replaced by two containers of chocolate: milk and dark. A shared plate held sliced bananas, de-stemmed strawberries, mini marshmallows, and cubes of pound cake to dip into the new pots.

We busied ourselves with dessert for a few minutes. I justified my ravenous eating by reminding myself that I was eating healthy by selecting only fruit to be coated in chocolate.

Alice stopped mid-nibble of her strawberry and peered at her coworkers. "I just thought of something. Have you guys heard about an official funeral or memorial service happening?"

The other teachers looked blank.

Alice placed her half-eaten strawberry on her plate. "There has to be one, right? Maybe Principal Lewis knows, but since I'm out for the next few days . . ."

Her colleagues avoided eye contact, and none of them volunteered to get the information. My sister turned to me and gave me a pleading look.

"Fine. I'll do it," I said and proceeded to stuff my face with more dessert—I needed some sweet reward to motivate me to go on a potentially awkward school visit.

CHAPTER

≈ fifteen ≈

DIDN'T FIND PRINCIPAL Lewis in the school office the next day. Instead, he stood in the staff room, near a table with a bakery box on it. He was arranging napkins into a fan-shaped display.

He'd dressed up in his usual professional attire, but the long-sleeved shirt looked a little wrinkled. Concentrated on arranging the goodies with flair, he hadn't heard me enter the room.

I tapped him on the arm to get his attention, and he jumped.

"Oh, Mimi." I remembered the effusive greeting from when I first met him, but this time, he didn't offer me a hug, a pat on the back, or even a handshake. In fact, he stepped about a foot's distance away from me. "You startled me."

Peering into the open bakery box, my mouth salivated. "Wow. Porto's," I said. The local Cuban bakery was known for its pastries, particularly the guava strudels I now eyed with glee.

"My wife got them for the staff," he said. "Everyone's under a lot of stress right now and could use a tasty pick-me-up." He adjusted his checkered tie as I grabbed a napkin.

"May I?" I asked, pointing at the box. "It'd be nice to take one for my sister."

Principal Lewis had the courtesy to look embarrassed. "I guess that's why you're here. I'm sorry your sister has to miss work. She's a wonderful teacher, but I believe it's in the best interest of everyone involved if we're proactive and try to avoid legal ramifications."

"Are you speaking from personal experience?" I remembered the legalese in Helen's note to him.

He took a napkin and mopped his brow. "I've recently learned to be more understanding."

Using a tactic from my college psych class, I stayed quiet. Sometimes people will fill in an uncomfortable silence with more information.

"I need to have clearer actions," he said.

He didn't seem to want to volunteer anything further, so I decided to broach another subject. "You must have a tough job." I gestured toward the window. "Like the other day, out on the lawn with Helen's father."

Principal Lewis crumpled his damp napkin. "I thought I'd met my share of angry parents, but he was of another scale."

"Why was he so upset?"

"Guess the authorities couldn't get ahold of him until really late. Then it took time for him to fly in from overseas."

Sounded like transference from Helen's father. He'd taken his rage at being informed tardy about his daughter's death and placed it on the principal's shoulders. "Having Helen die so suddenly must have felt awful. Did Mr. Reed happen to say when he'd be holding the funeral?"

Principal Lewis moved away from me and rummaged in the cabinet. He pulled out a mug and filled it from a nearby coffeepot. "No, and I didn't ask. I wasn't a personal friend of Miss Reed."

"Did Helen's father leave his contact info with you? I know that Alice would like to attend the service if possible."

The principal sipped his coffee and forced himself to swallow. "Lukewarm again." He fiddled with the button on the coffeepot. "You'd think Richard would've fixed this already."

I cleared my throat. "How can I reach Mr. Reed?"

Principal Lewis shook his head. "I'm not sure."

"You don't have a phone number? Or an address?"

"Well, he's staying at the extended stay hotel about two blocks from here."

I thanked the principal, but he seemed distracted again by his tepid coffee. He placed his mug in the microwave, failing to notice the "Out of Order" sign.

Naturally, it didn't work. As I left the room, he mumbled, "Sometimes I think Richard is sabotaging everything around here."

A joke of a comment, but might there be a smidgeon of truth? I remembered the broken glass in Helen's classroom and decided to search the school grounds for the janitor.

After ten minutes of looking, I tracked Richard down. He wore his usual down jacket and baseball cap combo and was wiping down the windows of the school library when I found him.

"Finally cleaned off the seagulls' crap," he said, as he threw a dirty wadded-up ball of newspaper away. The harsh scent of vinegar assaulted the air.

"Maybe you should clean the windows of Helen's classroom," I said.

"Why's that?" Richard fiddled with the brim of his Dodgers cap. "The birds don't typically fly through the hallways."

Perhaps he'd indulge me if I took a different tack. "I apologize. It's just that I really wanted to see her classroom, for closure."

"I didn't know you were such good friends with her, Alice." He shuffled down the hallway in his down jacket and jeans.

Again he'd called me by my sister's name. I shrugged it off. We did look alike, and perhaps I could continue to use the identity confusion to my advantage.

Richard paused before the door to Room 6 and fished out a pocket watch from his jacket. After holding it close to his face, he said, "You're not going to have very long until you need to get ready to teach."

"I promise to be quick," I said.

He put his watch away, but a frown crossed his face.

Remembering the napkin-wrapped guava treat I'd snuck in my bag, I took it out. My sister would never know, and I needed it to clinch the deal. "I got you something, Richard."

"For me?" He offered his hand, palm up, where I deposited the pastry. After unwrapping it, he said, "I do have a sweet tooth. Is this . . . a doughnut?"

"Even better," I said.

Smiling, he pulled out a giant brass ring of keys and unlocked the door to Room 6.

I stepped into a classroom of wonder. Cardstock clouds hung down from the ceiling, and suspended pretend raindrops the size of my palm hovered above the student desks. A large area rug, which covered one-third of the room, featured a detailed city map, complete with happy yellow buses traveling twisty asphalt roads. It even had a book nook with a mock rocket ship curtain door. The banner above the area said, "Reading Is a Blast."

"Wow," I said. "What a bunch of lucky kids. I wish I had a classroom like this growing up."

Richard shuffled in through the open doorway and sat down at the teacher's desk, munching on the strudel. "You didn't see her room before?"

"I never had the time to. Oh, how cute," I said, pointing to a lamp on the teacher's desk in the shape of a yellow pencil. The rubber eraser served as the bottom of the light, while the top looked like a lead tip. As I peered closer, I realized that the cord lay wrapped around the base of the lamp. "But why is it unplugged?"

"I haven't had time to replace it yet."

Busted microwave, semi-functioning coffeepot . . . A lot of things didn't work at the school. "What was wrong with the lamp?" I asked.

"The bulb broke," Richard said.

Shattered glass. I traced the length of the yellow pencil up to its pointed tip, where a bulb could be screwed on. The lamp wobbled at my light touch. "Kinda flimsy."

Richard nodded. "A hand-me-down."

"Did you clean up the glass?" I asked.

"I swept up the big shards. Those twisty bulbs, when they shatter, get glass everywhere."

Hmm. Despite Detective Brown's assertion, maybe some extra-sharp glass splinters had somehow hurt Helen?

I studied the lamp again and noticed chunks of rubber missing from its underside. No wonder it had wobbled earlier. I also saw something written there in permanent marker: "Property of Room 13." Interesting.

Richard pulled out his pocket watch. "Time to get going for the both of us. You need to teach, and I have to whittle down my long to-do list." He ushered me out of Helen's old classroom.

The janitor seemed like a kind but aging gentleman with a sweet tooth. I just hoped it wasn't only an image he projected to others.

I said goodbye to him. As I walked down the hallways back to the front of the school, I made sure to pass by Room 13. Peeking through the window, I saw it housed a bunch of laptops. A computer lab.

Disappointing. I'd hoped it'd belonged to a teacher, especially one of those on my suspects list.

In the parking lot, I did spot two people I wanted to investigate further. I saw Amy, dressed in a gray twinset, dangling a lucky clover keychain in her hand. She approached the driver's side window of a peach-colored sedan.

Based on the outline of the driver's high ponytail, I figured it had to be Jessie in the car. I walked behind her vehicle to get to my Prius and noticed she had a vanity license plate. The shortened combination of letters and numbers looked like it spelled "Number 1 Teacher."

How power-hungry had Jessie been to win the Teacher of the Year title? Enough to knock out the competition . . . permanently?

CHAPTER

sixteen

ACCORDING TO PRINCIPAL Lewis, Scott Reed's hotel was located down the street from the school. It took me a quick Google search to map out the directions to Angelic Suites.

I arrived to find a three-story taupe building. It reminded me more of an office building than a hotel.

Inside, the lobby felt tiny. I only had to walk a few feet from the entrance before running smack dab into the front counter. A middle-aged man stood behind it. He wore a fraying white dress shirt with its sleeves rolled up. And no wonder because it didn't feel like the AC worked in here. The whirring ceiling fans above made half-hearted turns to push around the warm air.

The man smiled at me and said, "Welcome to my wonderful hotel, the Angelic Suites. Are you here to check in?"

I shook my head. "I'm trying to find one of your guests, Mr. Scott Reed."

"Yes, a fine gentleman. I know all my guests by name. Unfortunately, he's stepped out. Would you care to leave him a message?"

He pushed some stationery across the counter toward me. A simple notepad with the hotel name printed in golden script and an accompanying cartoon cherub.

The owner positioned a ballpoint pen on top of the pad. What should I write to Helen's father? I'd never actually met him except for seeing him across the schoolyard yelling at the principal, and that didn't quite count. Besides, I couldn't give him a note asking for details about his daughter's funeral service.

I returned the paper and pen. "Do you know when Mr. Reed will return?"

The owner spread his hands in the air. "I'm sorry, miss, but he didn't say."

"It's just that I need to speak with him about something important." I drummed my fingers against the counter. "I had hoped to see him before he left the country."

The owner blinked at me. "You'll definitely have another chance. He's already paid for the entire month, a discounted rate. And, of course, he'll be at the upcoming crafts convention."

"Excuse me?"

The owner reached under the counter and gave me a glossy flyer. It outlined the details of the event, to be held in a few days' time at the hotel. The convention would feature a bazaar of international handmade goods.

"Did Mr. Reed say he'll be attending?"

"Oh, yes. He's going to sell his merchandise at one of the booths."

"Excellent." I made sure to put the date and time on my phone's calendar app, paired with an alert, to remind me of the event.

• • •

After picking up Marshmallow and Nimbus from home, I arrived at Hollywoof late. Thankfully, I'd left Nicola a set of spare keys for emergency's sake, and she'd already opened up the shop.

I had just settled the cats in their usual sunny spot when I saw my sister in the shadows of the interior hallway.

I turned to Nicola, who sat behind the cash register, flipping through an *Us Weekly* magazine. "Did you let Alice in?"

"Yep. Found your sister pacing outside the front of the store." She returned to studying her celebrity gossip.

Alice made her way over and grasped my hands in hers. "Please let me stay, Mimi. I've already cleaned the grooming tables with disinfecting wipes. I can be helpful here."

"You want to work at Hollywoof for the day?" I scrunched my nose at her nice blouse and slacks, but I also took in her bright eyes and eager look.

"Yes, please," she said. "It's so weird not being able to teach and having to stay home. I can't stand just sitting around, especially knowing why I'm not at work."

Marshmallow curled into an even tighter spiral in his sunny spot. "Mmm, lounging around all day sounds like the good life."

Ten minutes later, a woman with big hair that fanned around her face walked in with her Afghan hound. She approached the register and said, "I want to drop Belle off for a co-wash. Do you do those at your salon?"

Nicola snuck a puzzled glance at me, but I hadn't understood the lady, either.

I introduced myself as the owner of Hollywoof and asked the customer, "How can we help you exactly?"

"Belle needs a wash," the woman said. "A no-poo."

I stifled a giggle.

She continued, "Conditioner only."

I nodded. "Ah, I see. A co-wash."

The woman touched her own voluminous hair. "It works wonders on my tresses."

"Why, of course we can do it."

"Perfect. I have my own hair appointment soon, so I'll get going. Toodles," the woman said and handed over Belle's leash.

After the woman left, Nicola gestured to the price chart. "What should I charge her? We don't even have that service listed."

"Call it a wash-and-dry. It's about the same amount of work—minus the shampoo." I took Belle to the back room, and Alice followed me.

While we filled the industrial-size sink with water, my sister and I chatted.

"Must be nice being your own boss," Alice said over the gushing noise of the faucet. "Always coming in—or not—whenever you want."

"Very funny," I said. "For your information, I went to see Principal Lewis this morning."

Her eyes sought mine. "To find out about the funeral? When is it?"

I turned off the water and checked its temperature. "Not sure. I need to touch base with Mr. Reed directly to get the info."

Alice helped me place Belle in the warm water. I made sure to cover the dog's ear canals with cotton as a precaution.

As I lathered Belle with an oatmeal coat conditioner, I asked, "Can you tell me about the dynamics between Jessie and Helen?"

"What do you want to know?" Alice made sure I conditioned every inch of Belle's fur.

"Seems like Jessie and Helen were pitted against each other for the Teacher of the Year Award. No ill will there?"

Alice cocked her head at me. "Who makes a fuss over a plaque and getting your name plastered on the school's bulletin board?"

"Not everyone's like you." Turning on the spray nozzle, I started rinsing off Belle. "Do you know that Jessie's license plate translates to 'Number 1 Teacher'?"

"She does like being the center of attention," Alice said. "Jessie still tells people about being voted prom queen in high school."

I murmured, "She must have a competitive streak."

"I think she liked standing out in her small town." Alice named some tiny place in Central California I'd seen maybe once on a map.

"Big fish in a little pond."

"Right. She said she came to L.A. for better opportunities."

We carried Belle, who'd started shivering, to the metal table and hooked up her leash. Then I used the high-velocity dryer to finish grooming the pooch and warm her up.

I brushed her long fur until it shone. "Not too shabby, if I say so myself."

"She looks beautiful." Alice stroked Belle. "Like she's ready for a night on the town."

"Speaking of which, have you started planning the Ultimate Date Night for Ma and Dad?"

"Uh-huh. Just this morning, I called Roti Palace to check their prices."

"Great." I unhooked Belle from the table. "And how are we going to make their schedules mesh?"

"I'm on it," Alice said, as we returned to the main room. "Dad's always back by dinner, so I just need to convince Ma not to go to mah jong club that evening."

"Sounds like you've got it all under control, but let me know if you need any help." Similar to me, Alice liked handling tasks on her own—sometimes to her detriment—but at least I'd put out an offer of assistance.

CHAPTER

= seventeen =

THE OWNER OF the co-washed puppy came back, her hair looking even more like a lion's mane than before, and thanked me for a job well done. After that, we had several regular shampoo appointments.

When we finished the last one, I noticed Alice rolling up her sleeves. The material of her shirt had gotten soaked. Touching the damp fabric, I asked, "What type of fabric is this?"

"Silk blend."

I covered my mouth with my hand. "You can't wear stuff like that while grooming pets."

She shrugged. "This is the kind of clothes I usually wear to work."

I made her sit in the front room near the cash register, even though the space looked crammed with two people sitting behind the counter. The time seemed to drag by as we experienced an odd lull in business.

Nicola's glazed eyes stared without emotion at the *Benji* movie playing in a loop in the waiting area.

I clapped my hands to get her attention. "Good news, Nicola. Feel free to take the rest of the day off." Half the day had passed by already. How many more jobs would we get that required three people on the premises? As it turned out, none.

About fifteen minutes before closing, I urged my sister to go home. Most people wouldn't take their pet in for a shampoo without the adequate time to get it finished, and I could handle simple tasks like nail trimming without assistance. Besides, I'd managed to run the shop on my own before.

I waved goodbye to Alice and sat in the deep silence.

A paw tapped my ankle and brought me out of my reverie. "Now spill about the case," Marshmallow said. "Because curiosity never killed this cat."

He'd already heard about the fondue night, so I summarized everything else that had happened so far. First, I talked about the school visit with a standoffish Principal Lewis. Then I described Helen's classroom with its school-themed décor and my interesting chat with the janitor. I ended with a description of the parking lot scene, where I repeated Jessie's vanity license plate phrase, and Alice's reminder that her fellow teacher had enjoyed her reign as prom queen.

Marshmallow's whiskers twitched. "Priceless. You have to get a copy of that photo."

I pulled out my phone. "Will I even be able to find it?"

"Everything's on the Web, sweetheart." He flicked his tail. "Besides, it's not like you have anything better to do right now."

I took the bait. After several searches using various combinations of

her name, the town she'd grown up in, and "prom queen," I got a list of results. Picking one at random, I tapped the link to an archived yearbook,
while Marshmallow jumped on the counter and peered over my shoulder.

A version of a younger Jessie showed up, in a black taffeta dress
with a shiny bodice.

"There's got to be, like, twenty pounds of sequins on the top of that
gown," Marshmallow said. He started chuckling and almost rolled off
the counter.

I stopped his freefall by blocking it with my outstretched arm.

"Let's see another picture."

I went back to the search results and scrolled down.

"Hold on." Marshmallow extended a claw at the phone. "What's
that blog entry?"

I read the headline: "'Scandal at local high school.'"

We read the post together, which detailed how Jessie had been pitted against an auburn beauty for the prom queen title. Her rival had
been president of the class that year and captain of the cheerleading
team. Despite receiving more votes, the other girl ended up going home
right before getting crowned. Jessie had graciously taken over queen
duties for the night.

Marshmallow and I looked at each other. "What do you think happened?" I asked.

He didn't have time to answer before the front door swung open. A
customer so late in the day? I checked on who had entered. It was
someone who might be able to answer my nagging questions.

Detective Brown wore his typical sport coat ensemble when he
marched into Hollywoof with a straight back. His squared shoulders
relaxed as he caught sight of a dozing Nimbus, though. A small blip of a
smile crossed his face and then vanished when he caught me looking.

The detective turned his attention to me. "Mimi, I have an update for you."

My fingers twitched. When had the man ever brought me good news?

"An initial examination tested remnants of the ginger chews, and they turned out harmless. I left a message with your sister saying that she can go back to work—for the time being."

I almost sank down in the middle of the floor with relief, right on top of one of the golden stars that lined Hollywoof's Bark of Fame. Instead, I leaned against the front desk for support. "Thank goodness. Was there anything odd found during the autopsy?"

He rubbed the back of his neck, a sure sign he didn't want to tell me the exact details.

Something strange had been discovered about Helen then. Was there a toxic substance in her system? Or perhaps she had been pregnant at the time of her death. "Was it hCG?"

He gave me a blank look.

"Human chorionic gonadotropin. It's a chemical produced during pregnancy."

Detective Brown choked. "No, they didn't find any hCG."

"Huh." I peppered him with questions. "Is the case closed? Did Helen die of natural causes, then?"

"No and no. Everyone at that school is still on my suspects list. Plus, your sister had more motive than the rest since Alice got the pink slip threat last year instead of Helen Reed. There must have been ill will." His lips clamped shut, and he moved closer to the sleeping Nimbus. He'd talked too much but caught himself.

I followed the detective as he crouched down and examined the kitten. "How is she doing?"

"Nimbus is great." At the sound of her name, the kitty's eyes popped open. She focused on the man above her—and actually cooed.

"I didn't know cats could make that sound," Detective Brown said, his eyes lighting up.

"Well, she must like you."

From his spot, Marshmallow said, "For the life of me, I can't understand why."

Nimbus nudged the detective's leg. I swear I could hear a soft whisper from her: "Brown."

She'd memorized the detective's name. He must have treated her well and made quite an impression on her.

Detective Brown bent down and stroked the kitten's back. I suppose, who better than a cop to protect Nimbus? I chose my next words very carefully. "There might be someone dangerous at Roosevelt Elementary, Detective."

"Hmm. What's that?" He seemed to be lost in petting Nimbus.

"I saw a stranger in a weird jacket loitering near the campus."

Detective Brown stopped stroking the cat, straightened back up, and turned businesslike. I could almost see the sinister image I'd planted in his head.

A stalker in a coat near an elementary school? Any cop worth his salt would take that threat seriously. The stranger could harm the kids—or only as I knew, two beloved cats.

"I'll get somebody to check out the situation," Detective Brown said.

With any luck, the police would snatch the mad scientist—and perhaps Helen's murderer as well. After all, Nimbus had spotted the man nearby on the day of the crime.

CHAPTER

eighteen

THE DAY OF the international goods bazaar arrived accompanied by gray clouds and drizzle. Of course, I showed up to the hotel late. Driving in L.A. in any type of "rainy" weather added a spectacular amount of delay.

I hurried inside Angelic Suites. A large sign directed me down a narrow hall to the Grandiose Ballroom. The open doors led to an average-size room with dimensions not commensurate with its name. Indeed, it looked like it'd been an exercise room in its previous incarnation. One side of it even had a mirrored wall.

The ballroom could still, though, hold a large number of vendors. It looked like a local farmers' market stuffed inside a room. I passed by a table of carved jade figurines, a huge rack of sombreros, and a desk piled high with wooden clogs. It was like a global crafts tour.

Before I ended up at Scott Reed's station near the back of the room, I got distracted by an amazing display of pet toys. They came in different shapes and sizes: a striped tiger, a mini elephant, and even a sushi roll.

I picked up a stuffed toy that looked like a giant marshmallow. "Ooh, what beautiful material. Soft but hearty."

The vendor, a man with an oblong head, grinned at me. "It's a combination of peat fibers and softened hemp made by artisans from Eastern Europe."

"Can they withstand cat claws?"

"And dog bites," he said.

"Can you put this on hold for me? I want to check out some fabric over there first—" I pointed to the booth inhabited by Helen's father.

The vendor nodded. "Scott. I see him here every year."

I turned to the seller. "You've worked with him before? What's your impression?"

He shrugged. "Keeps to himself. I've heard he made a lot of international investments and owns a few manufacturing businesses overseas."

I thanked the pet toy vendor and moved toward Mr. Reed's table, where spools of fabric in a myriad of shades were spread across his table. Brilliant colors and soft pastels intermingled at the booth. The variety of hues on display reminded me of the dizzying array of paint swatches at the local hardware store. I caught a whiff of something musty as I approached the table and hoped the materials hadn't gotten soaked from the rain.

Helen's father extended his hand. He looked quite different from the yelling figure I held in my memory from the school function. Instead, he seemed very respectable in his expensive-looking charcoal suit with a white silk cravat.

His head of gray hair gave him a certain gravitas. He had shamrock green eyes set in a craggy face, and I imagined he might've been a looker in his younger years.

I stepped up and shook his hand. "My name's Mimi Lee."

"Well, you came to just the right spot, Mimi. I carry the finest in silks and other high-quality fabrics from around the world."

I reached for a turquoise material near me. What with the rich color, it almost felt like touching a flowing stream made of fabric. "That's amazing. It's surreally soft."

He grinned. "I guarantee that you won't find a better deal on these one-of-a-kind cloths . . . or my name isn't Scott Reed. And if you don't want to make your own creations from the fabric, we also sell scarves, bandannas, and wraps."

I touched a lavender scarf that called to me with its vibrant hue.

"That purple would be a great color on you. Really bring out your lovely eyes. And you can call me Scott."

An old warning from Ma rang in my head, and I frowned at Helen's father. Ma had told me about men with "flower mouths"—silver-tongued and too eager to flatter.

I removed my hand from the beautiful scarf and focused on my mission. "I've seen you before, Mr. Reed, at Roosevelt Elementary."

A flicker of wariness crossed his face, but he smoothed it away. "When was this?"

"At the Family and Friends Day. You were conversing with Principal Lewis in a rather, um, animated manner."

He gave a gentle chuckle. "Understandable, I hope. I'd just learned about my daughter's death and flew straight to the school after a long series of layovers."

I looked down at my feet. "I'm really sorry about what happened to Helen."

"Yes, it was all so sudden"—his voice caught, and he cleared his throat.

Despite the estrangement between father and daughter, maybe he had really cared about Helen deep inside. "My sister is a teacher at the school . . . and we were wondering if you'd arranged the funeral yet."

"There will be a private cremation," he said. "I'm planning on keeping the urn in my vacation home in Napa Valley."

"Oh." I tugged at my ear. "Well, what about a memorial service?"

"A nice idea, but . . ." His face clouded. "I'm afraid I don't know any of her friends here. Where would I even start?"

How sad to have missed out on the experience of knowing his daughter's community. But maybe in her death, there could be a chance for connection. Without thinking, I blurted out, "I could help set it up."

He startled. "You'd do that?"

"I would need your contact info—oh, here's your business card." I snatched one up from the pile on the table and tucked it into my purse while backing away. "I'll be sure to reach out with some ideas. Take care."

As I left his booth, my heart ached for the mourning father. How many times had my father said, "Family is number one"? Or as Ma put it in her Manglish, "Family is *satu*."

• • •

When I asked Alice to stop by my place, she readily agreed. "I'd love to," she'd said. "I've already gone to school to make sure everything is in place when I return, but I'm still anxious. A visit will help get my mind off things."

Then my apartment would be a good distraction for her. I did have two very cuddly cats. Although right now, they seemed entranced by the new toys I'd brought back from the crafts bazaar and didn't pay me any attention. (I couldn't help but get Nimbus her own soft toy, a cloud that I'd also spotted at the booth.)

The bell rang, and when I opened the door, Alice gave me a tight smile. She peeked over her shoulder.

"Everything okay?" I asked.

"My nerves are acting up," she said with a slight shiver. "Ever since I stopped by school, I've felt like I'm being watched. Maybe it's just my imagination running wild because the principal and other teachers might be looking at me with suspicion when I return."

Or perhaps it wasn't in her head. Could she be in danger? Then another more positive interpretation occurred to me. Maybe Detective Brown had acted on his promise and sent a cop to patrol the neighborhood to keep the school safe.

"Come inside," I said, pulling my sister into a hug. "And leave your worries out there."

Both cats came over at the sight of Alice inside the apartment. They started rubbing their bodies against her legs, and my sister smiled. "What a warm welcome."

"A minute ago," I said, pointing to the new toys, "they didn't even know I existed."

Marshmallow cocked his head at me. "Jealous much?"

I shrugged. Better that they lavish their attention on my sister, who really needed it. "I'll make you some tea," I told her. "Microwaved okay?" Ma usually did the whole nine yards when brewing: using real tea leaves, boiling the water in a kettle, throwing the initial practice batch out, and then making a whole new pot. I nuked my water and dropped a tea bag into a mug.

"I'm okay with instant tea," my sister said.

Cradling two mugs of hot Iron Goddess Oolong in our hands, we sat next to each other on the couch in the living room and chatted. The cats lolled beneath our feet and got rewarded with occasional pats.

As we sipped our tea, I filled Alice in on my conversation with Helen's grieving father and summarized the interaction by saying, "So I offered to help him set up the memorial service."

Alice almost sloshed her tea out of the mug. "You did?"

I gave her a quick grin. "With your help, of course. I bet you know all of Helen's close contacts."

"I don't think she had very many friends," Alice said. "Just school colleagues, her roommate, and her boyfriend."

"Then it'll be easy. I can talk to the people outside of school, and you handle the rest." I turned the warm mug in my hands. "We just need a last-minute venue."

"I'll check with the other teachers. They might have some good referrals."

"Thanks, Alice. You're the best."

Marshmallow purred in agreement but tilted his head at me. "You're not half bad yourself, Mimi."

I gave him an ear rub before turning to my sister. "Everyone knows you're the queen of event planning. Must be all those transferable organization skills from being a teacher."

She blew out a breath. "Maybe not. I've been having trouble calling Dad's buddy to check on their golfing schedule. My number must show on his caller ID, but he just won't pick up."

I drained the last dregs of tea. "Maybe I can call Walt. In fact, I'll do it right this minute."

"Good luck," she said.

I swapped my empty mug for my phone and asked Alice for his

digits. While my sister stayed cordial from time to time with Dad's cronies, I'd never talked to Walt on the phone before.

I wondered if he'd even answer after seeing the strange number pop up. The line rang several times, and I had almost given up when a woman with a sharp voice said, "Who's this?"

"Oh, hello." I stumbled over my words.

"Don't call here." She hung up.

"Oops." I glanced at my sister. "I think his wife thought I was a telemarketer."

We'd have to get moving on the arrangements, though. The days until Ma and Dad's anniversary were ticking away.

CHAPTER

nineteen

BEFORE THE ULTIMATE Date Night, a more pressing event loomed on the calendar. We needed to create a memorial event pronto for Helen. If not only for etiquette's sake, we needed to make sure to fit it in before Scott Reed had to leave the country.

My sister must have been on the same wavelength because she called me at Hollywoof the next morning while I was busy selecting a much-needed new film to show on the flat-screen television. (Nicola had been about ready to smash in the TV with one of the portable blow dryers.)

Alice said, "Okay. I've arranged a place for the memorial."

I stopped riffling through my selection of classic doggie movies. "Really? That was quick. How much did it cost?"

Alice hemmed. "It's free. Amy insisted on using her own home but didn't want young children running around at such a serious event and nixed any students. I didn't have the heart to tell her no."

Of course my sister had caved in. She had a hard time setting boundaries. A classic people-pleaser personality.

I sighed. "Give me the details."

"Can you call Mr. Reed and have him okay the date and time?"

"Yep," I said, rummaging through my purse to find his business card.

So what if Alice was a pushover? I softened my tone and said, "Thanks for making this happen. I'm sure Helen would've appreciated your efforts."

Alice made a tuneless hum down the line. She'd never been good at accepting compliments. "Text me once you confirm things with him."

We hung up, and after locating his phone number, I touched base with Scott. His schedule was clear, and he'd be able to make it on the tentatively planned date. Afterward, I texted my sister a thumbs-up emoji.

I should get started on inviting the two people on the guest list I was in charge of. Well, there was no better time than the present. Besides, I was due for a lunch break anyway.

As I got ready to leave, Marshmallow's head swiveled in my direction. "Where are you off to, missy?"

I turned to Nicola and said, "I'm headed to the beach. See you after lunch."

"Enjoy the sunshine," she said.

Marshmallow sidled up to my side and unleashed his kitty pouting power.

"Fine," I said, relenting. I asked Nicola to keep an eye on Nimbus and then my cat and I made our way to All Tide Up.

· · ·

When I got to the surf shop, Brandon was already out on his lunch break. The staff suggested I check out the nearby pier to find him since he usually took his lunch break there. Apparently, he liked having a view of the glistening waves. Thank goodness nobody enforced the no-pets policy on the boardwalk.

Despite it being the middle of the week, I found a large number of people dawdling on the pier. A number of them were sunscreen-whitened tourists wearing T-shirts advertising L.A. landmarks.

Benches were positioned all across the boardwalk so people could rest. I pinpointed Brandon at one of them. He sat facing the ocean, but instead of looking at the seascape, he seemed focused on the phone in his hand.

"Sucked into screen time," Marshmallow said.

I shrugged. "That's a common enough sight."

"Wonder if he'll notice if I do this . . ." Marshmallow crept to the side of the bench, in the peripheral view of Brandon. My cat did a fancy dance move, complete with swaying paws and bobbing head.

Brandon's eyes stayed glued to his phone.

"Huh," Marshmallow said. "Well, if he's not going to eat that fish taco, I think I'll help myself."

I saw the meal lying on a napkin next to Brandon. Marshmallow jumped onto the bench, but before he could place one paw on the lunch, I lunged forward.

Brandon startled and pressed the power button on his phone. He looked up at me in confusion before recognition dawned on his face. "Uh, Minnie, right?"

"It's Mimi, actually. I was just looking for you, but I guess my cat found you first."

Marshmallow twitched his whiskers. "Natural feline instinct. We cats know how to hunt down rats."

I choked a little.

"You okay?" Brandon's gaze shifted to the nearest lifeguard tower.

"I'm fine. Dry throat," I said. "I went by All Tide Up first and asked for you, and they said I might find you here."

Brandon nodded and scooted over. "Have a seat." He'd pocketed his phone by that time and reclaimed his taco.

I sat down on the sand-colored concrete bench and wrung my hands. "It's about Helen. There's going to be a memorial service for her."

He hung his head and murmured, "A shame I'm too busy to attend."

I furrowed my brow. "But I didn't even tell you the date and time yet."

He stared out at the distant water. "I really hate grieving in public. Especially in a large crowd."

"It's nothing formal and will be held at a fellow teacher's home." I told him the details.

"Still, I don't know . . ."

I again remembered the Kübler-Ross model of grief. Could he be in the denial stage? If so, going to a memorial might actually provide him a sense of closure. "It'll be a very small gathering, I swear. Her roommate, a few others from school, and her father."

He cocked his head at me. "Scott Reed will be there?"

"Yes. He's already confirmed."

Brandon rubbed the stubble on his chin. "I've wanted to meet him face-to-face for a long time. Count me in."

"Great." I pulled a paper from my purse where I'd written down the service details and passed it to him. "See you then."

Marshmallow still eyed the fish taco with longing, so I scooped him up. Inclining my head at Brandon's lunch, I asked, "Where'd you get that delicious food by the way?"

He pointed out the restaurant, located quite close to the pier.

As we walked over to grab a quick bite, Marshmallow said, "As well you should reward me, I got some great intel."

"On tacos?"

"No. I understand why Brandon's so keen to go to the memorial service because of Scott Reed."

"To meet Helen's father to pay his respects?"

"Please." Marshmallow stared me down. "I saw what Brandon was looking at on his phone when I jumped onto the bench—a hostile e-mail from Scott Reed."

"Are you sure?" I paused in front of the taco shop.

"No doubt about it. I got a look at part of the message. It said, 'Don't think you can get away with . . .'"

Uh-oh. That didn't sound good. "What do you think that means, Marshmallow?"

But my cat had already shifted his attention to the fish taco shop. He smacked his lips. "On to more important matters. You know, we can't think well without some brain food."

My stomach rumbled in agreement.

CHAPTER
≈ twenty ≈

After I'd finished the day's work at Hollywoof, I decided to stop by Marina's townhouse to invite her to the memorial service. It didn't make sense to drop the cats off at home first, though. Driving to my apartment would require doubling back on the route.

When we arrived in front of the spacious townhome, I warned the cats to stay away from Marina. I worried that Nimbus might trigger one of her migraines.

I rang the doorbell. Marina answered right away. She welcomed us in, but gave me a puzzled look. "Did you leave something here, Mimi?"

I shook my head as she led me to a couch. "I'm here to invite you to a remembrance event for Helen."

"Oh." She sank down on a sofa cushion near me, choking back a sob.

Out of the corner of my eye, I noticed the cats move away from the living room and creep into the kitchen. Marshmallow hid in the far corner of the linoleum floor, while Nimbus executed an elegant leap and settled on top of the refrigerator.

"Show-off," Marshmallow muttered.

The cats appeared to be out of the way, so I turned my attention to Marina. "Sorry to disturb you at home," I said, "but I'd hoped you might be in."

She rubbed her forehead. "Yeah, I'm just reorganizing and tidying up the townhouse tonight."

"Well, I won't take up too much of your time then. I just need to give you info about the informal gathering. It'll be at one of the teachers' houses." I offered her a slip of paper with the details, but she waved it away.

"I'll just lose that. Could you text it to me instead?"

So I got her phone number, typed up the info, and sent it to her.

Her phone chimed with the message, and she skimmed it. "Should be free then."

I reexamined the townhouse. It looked about the same as before. Remembering that Marina had mentioned maybe needing to pack up once Helen's father claimed the property, I said, "Are you tidying up because you might need to move?"

She bit the side of her cheek. "Actually, no."

"Oh, okay." I waved my hand around the townhome. "But your place already looks quite clean to me."

"Upstairs is a mess from when Helen's father stormed in here." She paused and hugged her arms around herself.

I placed a gentle hand on her shoulder. "Are you okay? I have a contact in the police department if you need official help."

"Her father hauled off half her stuff." Her eyes glinted. "Good thing Helen kept a few of her possessions stored in a safe place. He didn't get any of those in his greedy paws."

"Hey," Marshmallow said from his corner, "don't insult us cats."

My curiosity got the better of me, and I asked her, "What did you manage to keep?"

"Her personal stuff," she said in a happier tone. "Let me show you."

Marina got up and approached the staircase. Instead of going to the second floor, though, she went over to the secret closet, the Harry Potter nook that I'd noticed on my initial visit.

Pulling it open, she entered and returned with a rosewood chest in her hands.

"What's that?" I stood up and edged close to Marina before she'd even returned to the couch.

"Her mementos." Marina opened the box to reveal a stack of hand-written love letters, a bouquet of dried daisies, and a heart-shaped per-fume bottle.

She continued, "There's something else in here." Lifting up the let-ters, she revealed a small black velvet box.

"Is that . . ."

She nodded with eagerness. "Take a peek."

I touched the smooth contours of the box and then opened it gin-gerly. A shiny diamond ring lay nestled inside. "Wow, that looks huge."

"Over a carat, I imagine," Marina said. "He must have spent a for-tune."

I whistled and closed the lid.

She squirreled the box back underneath the letters and sighed. "If only her other belongings were as exciting. There are her clothes—sadly, not my size—to sort as well as piles of papers."

"Do you need a hand?"

"No, thanks. Besides, it'll give me a chance to remember all the good times."

Maybe it would help her heal to sort through Helen's things. "Please take care of yourself," I said.

She nodded, placing the rosewood chest on the floor, and pressed her palm against her forehead. "Maybe I should rest up first. I feel the beginnings of a headache."

That was my cue to leave. In the kitchen, I prodded a dozing Marshmallow awake. Then I called out for Nimbus, and she jumped off the fridge in a graceful arc.

I left a morose-looking Marina rubbing at her temples. She sat on the couch, leaned back, and shut her eyes.

With a pang of regret, I realized I'd have to leave the cats at home during the memorial service. Too bad, because Marshmallow could've done some excellent snooping at the event. Who else might I team up with? Well, I did know a special someone who always made a great partner.

CHAPTER

twenty-one

D ESPITE THE SAD occasion, my heart couldn't help but give a
leap of joy when I spied Josh at my door. He looked dashing in his
dark clothes, a fitted dress shirt with trim slacks.

He leaned forward and pecked me on the cheek. "It's so nice to see
you, but I wish it was for a happier reason."

I nodded and reached up to fix his bangs, which had swished out of
place when he'd kissed me. At my touch, his lips curved up into a gentle
smile. I longed to rest my palm against his cheek, to make his smile
deepen and his dimple appear. But I'd have to save that for another day.
It wouldn't do to be late to the service.

I grabbed the foil-covered treats that I'd laid out on Ma's special
jade platter. "Ready to go now."

Josh raised his eyebrows. "Was this supposed to be a potluck-style
gathering?"

"No, but my sister was in charge of the snacks, so I offered to help her." Besides, Ma always said it was tradition to offer something sweet at funerals to counteract the bitterness of death.

"How thoughtful," Josh said.

From the living room, I heard an internal groan from Marshmallow. "You call ditching us 'thoughtful'?"

He knew I couldn't take pets to a funeral, so I said goodbye and exited. I made sure to close the door firmly on his griping.

Josh and I spent the drive catching up on each other's lives. Though I made sure to stay away from the extra snooping I'd been doing, I did share my worries about Ma and Dad.

"What a shame," Josh said. "I know what might cheer them up. I'll make them some *furikake* snack mix. When will the next Family Game Night be?"

We had a wonderful tradition in the Lee household of playing card and board games as an excuse to eat snacks. The winner also got to claim a jar of loose change as the prize. "It's been indefinitely postponed."

Josh put his hand on my lap and patted it comfortingly.

As we drove down the cozy residential street, I checked the addresses until I found the right one. "Looks like we made it."

Amy's ranch home was painted in a pale blue-green shade except for the shiny red door. "Wah, so lucky," Ma would've said of the fortuitous color. The same brilliant shade used for lucky *lai see* envelopes.

Josh and I wobbled down a pathway strewn with dried beans before reaching the front entrance. It made for difficult walking. Thankfully, I didn't drop the platter I was holding.

Located at the center of her door where a knocker might have been expected was a giant horseshoe instead. I couldn't bang on that, so I searched for a doorbell. We had to ring it twice before Amy answered.

She looked hassled upon seeing us. "Is it time already? You're the first ones to arrive," she said. "And I'm still doing some last-minute cleaning."

I introduced Josh to her and asked, "Er, what are you holding?"

It didn't look like any typical duster I'd ever seen. If anything, it appeared to be a cylindrical bundle of weeds.

She hid the bunch behind her back and invited us inside. "Please go straight through that patio door and out to the yard with the food. I'll join you in a sec."

In the backyard, I saw a cloth-draped rectangular table. There was already an array of drinks on its surface, ranging from a large water cooler to a glass pitcher of orange juice with sliced strawberries floating around in it. An open bottle of champagne hid behind the juice.

I noticed a half-filled flute of orange liquid on the table as I placed my jade platter down. A smidgeon of magenta lipstick colored the rim of the glass.

Amy bustled out from the house and saw me staring at the drink. "Mimosas help me feel at ease," she said. "So, what snack did you bring?"

"Honey twists. They're sort of dessert-ish."

She clapped her hands in delight. "I can't wait to try them. And thank heavens you brought the food instead of Jessie. She always undercooks everything she makes."

Before we could talk further, the doorbell chimed. We headed back inside, and Amy opened the front door.

Principal Lewis stood on the stoop in somber clothing. An obsidian black tie completed his depressive look. He introduced himself to Josh, and they shook hands. Then he gave Amy and me a tiny head nod.

I moved toward the principal to chat with him, but he had already angled his back toward me. He started speaking to Josh in a loud voice.

After my boyfriend shared his profession, Principal Lewis leaned in closer and lowered his voice.

Meanwhile, Amy tugged on my sleeve. "Can you make sure I have everything set up properly?"

We left the foyer and entered the nearby living room, separated from the entryway by a low wall. Amy had lined up three rows of mismatched chairs. They faced a small wooden podium. She'd also commandeered a sound system for the occasion.

"Wow. Must have taken some time to organize all this," I said.

"It sure did." She smoothed her long black skirt and said, "The last to-do on my list is to check the sound system. Go and say something into the mic."

I crept over to the podium. "What do you call a frozen dog?" I waited a beat. "A pupsicle."

I could recognize the rumble of a laugh that floated my way, and I felt a sense of wonder at bringing Josh happiness. Too bad nobody else appreciated my punny sense of humor.

The men soon came over to the sectioned-off room. Principal Lewis must have unburdened himself to Josh because he flashed me a quick smile.

Now that I'd made certain the sound system worked, I stepped away from the podium to sit down in the last row. Sitting in the back made sense since I hadn't been that close to Helen.

Everyone else who'd been invited seemed to follow the same clock. They arrived at Amy's house in a huge mass. Alice wore a sensible black dress with kitten heels. Marina arrived with red-rimmed eyes and carried a large box with her. The two sat down in the front row.

Jessie showed up with a very made-up face wearing a poof of a dress while Brandon swept in with a dark T-shirt and jeans. Donna crept inside wearing a homespun dress accessorized with an antique cameo necklace. The janitor had on his typical down jacket, though he'd taken off his baseball cap in deference and displayed a mop of white hair.

Finally, Helen's father arrived, looking stiff in his collared shirt and pressed slacks.

As soon as she noticed Scott in the room, Amy stepped up to the microphone. "Let us begin."

Though she hadn't printed out a physical pamphlet, Amy seemed to have prepared a strict schedule. She first called Marina up to the podium.

Helen's roommate carried over the box she'd been holding and shuffled to the front. She placed it down and pulled out a phonograph. I didn't think I'd ever seen one of those machines in person. Marina must have borrowed it from the antique store.

After she set it up, she brought out an album. She took a deep breath and said, "This was one of Helen's favorite songs. I think it summarizes how I feel about her, too."

She slipped the record onto the phonograph, put the needle onto the vinyl, and let the music play. Then she stepped to the side.

Familiar strains of music began to play. When Nat King Cole's liquid voice filled the room, the song was undeniably "Unforgettable." From where she stood, Marina hummed the melody.

I glanced at the others around me. I'd selected a seat on the far end of the row and had a view of the handful of spectators. People whispered the words, bobbed their heads, or cast their eyes down, deep in reverie.

Josh, sitting beside me, distracted me from my observations by squeezing my hand. I looked over at him, and he gazed at me with a soft smile playing on his lips. To be fair, it was kind of a romantic song for a memorial service. My heart fluttered at his touch.

Then the song finished, and a screech sounded from the phonograph. Marina wiped away a tear, stepped forward, and stopped the player. She unplugged it and retrieved the machine.

After she sat down, Amy popped up from her seat. She opened the floor to any speakers who wanted to share a tribute. Josh and I remained seated, but I darted a glance at Alice.

She caught my look and gave me a quick head shake. Though she could command a class of rowdy kindergarteners with ease, she disliked speaking in front of adults. Principal Lewis, who sat beside her, started brushing invisible lint off his suit jacket. The other teachers looked away from Amy. Richard the janitor fidgeted in his seat. I mean, who had really known Helen well enough to speak?

After a long stretch of silence, Brandon volunteered and walked over to the podium. He held the microphone in his hands like he was about to kiss it. "I just want to say that Helen . . . Well, she was my soul mate."

I heard a few *awws*. I wasn't sure if people were moved by his sugary turn of phrase or his sweet looks. Josh snaked his arm around my shoulder, and I patted his knee in reassurance.

Brandon continued, "When I first saw Helen at the beach, I ended up jumping into the waves to save her . . . graded papers. And that's when we knew we were meant to be—"

Helen's father let out a huge cough that sounded almost like a snort. He covered his mouth with his fist and coughed some more.

Brandon gave a pointed look at Scott. "But we were like Romeo and Juliet. Star-crossed until the very tragic end." He hung his head, and Amy managed to get him away from the podium by taking him by the elbow and leading him back to his seat.

Even before Brandon sat back down, Scott sprang up and marched over to the podium. He snatched the microphone in a death grip. "Let me tell you something. Helen was the best surprise of my life, a blessing of a baby girl." His voice shook. "And sure, I didn't realize it as a young ambitious businessman, but I amended my ways recently. I strove to *protect* her, like any loving father would do." He paused and glared at Brandon.

The temperature in the room seemed to drop by several degrees. Josh must have also felt the chill because he pulled me closer to his side.

Scott continued railing. "And just when I had a second chance to make things better, she was taken from me." He shook his fist at the ceiling before clambering back to his chair.

Amy pushed her way up to the podium. "That's all the time we have for speeches. Now, let's calm our energy and observe a moment of silence for Helen."

A deep hush crept over the room. After the short silence, the impasse between Brandon and Scott seemed to have subsided.

Besides, Amy then invited us all to the backyard to grab a bite to eat. That would definitely create a better mood over the whole event.

I'd walked only a few steps toward the patio when somebody stumbled into me. I caught Richard before he fell.

"Sorry," he said, giving me a sheepish grin.

Without his baseball cap, I had an unobscured view of his face. He had a broad forehead, eyes of cloudy blue, and thin lips. "No worries," I said.

I turned to locate my boyfriend and saw that Principal Lewis had cornered him again. "I'd appreciate getting your business card," the principal said to Josh.

Richard looked left, right, up, and down. "Where are the refreshments?" he asked me.

"I'll take you there," I said.

He clung on to my arm like a leech as I led the way outside. I passed by Alice and her teacher associates, several munching away on my honey twists.

Jessie took a moment to twirl before the ladies in her taffeta dress and show off the sequined bodice. "I wore this same gown to prom when I was crowned queen. And, of course, it still fits."

At the food area, I helped Richard pick up an empty plate. I saw Scott and Brandon glaring at each other across the same long table. If Helen and Brandon had gotten married, I wondered what kind of crazy father and son-in-law disaster would have resulted.

Richard took his time getting his snack. He asked me about the ingredients in the honey twists and how the wonton wrappers ended up getting so intertwined.

Finally, Scott strutted off and disappeared inside the house, and I didn't have to endure the angry vibes between him and Brandon. When he reappeared outside, he held a large bag in his hands. In a booming voice, he said, "I appreciate everyone attending this service in memory of my daughter. Can someone help clear a space on this table?"

Like usual, Alice volunteered first and reorganized the snacks and drinks.

"Here's a little parting gift to thank you all," Scott said, laying out a spread of beautiful shawls in a wide array of colors.

Brandon retreated from the display and Josh opted out, but Principal Lewis quickly selected a gray shawl. We ladies took our time, fawning over the luscious fabrics. Alice selected a dark purple, her favorite shade, while the other teachers picked muted colors. I opted for lucky red (Ma would've been proud).

Everyone said their goodbyes, and I escorted Richard to the front door. I also managed to pry Josh away from Principal Lewis, who seemed intent on getting a few last words in with my boyfriend.

After Josh and I buckled into the car, I said, "What were you and the principal talking about for so long?"

"He needed some legal advice." Josh started the car and pulled away from the curb. "Too bad we chatted so long I didn't get a chance to try one of your amazing-looking honey twists."

"Oh no." I clapped my hand to my forehead. "Ma's gorgeous jade platter. I need to get it back."

Josh reparked, and I sprinted to Amy's house. I had to repeatedly ring the bell before she opened up. And when she did, Amy held a bunch of smoldering sticks in her hand.

CHAPTER

≈ twenty-two ≈

"WHAT ARE YOU doing?" I asked, gesturing to the smoking branches in Amy's hand.

She tried to hide the bundle behind her back, but I could still see the smoke snaking up in the air. A heavy earthy fragrance filled the house.

"Kind of smells like, er, Mary Jane."

She sighed and brought the branches back out. "It's sage. Meant to clear the air of vengeful spirits."

Spirits? I didn't believe in the supernatural much, but owning a psychic cat had definitely expanded my beliefs. I missed Marshmallow; his dry wit would've alleviated the tension at the service today.

"Do you have some sort of haunting?" I asked, peering around her home, particularly at her television. Did she have a poltergeist lurking behind the screen?

"It's not that." She pointed to the living room, where the chairs were still set up for the memorial service.

"Wait, are you talking about . . . Helen's ghost?" I stared at her in disbelief. Then again, the woman did carry a lucky clover keychain and had practically *hissed* herself when she'd spotted my cat.

Amy crisscrossed the house, all the while waving the sage. "I just don't feel like Helen's at peace."

Was she saying that as a general comment, or had she witnessed something untoward the day of Helen's death? I stepped into the middle of her weaving path. "Do you know anything that might help the case?"

She stopped moving the bundle of sage, and her left hand stroked her stomach. "Of course not. Don't be ridiculous. I *belly* knew her."

"You what?" Even as an untrained psychologist, I'd caught her Freudian slip. "Did you say 'belly'?"

"Ha." She laughed it off. "You must have misheard me. I said I barely knew her."

Nice try, Amy.

Her free hand fluttered in the air. "Anyway, why'd you come back?"

Gesturing to her backyard, I said, "I left my favorite platter."

"I'll go get it for you." She placed the sage down in a decorative glass bowl on an end table and bustled outside. It felt like she had wanted to get away from me—and my probing.

While I stood waiting, I wandered over to a nearby bookcase in her front room. I loved checking out what people read. Their taste in books often gave me insight into their character. I myself read young adult fiction. Did that mean I was a teen at heart? Amy's shelves were lined with tomes on the esoteric: the magic of Stonehenge, voodoo rituals, and ancient Egyptian animal familiars.

She soon returned with my jade platter and thrust it at me. "There you are. Bye now."

How awkward to end the visit this way. "Thanks again for hosting the service," I said.

She shifted from one foot to the other. "It was the least I could do."

I said goodbye, and she shut the door behind me. What secret knowledge could she have? Amy had mentioned the word "belly," and it didn't seem like a coincidence that Helen had suffered an upset stomach the day she'd died.

I found Josh still sitting in the car where I'd left him. However, he wasn't wearing his usual smile. A deep furrow creased his brow instead.

I slid into the passenger's seat and asked, "What's wrong?"

Josh fiddled with his own business card. The prosperous-sounding name of "Murphy, Sullivan, and Goodwin" flashed up at me.

I touched him on the shoulder. "Didn't you get a rave review during your last performance meeting?"

He turned to me in slow motion. In the sunlight, a hint of gold reflected in his deep brown eyes. My breath caught at the beauty of it.

Josh shook his head, and his bangs swished away. "It's not about work. Or rather, it's about getting more work."

"That sounds like a good thing."

He jerked his thumb back at Amy's house. "Principal Lewis asked me for a favor."

I searched my memory. Why would the principal need legal advice? "Is it about that mysterious note he got from Helen?"

"Yeah. The code is actually CFR Title 29 Part 1604.11."

"Oops. I couldn't remember the entire train of numbers." Detective Brown had said they hadn't found any hCG in Helen's system, so I ventured a guess. "The legalese isn't even related to pregnancy, right?"

"The regulation covers sexual harassment. The principal's worried because Helen had threatened to file a claim. He asked me to check up on that."

I gazed into Josh's earnest eyes. "Are you worried you'll pull up something unsavory?"

He put his hands up. "It's really not my area of expertise." Josh's familiarity with legal patents didn't make him an expert on workplace discrimination.

He scratched the back of his ear and continued, "I'm going to ask around my alumni network and see if she filed anything. And I'll be scrutinizing the principal's résumé on his LinkedIn account to cover the bases."

"Why?"

"To see how long he lasted at his old jobs. For Alice's sake."

I nodded.

"Maybe you should talk to her and get her perspective on the principal's behavior. Just in case."

He was probably right. I scrunched my nose. But I should ask her in a lighthearted location, to make it a less intense experience.

It was going to be an icky conversation, especially if I did find something off about the principal. I should bring Marshmallow along, too—we might need some pet therapy, what with the sure-to-be-uncomfortable talk.

CHAPTER

twenty-three

ALICE AND I met up at a cat café called Just for Licks. It was located in Century City, near various production studios. I'd often wanted to make the drive there to watch a live show taping.

Instead, I'd finally made it so I could check out the opening of a new cat café. The painted sign outside showed two calico cats playing tug of war with a giant ball of yarn.

"Cute," I said to Marshmallow as I walked in with Nimbus in my arms.

"Kitschy," Marshmallow said, following me in with plodding steps.

The spacious lobby boasted a feline theme with mock famous artwork on the wall, including a cats-playing-poker print. A tiger-striped carpet blanketed the ground beneath our feet.

Marshmallow froze. "Did they really think a rug made to resemble a skinned cat was a good idea?"

"Be happy you didn't have to stay inside my purse this time." We'd done some sleuthing in secret before, when I'd had to sneak him into some pet-unfriendly places.

We walked over to a fenced area where I saw people mingling with a number of rescue cats up for adoption. Folks looking for a furry companion could pay an admission fee to play with the kittens—and hopefully adopt one. I saw a tall man clucking his tongue and dangling a stuffed mouse toy and cooing to a nearby kitty.

Marshmallow murmured, "And who said humans couldn't be trained?"

"Mimi, over here." I heard my sister calling me from the other side of the lobby.

We went to the far end of the lobby to the café side. Alice held the gate open for us to enter the space. Tables took up a third of the room, but the rest of the space was designated as a deluxe kitty playground. Owners got to sit down and eat at metal mesh tables while their pet cats had the chance to explore a wonderland of ladders, tunnels, and even a spiral staircase.

In fact, Nimbus jumped out of my arms and scampered up a ladder to reach a ledge that ran the perimeter of the ceiling. Marshmallow blinked at the cat-opia and said, "I'm a cat, not a rat to put in a maze."

He chose instead to greet Alice with a gentle head butt. She crouched down and opened her arms to him, and he jumped into them.

We made our way to an empty table and sat down. Then Alice proceeded to pamper Marshmallow. He welcomed the petting fest.

"This is the life," he said. "Can you also scratch an itch I have? A little more to the right . . . ahh."

I slipped the menu out of the plastic holder on the table.

"I'm going to order the vanilla cat-puccino," Alice said.

My tummy growled. I'd need something more substantial than coffee to tide me over. "I'm digging the Hello Kitty hotcakes."

We called one of the waitstaff over and placed our orders.

I watched Nimbus scale up a brick wall for a few moments before turning my attention to Alice. "I need to ask you a delicate question."

"Um, may I be excused?" Marshmallow said, but Alice had a tight grip on him.

My sister held my gaze. "You know we don't have any secrets between us."

I took a deep breath, held it briefly, and exhaled. "It's about Principal Lewis. He confided in Josh at the memorial service. Have you ever seen him do anything, er, unprofessional?"

Ma had given her own version of the birds and the bees—the cranes and crickets—to a teenaged me. The talk had been shrouded in so many allusions that I hadn't understood a thing. And Dad had failed to enlighten me at all; he'd stammered and turned beet red every time he'd tried. In the end, he'd abdicated all responsibility to Ma.

But Alice still caught my drift. She looked appalled. "What? No," she said.

I kept pushing the issue. "Has he ever been too touchy, particularly with Helen?"

My sister blanched. "Why would you ask that?"

I lowered my voice. "This is confidential, but Helen might have started a harassment case against the principal because of his, uh, huggy ways."

Alice frowned. "I haven't heard any complaints. Probably because he's like that with everyone. He seems to view us staff like his surrogate grandkids."

"Oh, okay." I averted my gaze and glanced in Marshmallow's direction, where I noticed him dozing off.

Thankfully, the staff appeared with our order, so we could avoid an awkward silence. Alice busied herself sipping her coffee, and I devoured my Hello Kitty–shaped pancakes. The plate even came with two eggs sunny-side up.

I changed topics. "How was the memorial service for you? Did you get a chance to process?"

"Kind of. Thanks for being there with me."

"Of course, I'm your *jiejie*," I said.

"I'm glad I got to celebrate her life." She paused. "Hope I wasn't making a big scene by bawling my eyes out."

I nodded. "Nope, and your mascara didn't even run."

"Well, Jessie lightened the mood by showing off her dress." Alice adopted a royal British accent. "You know, she was crowned prom queen."

I stopped short of rolling my eyes. "I may have heard that once or twice before, but she seems like someone who would enjoy being in the limelight."

My sister shook her head with emphasis. "Oh no, you're wrong about that. Jessie wasn't supposed to be crowned queen—it just happened. She told us all about it."

I'd read the blog post, but maybe Alice knew more of the story. I leaned in. "Do tell."

Alice fiddled with her coffee mug. "Jessie's classmate got sick that night—a bout of food poisoning, so Jessie got boosted from runner-up to queen at the last minute. She helped keep the festivities going."

Food poisoning? I pushed my eggs with their oozing yolks to the side. No salmonella for me, thank you very much. They reminded me of something I'd heard from Amy . . .

I dropped my fork with a clatter, and Marshmallow groused at me. "Just when I was getting some good shut-eye," he said.

"Forgot I needed to make a phone call," I said as I excused myself from the table.

Marshmallow's ears pricked up. "Is that code for contacting the fuzz?"

I gave him a head bob before I moved back to the lobby. Scrolling through my contacts, I dialed Detective Brown's direct line.

By the gate overlooking the eating area, I watched my sister petting Marshmallow without a care in the world.

The cop answered in his gruff way. "Brown here."

"Detective," I said. "It's Mimi Lee, and I've got a lead for you."

He groaned. "Do I have to remind you what happened the last time when you didn't leave things to the professionals?"

The killer had confronted me at Hollywoof, but I'd prevailed in the end and managed to clear my name. I puffed out my chest. "I've got an excellent theory. Helen Reed complained about a stomachache, right? Well, it turns out that Jessie *undercooks* everything."

Detective Brown remained silent. As I waited for his reaction to my brilliant revelation, I snuck a glance at Nimbus. She had stopped in front of a mirror.

"Tell me you've got more than that, Miss Lee."

"Of course I do. Jessie has a history of sketchy behavior. She got her high school rival out of the way to become prom queen. And she's had her eye on that Teacher of the Year Award at Roosevelt Elementary. She'd been competing—against Helen." I saw Nimbus cock her head at the "other" cat in the mirror.

I continued, "Helen ate some of Jessie's poorly baked cookies that day—"

"Irrelevant," he said.

Nimbus arched her back and bristled at the cat in the mirror. I felt like acting in the same manner with Detective Brown.

"Just hear me out—"

"No. The victim's cause of death wasn't due to her stomach contents. Those all checked out."

"Oh." My theory had been like Nimbus's reflection: an illusion. "What happened then?"

"She may have felt nauseated, but . . . All I can say is it wasn't *food* poisoning."

I gazed over at Alice, who was rubbing Marshmallow's ears. "So my sister is totally in the clear?" I held my breath for his response.

"Not quite. Anyone at the school that day with access to the substance could have poisoned Helen Reed. This investigation is still ongoing."

I stammered. "I don't understand, Detective."

"Miss Lee, the fact remains that your sister was still the last person to see Helen Reed alive."

This wasn't the way I had wanted the conversation to go. I ended the call feeling less sure of everything.

CHAPTER
≈ twenty-four ≈

THEY SAY THAT pets and their owners sometimes look alike, and the following afternoon, my client insisted on making that twinning happen on demand. A lady with her hair in tight ringlets and boasting a face full of bronzer walked in, bringing a wave of overpowering perfume with her. She steamrolled through the door, leading a toy poodle on a leash. Nicola was off to the side, placing a DVD in the player, so I decided to greet this new customer.

"My dog's fur needs to match my hairstyle exactly," she said to me.

Nimbus continued sleeping in her corner, but Marshmallow sneezed and blinked open his eyes. Then he shut them again. "I didn't know I would be waking up to a nightmare."

"I'll be back in a while for my lovebug," she said. "Be creative with your cut, but go for a Sofia Vergara type of look. That's what I told my stylist when she did my hair."

She left with a "Ciao" and wiggled her fingers at us. Nicola and I exchanged a look.

"She may have asked for Sofia Vergara," I said, "but that lady got Shirley Temple instead." *Hiss*. My cat's snarkiness must be rubbing off on me.

Nicola sprang a Hollywood factoid on me: "Did you know that Shirley Temple always had exactly fifty-six curls in her hair?"

"Um, how is this helpful?" I wasn't about to count out the curls on the dog's body.

She shrugged. "You never know . . ."

I took the toy poodle to the back room. Thank goodness I didn't need to actually put rollers in the dog's fur to create curls.

Instead, I used the natural curliness of the poodle to my advantage. I trimmed the fur of the body and left a mop sticking out on top. Now, it looked like a matching set of curls on both pet and owner.

When the perfumed lady returned, she was delighted with her pooch's new 'do. She insisted on posting a selfie with her pet on Instagram and tagged my shop in it.

"How did you make those curls?" she asked.

"With some fancy scissors work."

She clapped her hands. "Wonderful. I usually spend *hours* at the salon, and they put all this stuff in my hair to make it curl."

I touched the poodle's curly mane. "No chemicals needed. This is all natural."

As the owner left after blowing kisses to Nicola, me, and even the cats, I thought back on my own words. Chemicals.

Detective Brown had said Helen hadn't suffered from food poisoning. Could it have been a chemical of some sort instead?

And that's when my sister burst in through the door. I gaped at

Alice and checked the time. She must have rushed over right after school had ended.

I hurried toward her. "Is everything okay?"

She clutched a piece of paper in her hand, and her gaze flitted around the store.

"Talk to me," I said, leading her over to rest in the waiting area. "Nicola, can you refill the dog biscuits?"

Nicola raised her eyebrows at the glass jar. It looked three-quarters full, but she still left to give us some privacy.

On the cream pleather bench, Alice shivered. "I had the strangest feeling all day long. Kind of like when someone's watching you and the hairs on your neck rise up?"

"Did you see anyone odd around?" I asked.

"No. I even walked up and down the sidewalk in front of school to check. Nobody in sight."

"Then maybe it's just your imagination."

"You're probably right." She bit her bottom lip. "I even noticed a police car across the way, so I shouldn't feel anxious."

Excellent. Detective Brown had kept his promise.

"I also found this paper stapled to a utility pole." She dropped the flyer into my hand.

Smoothing it out, I read, "'Have you seen my cat?'" A short description of a fluffy gray kitten followed.

Alice tapped at the photo. "Is that Nimbus?"

"Can't make out much from this blurry image."

She wrung her hands. "I thought maybe you could tell offhand since you've been around her a lot."

I squinted at the picture. "Looks like a fuzzy Rorschach blot to me."

"I'd hate it if the flyer was from her owner. Maybe I should call the number and double-check."

"No," I said, folding up the flyer. It might actually be from Edgar, and I wouldn't want my sister anywhere near that creep. "I'll look into it."

Alice seemed like she wanted to argue with me over who should take responsibility, but she got distracted by Marshmallow and Nimbus. They'd woken up, and the cats scampered over to nuzzle Alice's legs.

After my sister left, Marshmallow glared at me. "I've told you before. Wake me up when something good happens."

"Sorry," I said. "I was more concerned about dealing with this flyer."

I showed the cats, and Nimbus meowed at the gray blur of a shot.

Marshmallow's fur bristled. "That's the old captor's handiwork all right."

"How are you so sure?"

Marshmallow extended a paw at the phone number. Besides the usual area code, the seven digits had been made into a mnemonic: "ALL-4-POE."

I raised an eyebrow. "Gothic lit lover?"

"Why do you think he goes by the nickname of 'Edgar'?"

"A Poe fanboy, huh?"

I had to find a way to keep the man away from Alice and the cats. In fact, I'd just remembered one of Poe's scary stories involving a murderous narrator: "The Tell-Tale Heart."

Could Edgar have exacted revenge on Helen? I snuck a glance at Nimbus. Maybe for her inadvertently stealing his talking cat? And might I be his next victim?

CHAPTER

twenty-five

TO UNDERSTAND WHAT possible threat I needed to prepare for, I had to figure out what kind of poison Helen had been exposed to. Her autopsy report would spell it out. Detective Brown had all the answers, but he guarded them like a Doberman. So, I came ready to meet him on his home turf, with not one, but two bribes.

Upon Josh's recommendation, I'd grabbed a dozen mochi doughnuts from the local Hawaiian bakery earlier this morning. I'd also brought along Nimbus, whom the entire police station had obviously adored before. Marshmallow tagged along, too, but said, "Remember, nobody touches this *mahvelous* fur."

I soon arrived at the station with the treats. Detective Brown watched as I put Nimbus down several feet from him and placed a doughnut box on top of his desk. "Thanks for getting someone to monitor the school," I said.

He grunted. "The officer will only patrol the neighborhood on week-days. At three in the afternoon." Then he continued with his paper-work.

A crowd soon gathered around Nimbus. From my purse, I pulled out a cat toy: a wand with a long rainbow swirl of cloth. One eager police-man grabbed the stick and waved it at Nimbus.

She caught it and tugged at the colorful fabric. The policeman laughed and tried the same trick with Marshmallow, who blinked back and said, "Excuse me. Why are you dangling that in my face?"

Nimbus kept getting petted, and her purring grew louder over time. Detective Brown finally broke his concentration and peeked over to where Nimbus lay on her back, with multiple police officers giving her massages.

"Maybe I'll take a peek at the kitten," Detective Brown said, "to make sure she's doing okay. She still doesn't have an owner?"

"Not yet . . ."

As he ambled toward the kitten, I snuck a glance at the file folders on his desk. Pretending to lean over the doughnut box, I sifted through his paperwork. There. I spotted one marked "Reed."

Looking over my shoulder, I saw Detective Brown busy stroking Nimbus's ears. I made an exaggerated motion to open the doughnut box and reach for a sugar-coated treat. In the process, I also happened to knock down the folder. "Oops."

I crouched down to examine the papers. One scribbled sticky note read, "School's camera footage shows only staff and students interact-ing with the victim on campus that day."

Detective Brown's voice practically growled. "What's going on over there?"

I froze while Marshmallow crept close to my side. Detective Brown saw the papers spread on the floor and frowned. "You should know better, Miss Lee."

"What?" I said, trying for a straight face. "I'm naturally clumsy."

"True," Marshmallow said. "Just ask my tail."

"I'll pick those papers up without your meddling assistance," Detective Brown said as he returned my way. He shielded my view of the documents as he gathered them up. Then he kept a tight grip on the file folder as he asked me to leave the station in a firm voice.

I took Nimbus and slunk off.

At the car, I started settling the cats in the back. "What a waste of time. I was so close to reading those papers. And I didn't even get a doughnut out of this whole mess." My mouth salivated as I thought of the ringed dough made with the slight chewy give of mochi rice flour.

Marshmallow narrowed his eyes at me as I placed him in his carrier. "Like humans are the only literate ones around."

"No offense," I said as I clicked his cage shut. "I really wanted my plan to work, and the cause of Helen's death was within arm's reach."

Marshmallow licked his paw. "Oh, you mean, the one listed on her autopsy report. Like I said, people didn't corner the market on reading."

My mouth dropped open. "Did you happen to see the document?" He had been by my side near the scattered papers.

"While you and the detective were having a verbal cat fight, I had plenty of time to spy the chemical responsible for Helen's death. Mercury."

Mercury? Something about the element tickled the back of my brain, but I couldn't quite remember. What I did realize, as I looked at my car clock, was that I needed to get a move on to open up the shop on time.

• • •

Five minutes after I unlocked Hollywoof for business, Nicola sailed in with stars in her eyes. Registering her dreamy face, I asked, "Did you land a role?"

She'd mentioned several recent auditions, and I wondered if she'd gotten her big break.

Nicola dazzled me with her halogen smile and said, "I did. I'm going to be an extra."

"An extra what?"

"You know, a person who's in the background in a scene."

From his usual napping spot, Marshmallow turned his head our way. "If you can get paid for lying around, count me in."

Beside Marshmallow, Nimbus played with a ball of yarn.

Nicola rubbed her hands. "I'll get an acting credit to my name."

"Congrats," I said as the shop bell jingled. Impeccable timing. It had added a celebratory chime to my remark.

Indira glided in, exuding her usual Bollywood star power. Dressed in lycra and wearing her typical fanny pack, she radiated a healthy glow. With one hand, she rolled in a suitcase. In the other, she held a leash attached to a very excited tan Chihuahua.

The little dog started yipping and almost tangled herself in the lead trying to reach Marshmallow. Indira let go of the rolling bag and unclipped the puppy.

Ash rushed toward Marshmallow, and Nimbus shrank back from the excitable dog. Marshmallow meowed, perhaps introducing the puppy and kitten to each other.

I turned to Indira. "Lovely to see you. And Ash is looking wonderful."

She pointed to her suitcase of merchandise. "All thanks to my popular line of puppy pouches. The profits allowed me to fund Ash's leg surgery." The poor doggie had suffered from patellar luxation, a knee condition.

Nicola murmured hello from the side of the room, and Indira gave her a quick nod. "You seem to be enjoying this position more than your last one."

Nicola turned pale and excused herself to tidy up the back room. No doubt she didn't want to relive memories of how she'd been let go during her last job as Lauren Dalton's assistant. The famous producer's wife also happened to be one of Indira's acquaintances.

"She's still sensitive about that," I said in a low voice.

"Best to toughen up if she wants to survive in this town," Indira said. "By the way, kudos to you for trying to renegotiate our deal. I'll agree to the fifty-fifty split for bag sales if you'll carry my latest versions."

Wow. I couldn't believe I'd stood up for myself and gotten my way with Indira. Even though she respected me as a fellow entrepreneur, she was also a skilled businesswoman who always focused on the bottom line.

Indira laid down the suitcase on top of Lassie's golden star on the Bark of Fame floor. She zipped it open and said, "Tah-da. My latest batch."

Indira's hit merchandise were bags made to carry puppies nestled against the chest. However, the new supply she wanted me to stock at Hollywoof didn't display her usual appealing shades. One looked vomit green. Another—

"Is that the lovely color of armpit stain?" Marshmallow said from his corner.

I rubbed my eyes. The pouches also looked uneven in their coloring. "Why are there spots and streaks on them?"

Indira jutted her chin out. "Can't you tell art when you see it right in front of your face?"

"Uh, sure." Though, to be honest, I'd never been one to understand paintings made with splatters and blocks of color. No wonder she'd agreed to a fifty-fifty split with me for these latest designs. "But why the new stock? We still have a few of the other ones left."

Indira pointed at the suitcase's contents. "I had a light bulb idea to use naturally derived colors, like beet juice. You can market them as eco-positive bags."

"That does have a nice ring to it." I hung up the streaked pouches on the wall rack.

Indira zipped her suitcase shut. "Nice doing business with you, Mimi."

After she'd left, I turned to Marshmallow. "She's on top of the latest environmental trends."

"And alert about her pocketbook. I'm sure beet juice has to be a cheaper alternative to artificial dye."

Cheap and marketable. That sounded like a winning combination right up Indira's alley. "A light bulb idea," she'd called it. And that's when something shifted in the murder case for me.

CHAPTER

twenty-six

I MANAGED TO DO a series of shampoos and even a nail trimming after Indira's visit, but during a break in business, my mind returned to the phrase she'd used: "light bulb idea." The term had reminded me of the mercury bulb and broken glass from Helen's classroom.

Did Helen have direct skin contact with the mercury from the bulb? I wondered if the janitor, Richard, might shed some light on the matter. After all, he'd cleaned up the classroom with the broken glass.

Turning to Nicola, who sat on the stool near the register, I said, "It's pretty late in the afternoon. Do you think you could close up shop by yourself this evening? I want to swing by my sister's school and would like to beat the rush hour traffic."

"Sure," Nicola said. "But do you want to hear about my celeb sighting first? It was the back of his head, but I think I'm an expert on the nape of Gosling's neck."

"Spare me from this torture," Marshmallow said, springing over to my side.

"Maybe next time you can tell me more about Ryan, but I should go now. And"—I scooped up Nimbus and nodded at Marshmallow—"I'll take the kitties with me."

I held the door open for Marshmallow to exit. "After you, Sour Puss," I said.

Marshmallow whipped my leg with his tail as he passed by.

We had a smooth drive over to Roosevelt Elementary, zipping along the highway. When we arrived at the parking lot, only the spot labeled "Principal" was filled.

I hurried down the hallways carrying Nimbus in a doggie pouch and hoped I wasn't too late to catch Richard. But Alice had mentioned that the janitor took public transportation to work, so the lack of another car in the parking lot didn't mean much.

"Tell me if you spot him," I said to Marshmallow.

We decided to split up for efficiency's sake. My cat headed in one direction while I bustled the opposite way.

I soon heard a plaintive mewl. "Found him," Marshmallow said.

Doubling back, I ran down the corridor and spied Marshmallow at the end. Huffing after the quick sprint, I took a break, leaning on a nearby ash tree planted on the strip of green lawn.

I wondered if I should take up spinning class like Pixie—or even golf, like my dad. I frowned. He spent way too much time on the course instead of being at home with Ma.

A supplies cart sat in front of an open classroom. A construction paper poster on the inside of the door read "Miss Amy's Domain."

The janitor strolled out of the doorway, a gray wastebasket in his hands. As soon as he saw me, Richard set the trash can down. Meanwhile, Marshmallow darted into the classroom, saying, "Ah, time to relax in the AC."

Richard didn't seem to notice Marshmallow. Instead, he adjusted the brim of his baseball cap and spoke to me. "Alice, are you still here? Do you need something?"

Nimbus wiggled in the pouch, so I removed her from the soft carrier and placed her on the ground to better focus on my conversation with the janitor.

I tried to make my voice sweeter and higher, to match the dulcet tones of my sister. "I really liked that pencil lamp Helen had in her classroom. Could I take a look at it again?"

Richard frowned. "The new teacher got rid of it. Said it was too wobbly for her to use, a safety hazard."

"Oh." I couldn't keep the frustration out of my voice. What a dead end.

Richard must have noticed my dismay and started rubbing his chin in thought. After a few moments, he said, "You could ask Donna."

"Excuse me?"

"If I remember correctly"—here he adjusted his cap—"she was the one who gave the lamp to Helen in the first place."

"She didn't need it anymore?" Then again, maybe her class of fifth graders wouldn't have appreciated the kiddie pencil shape. "I thought the lamp came from Room 13. The computer lab?"

"When she switched grades, Donna also asked to change rooms." Richard coughed into his hand. "She never liked that number." Of course, unlucky 13.

Had Donna poisoned Helen with her Trojan pencil? She might have done it out of spite, providing the fatal lamp to the upstart teacher who'd booted her out of the younger grade she'd wanted to teach.

Richard continued standing before me, as though waiting for a response.

"Er, I'll go ahead and ask Donna tomorrow," I said, taking on the role of my sister.

I heard a loud meow as Nimbus leaped into the trash can. She tossed around in it and eventually knocked it over. A jumble of broken crayons, crumpled papers, and pieces of yarn fell out.

"Sorry about that," I said as I cleared the debris off Nimbus and placed her back in the pouch.

"Did you bring your kitty to school?" he asked, frowning at me.

"It was for, uh, a special Show and Tell."

"Just this once then," Richard said. He picked up the mess and placed it back into the wastebasket. Then he dumped the whole load into a larger trash can attached to his supplies cart.

"Here, you missed a few," I said, crouching over to pick up the stray crayon bits. Could he have accidentally left some mercury behind because of his failing eyesight?

Richard grunted and bent down to replace the trash bag. In the process, his back popped. The poor old man.

I heard a loud purr of delight coming from the classroom. Soon after, Marshmallow sauntered out with something in his mouth. From the shape and size of it, I sure hoped it wasn't a dead mouse.

"Quick. Open up your purse," he said. "Before Richard straightens up."

I shuddered but did as he asked, and Marshmallow dropped the item inside. As it plopped down, I breathed a sigh of relief. The object I'd seen had been made of cloth. I wondered what Marshmallow had discovered.

"Thanks for your help, Richard," I said, excusing ourselves and going around the corner.

"What did you put in here?" I said as I placed my purse on a wooden bench with a view of the nearby concrete handball wall.

I slipped out the item and noted a silver ball head pin in the middle of it. Was it a pincushion? But as I paid more attention to the object, I realized it looked kind of like a crude doll. "What exactly am I holding?" I asked Marshmallow.

He twitched his whiskers. "It was hidden in the back of Amy's desk drawer."

I examined the simple features of the doll: wide eyes, flushed cheeks, and pink lips drawn in permanent marker. Given Amy's reading preferences from her home library, I made an educated guess and shivered at the creepiness of it. "I think this is a voodoo doll."

"Made to resemble Helen, I bet," Marshmallow said. It did have a familiar shade of light brown yarn for the hair.

"No wonder she wanted to burn sage after the memorial service," I said. "Helen's ghost *would* be furious about this."

Marshmallow unsheathed his claws and pointed at the cloth figure. "The question is: Did Amy do the same thing in real life as she did to this doll?"

I didn't believe in black magic, but I couldn't leave the pin in the doll. "We'd better put this back before the door gets locked, and Amy discovers it's gone."

Creeping around the corner, I was relieved to see Richard's cart still there. Except the janitor seemed to be inside the classroom now. "If only I had a good distraction," I mumbled.

"I know just the thing," Marshmallow said. "Put Nimbus down."

I placed Nimbus on the ground, and they meowed at each other. Then Nimbus scrambled up the branches of the ash tree.

Running inside the classroom, I said, "Richard, my kitten's stuck in the tree. Can you fetch a ladder?"

He stopped wiping down a student desk. "Of course."

I watched him shuffle down the corridor to get a ladder. Then I nodded at Marshmallow, who directed me to the appropriate drawer in Amy's desk. I placed the doll and pin down gently.

"Wow," I said to Marshmallow. "How ever did you manage to open this?"

"Practice makes perfect," he said.

"Wait a minute. Is that why the cat treats have been disappearing so quickly from the kitchen?"

Marshmallow puffed up his fur. "I need to eat well to keep up this fab physique."

I sighed but decided to save the reprimanding for later. Hearing a commotion from outside, I went through the open doorway. I saw Richard dragging a ladder down the hall.

Right before he reached the classroom, Nimbus made a graceful jump and landed safely in the grass.

"Oh," I said. "Guess she was able to make it down on her own."

"Well, I'm glad your kitten is fine," Richard said.

He had such a kind soul. I really didn't want him to be involved with Helen's death.

When I returned to the parking lot, I spotted Principal Lewis near his car. I waved at him and assumed he'd stop to chat. Instead, he hurried to unlock his car and hopped behind the driver's seat. He screeched out of the parking lot as though I'd chase him down.

Why was he so scared? Could it have anything to do with Edgar lurking around campus?

"Do you smell cigar smoke right now?" I asked Marshmallow, hoping he wouldn't detect the telltale scent. He and Nimbus conferred, but both of them shook their heads.

I checked out the school's surroundings and didn't see anyone. However, I did spy a familiar-looking flyer on a utility pole across the street. Edgar probably thought the cat rescuer would come to him. At least that meant he would bide his time before disturbing Alice or anyone else at the school.

We got into my Prius. As I turned onto the residential streets, I didn't see any sign of the principal's car. He really had sped away from Roosevelt Elementary. If it wasn't fear about Edgar, why was he leaving his workplace so quickly? Maybe he'd wanted to ditch the bad memories— either of Helen's death or her discrimination accusations.

Or perhaps it was something more innocuous. Maybe he'd been rushing home to see his wife for date night. Speaking of which . . .

I had my own outing planned for this evening. I'd be treated to a gem of a theater that specialized in playing old films with my very own diamond of a man.

I made sure to tuck the cats into their beds before I left. The temperatures had started dipping lower at night, and I draped the shawl gift I'd gotten around Nimbus. Marshmallow watched with wide eyes as I fussed over the kitten.

"Do you want a blanket, too?" I asked Marshmallow.

He shook his head. "I'm never cold, Mimi. As expected, since I'm so sizzling hot."

"Yeah, you're full of fire and vinegar."

Marshmallow grumbled, and I patted him on the head. "But I wouldn't have you any other way."

He harrumphed at me but settled down in his bed and closed his eyes.

• • •

Downtown El Segundo looked charming with its quaint row of shops. Even though it was located right next to the LAX Airport, it felt like a small town—except when the jet engines roared in the sky overhead.

Josh and I strolled hand in hand toward the small movie theater. We'd found the venue through Yelp and had been excited to hear about the black-and-white films it regularly featured. They even offered silent movies once in a while, complete with an accompanying Wurlitzer organ player.

Though the outside looked like nothing more than a solid brick building, the inside theater held faded plush velvet seats. The high ceiling and the ornate columns throughout the space brought to mind the Golden Age of Hollywood. I made a mental note to tell Nicola about the theater on the next workday.

Josh and I happened to be two of only a handful of moviegoers, so when the lights dimmed, we grabbed seats in the front row. Darkness fell, and a beam of light shot forth from the back of the room and settled onto the huge screen before us. I heard the whir of the movie projector.

We'd selected *Sabrina* to watch, a classic romantic film. But then the machine behind us started clunking. The image onscreen flickered.

A disembodied voice announced: "Sorry. Technical difficulties, ladies and gentlemen. While we fix this problem, go ahead and visit the concession stand for a free snack of your choice." The lights turned back on to full blaze.

Josh squeezed my hand. "What would you like, Mimi?"

"Popcorn would hit the spot."

Josh quickly returned carrying an overflowing bucket of popcorn. Grinning, he also produced a box of Goobers.

"You remembered." I'd told him once that I liked mixing the two snacks together. The rich buttery flavor of popcorn paired well with the sweet chocolate-covered peanuts.

I mixed the treats together and started snacking. Sometimes, I scooped up an extra portion just so our hands could collide in the tub.

After five minutes had passed, I frowned at the screen. "It's not fixed yet?"

I noticed other people grumbling. A few even walked out.

With no movie to watch, Josh leaned toward me and asked, "How was your day?"

"Well, I happened to see Principal Lewis"—I didn't mention I had been *snooping* at Alice's school—"and he didn't seem very keen on talking to me. In fact, he practically ran away."

Josh furrowed his brow. "He must still be worried about that potential lawsuit."

I glanced around the mostly empty theater but lowered my voice anyway. "Did you find out anything more about the threat?"

He traced the rim of the popcorn tub. "Actually, I did track down the lawyer Helen consulted with. The guy was pretty forthcoming . . . once he found out I was a fellow Trojan."

I groaned. A buddy from the University of Southern California, rival college to my UCLA alma mater. But at least the brotherly connection had made the other guy spill. "What did he tell you?"

"He advised Helen to speak directly to the principal. Though she always refused Principal Lewis's hugs, and he complied, she felt uncomfortable saying no to him all the time. Sounded like the old man maybe had no clue about business protocol, especially about hugs in the workplace."

Reflecting on the age of Principal Lewis, I realized he came from a different cohort, people born in a specific generation, than Helen. Maybe he'd even heard of the Harlow monkey study, which showed that touch was needed for humans to thrive. Or perhaps all those years of seeing little kids run up and embrace their teachers with joy had rubbed off on him.

I munched as I thought. "Do you know if they ended up hashing it out?"

"Well, during their consultation, the lawyer mentioned the legal code, how she could file something pursuant to CFR Title 29 if things got worse. But there was never any official lawsuit. Instead, Helen told the lawyer she'd proactively write a note to the principal and nip the issue in the bud before it turned into something creepy."

"Huh. Her aggressive threat to the principal must have been her way to prevent a future problem." Perhaps the apple didn't fall far from the tree. I bet her father had done the same thing, leveraging his funds to keep Helen from being given the pink slip last year.

"Let's talk about something else," Josh said. "We're here to get out and have fun . . ."

"Right." I smiled up at him.

He touched my fingertips with his, and I didn't mind their buttery slipperiness. "Even though there are technical difficulties, I'm still glad I get to do this with you, Mimi."

My heart bounded like an excited puppy with a slipper to chew.

"My parents are extremely excited about our new relationship," he said. "They actually mentioned wanting to meet you through video chat. What do you say?"

My voice croaked. "Sure." Though we'd been together for months, Josh's parents had been so busy running their business in Hawaii that I hadn't met them yet. "Do you think they'll like me?"

"They'll love you," Josh said, his wide grin putting some of my fear to rest.

I nestled closer to him. I looked forward to the upcoming romantic flick, even though I knew it couldn't compete with my real-life relationship.

The speaker in the theater blared, and the announcer said, "Our apologies, folks. We have to switch out the movie."

The new film started playing, and we soon realized it wasn't a romantic movie. The popcorn kernels scraped at my throat. The film, *Gaslight*, depicted a man who was trying to convince his new wife she was going crazy, all in order to gain access to valuable jewels. I suddenly recalled how I, too, thought I'd been going insane when my cat had started talking. But in my case, his talent had turned out to be very real.

Near the end of the movie, I realized I was so freaked out I hadn't eaten very much. We still had half a tub of snacks left. After the police finally arrested the villainous husband, I felt a wave of relief.

When the credits rolled, I started smiling. The villain's capture, along with the entire gaslighting situation, had planted a new idea in my head on how to deal with Edgar.

CHAPTER

= twenty-seven =

I PREPARED FOR MY confrontation, scheduling it on a teacher in-service day, so students wouldn't be around. Well before the appointed time with Edgar, I leaned against the elm tree in front of Roosevelt Elementary. Nimbus lay cuddled in my arms, and a brown grocery bag lay at my feet.

Edgar came fumbling around the corner, but at least he'd arrived on time. I saw the edge of a cloth sack peeking out from the tailcoat pocket of his massive black frock coat. Nimbus stiffened in my arms, although Marshmallow had already explained the plan to her multiple times.

A whiff of stale cigar smoke carried on the wind as Edgar came closer and extended his hand to me. I refused to shake it.

Up close, he had a face with a prominent forehead, dark beady eyes, and a neat square mustache. "You found my precious," he said.

I startled at the nickname. (One cat to rule them all.) "How do I know this is your kitten?"

He spoke to Nimbus. "Come here, EFV2." The kitten snuggled deeper in my arms.

I blinked at Edgar. "That's what you call your pet?"

"I don't know why she's not responding," he said. "She's the spitting image of my cat."

"Well, let me give her a snack. Maybe she's not cooperating because she's hungry."

I put Nimbus down and extracted a can of sardines from the grocery bag.

Nimbus riveted her eyes on the treat. "Fish," I heard her say in a clear, sweet voice.

Edgar's dark eyes glittered. He blurted out, "Yes, that's my cat. I heard her speak."

"I'm sorry. I don't quite understand."

He looked at me with wide-eyed wonder. "My cat used to say 'fish' every time I gave her sardines. And this kitten talks, too."

I waited a beat and then gave a slow nod. "Oh, I get it. It's a Pavlovian response. Studied it in psych class. The dog salivates in response to the bell. Maybe your cat made a hissing noise that you misinterpreted as speaking."

His mustache quivered. "No, I clearly heard her. Like I did just now."

I shrugged. "So tell me why I didn't see a collar with your info on it when I first found this kitty."

He coughed. "She, uh, got loose from my house. Must have tangled the collar in a bush."

"I looked for a microchip. There was some sort of device, but it didn't get picked up by the scanner correctly."

"It's a high-frequency emitter meant to—never mind."

I tilted my head at him. "You actually look very familiar. Did I see you around the school the day before Valentine's?"

"What? No." He edged away from me. "I didn't set one foot on the campus."

At least he hadn't during the Family and Friends event. I stared him down.

He tugged at the collar of his coat. "Really, I didn't have anything to do with that ambulance showing up."

I raised my eyebrows at him.

"I swear." He lifted his chin up. "All I did was find my cat's collar on a bush outside of the school. I didn't touch that woman."

"Fine. I believe you. Now let me feed this kitten." I opened the can of sardines. No sooner had I popped open the tab than a hearty flapping noise sounded. A dark shadow swirled overhead.

Edgar watched as a raven landed in the branches of the elm tree. His jaw dropped.

The sleek bird opened its beak. "Nevermore," it croaked.

Edgar whispered, "That bird can talk."

"Right," I said slowly as if talking to a child. "It's cawing at us."

I could see his Adam's apple bob up and down.

The raven spoke again. "Nevermore."

"This is impossible," Edgar said, but he rubbed his hands with glee. "I've discovered more talking animals."

The bird's beak opened. This time, it quoted an entire passage from "The Raven" by Poe.

Edgar's eyes glittered with greed, and he lunged for the bird.

Too quick for him, the raven flew off, landing on the blacktop expanse behind the locked school fence. Nimbus let out a startled purr of delight.

She slipped under the gate and followed the bird on silent paws. Then the animals stood frozen on the blacktop, staring at each other.

"This is my chance to get them both," Edgar mumbled. He tiptoed toward the fence and started climbing it. The animals appeared oblivious to his movements.

In the meantime, I distanced myself from the situation and slipped into the shadow of the tree. Soon, I saw the patrol car rolling down the street. This officer was prompt about following the three o'clock schedule Detective Brown had told me.

The police car flashed its sirens, and the officer spoke into his bull horn. "Stop right there, mister."

Edgar paused halfway up the fence. With his great frock coat billowing in the wind, he looked extremely suspicious.

The policeman got out of his car and called out, "I'm going to take you into custody."

Edgar climbed down, and I watched the officer manhandle him into the police car. The policeman shoved the door shut hard.

I hoped it meant double trouble for Edgar. After all, he'd been found in the act of trespassing. And not just at any elementary school, but one where complaints of a lurker had previously been reported.

Once I couldn't see the police vehicle anymore, I said, "You can come out now."

Marshmallow emerged from behind the tree. "Told you I could do it. Convincing, right?"

"You'd make a great ventriloquist."

I patted him and gave him a sardine. Meanwhile, the raven flew over to a branch of the tree, and Nimbus also returned. I tossed a sardine to the raven, who gobbled it up.

Kneeling before Nimbus, I offered her a fish. She didn't eat it but trembled by the base of the tree.

Too much shock maybe. "Don't worry, Nimbus," I said. "That man will be too busy dealing with the police to bother us. And he won't be able to step anywhere near here."

With a smile on my face, I dialed up Detective Brown to let him know Roosevelt Elementary wouldn't need a security detail anymore.

Once he picked up, I shared the good news with him. The detective didn't congratulate me. Instead, his voice rumbled over the phone. "How do you know the situation got resolved, Miss Lee?"

I kept the laughter out of my voice as I looked up at the sky. "Let's just say a little birdie told me."

He let out a loud exhale on his end. "You shouldn't try to fix things on your own so much. And the patrol will stay put since there *is* an active murder case going on."

"Speaking of solutions, I've got two great suspects for you to follow up on, janitor Richard and teacher Donna."

"Why those people specifically?"

"Because the autopsy report mentioned mercury—"

"Don't tell me you caught a glimpse of the report that day you came by. How could you have possibly read it so quickly?"

I winked at Marshmallow. "What can I say? I have sharp cat eyes." He preened himself at my praise.

I continued to share my intel with Detective Brown. "The lamp that broke in Helen's classroom was given to her by Donna and cleaned up poorly by Richard."

"Are you implying something?"

"The broken bulb released dangerous mercury and poisoned Helen."

"I'm afraid your allegations are incorrect," the detective said.

"Excuse me?"

"There isn't enough mercury in a small light bulb to be fatal."

"Oh." I kicked the trunk of the tree with my sneaker. "Well, shouldn't it be easier to narrow the list then? Who would have access to mercury? Certainly not my sister."

Detective Brown's voice hardened. "Investigations don't get solved by snap decisions. I will do my due diligence to get to the bottom of this case and bring justice to Miss Reed. I'll catch the killer." He paused. "Whoever he—or *she*—may be."

After the detective clicked off the phone, I stared at it. My big sis alert went into overdrive.

CHAPTER
twenty-eight

THE NEXT WORKDAY, I had to drag both cats into Hollywoof. I dumped them into their sunny spot to continue on with their dozing.

Nicola stepped through the door, her eyes fixated on a piece of paper while she mouthed words under her breath. She plopped onto a pleather bench, deep in concentration.

Before too long, the first customer arrived. A frazzled woman stepped in, cradling a Maltese puppy in her arms and crooning at it.

Nicola peeked up from her paper when she heard the woman's humming. She looked ready to rise, but I put my hand up. "Don't worry, I've got this." Nicola seemed immersed in prepping for an audition.

Turning to the woman calming her little dog, I said, "What can I help you with today?" I doubted it'd be a standard shampoo since the puppy's white fur looked like fresh cotton.

The owner turned to me, and her lips trembled. "My poor baby. She has tear stains."

I peered at the dog's face and saw the telltale reddish-brown trails near her eyes. Snapping my fingers, I said, "I've got just the thing for her."

"Really?"

"Yes, a blueberry facial." I didn't explain that I'd gotten the sample from a pet-pampering company and her dog would be the first to try it.

"That sounds incredible." She handed her dog over and said, "I'll just hop over to Whole Foods while you work your magic."

I silenced my inner critic. To my finance-focused dad, he'd called the store "Whole Paycheck," particularly when compared to Ma's bargain Asian grocery store finds. A twinge of guilt surfaced; I hoped Ma and Dad were doing okay. But I knew Alice was on the job, having already preordered the food for the upcoming Ultimate Date Night.

In the back room, I hooked the leash to the grooming table. "You'll look dazzling after this spa treatment," I told the puppy. "At least that's how the company marketed the product."

I squeezed the bottle, and a spray of blue lotion landed in my palm. Rubbing the cream into the puppy's fur, the delicious scent of blueberry pie floated in the air. I took my time when massaging around her face, making sure to cover the reddish tints but staying away from her sensitive eyes. I let the formula steep for a full five minutes per the instructions on the bottle before placing the doggie in the sink and rinsing her off.

I'd definitely stock up on the blueberry facial because not only did the dog smell scrumptious afterward, but her tear stains had disappeared. Her fur even shone brighter than before. To complete her polished look, I used the high-velocity dryer to fluff out her fur.

We managed to return to the front room right when the owner returned. The woman grinned and gave her puppy several kisses before paying attention to me. "Luxury treatments for our precious pups. I'm going to tell all my friends in the local MOM—Mothers of Mutts—Club."

That recommendation sounded lovely to me, and I thanked her as she left.

Nicola had put away her notes by then and sat ready by the cash register.

"Finished studying?" I said.

She pulled a face. "I've spent the last few days trying to memorize lines for a callback, so I didn't do anything this weekend. Tell me you had a more exciting time."

"Well, Josh and I had a date. You would've loved the spot. It's an old-fashioned movie theater in El Segundo—"

She whistled. "The city informally known as the Mayberry of the West."

"Come again?" The word "berry" had made my mind return to the recent dog facial.

"Mayberry. That small town from *The Andy Griffith Show.*"

El Segundo was known for its tight-knit community. People paid high prices to live in its insular embrace. I'd probably never be able to afford to rent or own anything there, which left me with my tiny apartment by the freeway. But at least I had a cute neighbor.

My cheeks flushed with heat, and Nicola asked, "Hmm, did you even watch the movie?" She gave me a sly grin.

I stumbled over my words. "We did. Actually, it was *Gaslight.*"

She arched her plucked eyebrows. "Interesting choice. Which version—1940 or 1944?"

"Uh . . ."

"Did it have Ingrid Bergman?"

I nodded.

"'Forty-four then. Directed by George Cukor."

"If you can memorize factoids like that, then you should have those lines down pat."

"From your mouth to the director's ear," Nicola said.

"What are you auditioning for now?" I asked.

Before she could answer, a loud snuffling sounded in the shop. It seemed to be coming from the cats' area. And it didn't sound like the usual snoring.

I traced the source to Nimbus, who had her eyes half open. She gave a disgruntled mewl. "Are you okay, little one?"

In response, she closed her eyes and snuffled again.

I nudged Marshmallow, who awoke and grumbled at me. "Why do you always insist on interrupting my beauty sleep?"

Bending close to Marshmallow, I whispered, "Nimbus looks sick. Can you find out what's wrong?"

I straightened up, and in a louder voice, I said, "I'm going to call the vet just in case."

After speaking with Dr. Exi's staff, I managed to snag a spot for the following day. I gave Marshmallow a questioning stare after setting up the appointment.

He twitched his nose at me. "She said she's just tired and not to make a big fuss about it."

I glanced at the almost comatose kitty. Sure, she could have been overwrought from the confrontation with Edgar, but could it be something more than that? Nimbus usually enjoyed scaling things and chasing spools of yarn. This level of inactivity was suitable for Marsh-mallow but not for a typical active kitten.

In my worry, I bit my fingernails, creating jagged ridges. I needed to distract myself tonight, or I'd spend the whole evening worrying about Nimbus—and be left with no fingernails. Who could I call on at the last minute?

I texted Alice.

Me: Sister hangout tonight? XOXO

Alice: Can't. Amy, Jessie, and Donna want to meet up.

Me: NVM then.

Alice: Let me check with Amy if you can join.

Me: Why Amy?

Alice: She's treating us . . .

A moment later, Alice sent me a happy face emoji and the details for dinner at Roscoe's.

• • •

Every branch of Roscoe's is famous for their chicken and waffles. The two items sound like potential opposites, but they create an amazing sweet and savory contrast. The restaurant chain is an institution in the Los Angeles area.

Once I'd stepped inside Roscoe's, I could smell the chicken frying. I found the teachers around a sticky wooden table and greeted them all by name. A few moments after I'd settled into my round-backed chair, the waitress came by for my order.

When we got our beverages, I stared at my glass of Sunset, a pretty concoction of fruit punch and lemonade. Though the drinks had arrived, I knew better than to fill my stomach before the enticing main course.

"Cheers," Amy said, lifting her glass up.

We clinked cups with one another. "What are we celebrating again?" I asked.

Amy lifted her shoulder in a nonchalant half shrug, but I noticed a smile playing on her lips. "Just having a teachers'—er, ladies'—night out."

Jessie's strawberry-glossed lips pursed. "But why did you bankroll it?"

"I appreciate your friendship."

"Um, I'll pay for my own plate," I said, feeling like an awkward third wheel.

Amy patted my hand. "Any sister of Alice is a friend of mine."

All of the teachers, including Alice, seemed surprised by her generosity and burst out with spontaneous guesses:

"I know what. You've come into a large inheritance."

"We're celebrating because you met someone special."

"Family member discount?"

"Principal Lewis selected you to be a new last-minute Teacher of the Year nominee."

Jessie took a giant swig from her beer bottle at that last remark.

Amy stayed mum. The ladies looked at one another as Jessie announced that she needed to powder her nose. Donna volunteered to tag along and tugged on my sister's elbow to follow. No doubt the trio of ladies would create some new hunches in the restroom.

Once they'd left the table, Amy took a huge swallow of her wine. "Want to know a secret?"

"The juicier the better."

"Burning the sage worked."

I remembered the bundle of smoking herbs at her house. "You got rid of the negative energy?"

Amy tipped her almost empty wineglass my way. "That's right. She forgave me."

My heart skipped a beat. The alcohol had gone to her head. Was she about to confess? "What did she have to forgive you for?"

Amy used her finger to circle the rim of her glass and giggled. "Let's say, she got *unstuck*. My conscience is no longer *pricking* at me."

Wait a minute. Could Amy be referring to the pin I'd taken out of the doll? Did her guilt come from the voodoo ritual? If Amy had actually committed a serious crime, surely her mind wouldn't be so easily appeased.

The others returned from their restroom rendezvous. Just in time, too. The dishes also arrived at that moment.

My mouth watered as I stared at the crispy poultry and the accompanying waffle with its little mound of butter. I felt a sudden giddiness in getting away with breakfast for dinner and added a drizzle of maple syrup to complete the decadent combination. For a few minutes, I escaped into my juicy chicken meal.

Then I focused my attention on Donna, who'd started wielding her fork and knife like weapons. She sliced her chicken into bite-sized pieces with force.

Maybe the mercury bulb hadn't done Helen in, but wouldn't Donna know where to find more mercury? I turned to her and said, "You know, I couldn't help but admire that pencil lamp Helen had in her classroom. I heard it used to be yours."

She speared a piece of chicken, chomped on it, and swallowed. "I didn't have any use for it once I switched grades. Fifth graders would have called it babyish."

"Do you know where I might find one myself?"

"It's an old model. Been in my family for ages." She paused. "I'd imagine it'd be hard to buy a brand-new one."

Her answer struck a chord in me. I realized there was another place that could clue me in about mercury. The antique store, Déjà Vu.

CHAPTER

twenty-nine

SINCE I'D ALREADY taken the morning off for Nimbus's appointment with Dr. Exi, I figured I could squeeze in a quick pit stop before the vet's office. I entered Déjà Vu, and the antique store appeared as cluttered as it had the last time. The stained glass windows hanging from the ceiling seemed to have faded in color, maybe due to a new layer of accumulated dust.

Instead of Marina behind the register, I found a wizened old man, who could serve as Dumbledore's twin—except he was shy of a full beard with his extended goatee. He stopped fussing with a large cardboard box of what appeared to be piles of receipts and invoices clumped together in a disorderly mass.

I approached the counter with my large Hello Kitty tote, careful not to bang it against the glass. After all, I had precious cargo inside.

He looked at me through his wire-rimmed glasses and said, "May I help you, miss? Although you're helping me by being here. I'd rather be with a customer than deal with this mess of an accounting system."

A snore came from my tote, where I'd hidden Marshmallow. My cat had insisted on coming along and leaving behind the "kitten coo-ties." He'd already given me an earful after missing out on the juicy gossip during my Roscoe's outing even though I'd managed to catch him up to speed.

I danced my fingertips along the side of the bag.

"You don't have to poke my eye out to wake me up," Marshmallow said.

I snorted.

"Not my fault I conked out," he said. "This bag practically suffo-cated me."

Dumbledore's clone widened his blue eyes at me. "Go ahead and laugh. The finances are kind of a joke around here."

I gestured to the cluttered aisles in the store. "Someone I know has an adorable mercury lamp. She said it was passed down to her. Do you carry those here?"

"Can't say that I do, but let me check the inventory list." He plunged his hand into the large cardboard box, shifted some crinkled papers, and finally gave up. "Maybe it'd be faster to walk through the aisles."

He came out from behind the counter, shook my hand, and intro-duced himself as Merlin. I wondered if he'd gone the wizard route be-cause of his name and thought he had to live up to it. Although he had the white hair and goatee going for him, he didn't wear a magical robe. Actually, he looked more like a tourist with his loud Hawaiian shirt and Bermuda shorts.

We moved down the aisles at a slow pace due to Merlin's slight limp. He favored his right leg when walking.

Passing by various odds and ends, we managed to stumble upon a shelf of gorgeous Tiffany lamps. Their variegated colors shone brightly when plugged into a nearby outlet. No mercury lights or bulbs in them, though.

Sucking his breath in, Merlin hobbled down a different row. "You're looking for a *mercury* lamp . . . I have some scientific instruments that have mercury in them. Here are some old barometers and thermometers. But I don't see a lamp."

I glanced at the instruments. "Do people still use measuring tools with mercury?"

"Not really. Everything is digital nowadays. In fact, I got some of these donated from a university cleaning out their storage."

I wondered if Roosevelt Elementary had their own science lab. My sister ran experiments in her kindergarten class, but she didn't do much more beyond making flowers drink colored water and showcasing stem absorption . . . But I thought she'd mentioned before that upper grades did more complex experiments in a separate classroom.

"Is there anything else I might help you with?" Merlin asked.

"I don't th—"

Marshmallow's head butted me from inside the bag.

"Oof," I said.

"Can you speak up?" Merlin cupped a hand behind his ear.

"Marina has access to mercury here right under my whiskers," said Marshmallow. "Get the lowdown on Merlin's employee. Bosses love gossiping about their hires."

Being an employer myself, I wouldn't quite put it that way. Still, I turned to Merlin. "Actually, Marina referred me to your store."

"Oh, she's a great worker."

"He's being polite," Marshmallow said. "Dig deeper."

"How *is* she doing?" I asked. "I don't know if you realized, but her roommate passed away recently. It was quite sudden. A shock to all of us who knew her."

Merlin stroked his tapered goatee. "Marina did ask me to extend her hours at the shop a few weeks ago. Said she wanted to avoid the stress at home."

"Maybe the extra work helped her cope with the loss."

We'd looped back to the register area by then, so Merlin sat down once more behind the counter. "She recently reduced her hours helping out here, though."

"I guess she's processing the grief better now."

"I'm still worried about her expensive rent. She used to complain about it all the time. I told her I could try increasing her hourly wages."

"That's very generous of you."

He spread his wrinkled hands across the countertop, covering the antique coins beneath the glass surface. "Can't take it with you to that great bank in the sky."

Wise words. "So, did she take you up on your offer?"

He let out a deep sigh. "Refused to even consider it. She said she didn't need it. Wasn't worried at all about finances."

Really? I thought the townhouse cost a pretty penny. "That's a positive attitude," I said.

"She's got a fighting spirit."

Indeed. I said goodbye to Merlin and thanked him for his time.

We exited the store, and I took Marshmallow out of the tote on the sidewalk.

"Freedom," he said, stretching his limbs.

"Do you find it odd that Marina doesn't seem worried about money? Alice and I had even suggested she get a new roommate to split the rental cost."

"It is strange," Marshmallow said, "but her general behavior is so weird. Who won't take in a stray, even if said kitty gives you a headache now and again? I mean, humans give me migraines all the time."

"Present company excluded, right?"

He didn't answer for a moment, but then he stuck his tongue out at me.

"Very funny, Marshmallow. But speaking of cute kitties needing help . . ."

We rushed back home to get Nimbus, just in time to get seen by Dr. Exi.

· · ·

In the sterile examination room, I twiddled my thumbs waiting for the vet to appear. Even Marshmallow paced back and forth in the small space. Only Nimbus looked devoid of energy, lying flat on the examination table.

Dr. Exi strode in with a worried expression on his pale face. "What's wrong with the cute kitty?"

Marshmallow widened his blue eyes. "Why, I'm totally fine. Thanks for asking."

I cleared my throat. "Nimbus is acting differently these days. She's a lot less active than before."

He quickly checked her body. "Nothing appears out of the ordinary. Anything happen recently to zap her energy?"

I tapped a staccato beat on the polished floor with my shoe. "She hasn't been sleeping well, been shivering at night."

He looked out of the window at the gloomy sky. "Could be the nippy weather. Keep her well covered at night."

I made sure to tuck in Nimbus nice and tight in her cat bed every night. Marshmallow, on the other hand, hated being covered and would claw any blanket to shreds.

"And be sure to keep her hydrated," Dr. Exi said. "Makes a real difference in energy level."

Marshmallow piped up. "She's been having some nightmares. Tossing and turning. Whining about Edgar being on the lookout for her."

I turned to the vet. "Could it be psychological? She did have a scare a few days ago."

Dr. Exi assessed Nimbus with piercing eyes. "Maybe. If so, the symptoms should pass over time. Keep maintaining a peaceful environment and a consistent schedule."

My fingers twisted together. Maybe I shouldn't have brought her to the facedown with their previous owner, but I'd needed Nimbus to provide a believable cover for the meeting.

I gave Dr. Exi a trembling smile.

"One more thing," he said, "she hasn't felt warm or anything, right?"

"Not that I noticed."

"Let me do a quick check. Please hold on to her." Using a rectal thermometer, Dr. Exi measured her temperature. After reading the display, he declared it normal.

At least she wasn't running a fever.

Dr. Exi rubbed Nimbus's back. "Give her a couple weeks to recover.

If she still has really low energy, come back in. We can run some tests then."

I thanked the vet for his time and left him cleaning his instruments. Seeing him with the thermometer reminded me to check on Roosevelt Elementary to see if their science equipment still used mercury.

CHAPTER

thirty

ALICE GOT PERMISSION from Principal Lewis for me to visit the school's science lab during lunch break after I told her my reasoning. Still, the request must have sounded odd to the principal. Why would a pet groomer want to scope out a school classroom? Although Principal Lewis let me on-site, he insisted that Richard accompany me the entire time. Alice also volunteered to tag along.

When the janitor saw me, he said, "I never realized Alice had a sister." Swiveling his head back and forth between us, he said, "You two could be twins."

I didn't tell him that he'd confused me with Alice multiple times before.

My sister and I followed Richard to a bungalow at the back of the campus. When we entered the dark classroom, the first thing I noticed was the stench of chemicals in the air. It reeked of surgical procedures, and I had to pinch my nose. Even Alice rubbed a hand over her face for a moment.

Richard flicked on the lights and must have noticed the grossed-out expressions on our faces. We probably looked like we'd smelled some stinky tofu. "There might be an odor left from the recent frog dissection," he said.

Thank goodness I hadn't eaten much before visiting the school. I peeked at my sister, who pasted a bland smile on her face.

"This will take ten minutes, tops," I said to the both of them.

As I glanced around the room, my gaze slid past the long tables with their shared microscopes. What I sought would lie hidden inside the cupboards. I opened their doors to find stacks of measuring tools: glass beakers, calipers, and pipettes.

Turning to Richard, I said, "I'm looking for things like thermometers."

He shrugged. "I only clean up around here. Keep on looking, but everything must stay inside the classroom."

I agreed to the restriction. My sister and I split up to examine the lab, pulling open various drawers. After five minutes of intense searching, I hit the mother lode. I'd found a stash of glass thermometers.

My voice cracked. "These have a red tint to them. They must be mercury-based."

Alice gasped from her corner, where she stood holding a clipboard.

Richard shuffled over to my side and peered at my discovery. "Actually, the thermometers with red liquid are newer. The old ones I used as a kid with mercury in them always had a silver line. But that was ages ago . . . when dinosaurs roamed the earth." He chuckled.

Silver, really? I did a quick search on my phone and verified Richard's comment.

Alice raised the clipboard she was holding into the air. "I found a master list of the lab's supplies. Maybe you should look at the inventory."

Scurrying over to her side, I scrutinized the list. Not only did it itemize all the equipment, but any teachers who wanted access to materials had to initial, date, and time stamp whatever they used for their science experiments.

"The equipment is shared," I said. "Can people borrow the stuff they want and use it inside their classrooms?"

Alice ran her finger down the sheet and pointed to the fine print at the bottom. All the supplies were deemed school property and had to stay in the science lab. A warning indicated that Principal Lewis himself would cross-check the list and make sure the classroom's equipment remained in working order at the end of the school day.

Anyway, it didn't look like there were even any supplies containing mercury in the inventory. On the flip side, the strict regimen could be a step in the right direction in keeping Alice off Detective Brown's radar.

Relieved, I took a deep breath in—much to my dismay. The dissection fumes shot up my nose, and my stomach recoiled. I rubbed my tummy in a soothing circle.

Alice followed the motions of my hand. She snapped open her purse and offered me a packet. "Ginger chew?"

The offer only reminded me again about her precarious situation with the cops. I really needed to find out who had hurt Helen and dispel any lingering cloud of suspicion over Alice.

"No, thanks," I said, nudging away the ginger candy.

But my sudden wave of nausea wasn't done with me yet. Another stomach spasm hit. Maybe I should've eaten more today. Perhaps these were actual hunger pangs.

Alice guided me out of the science lab with her hand on my back. "Are you sure you're okay?"

"Yes, and the fresh air should revive me." I took in a giant gulp for good measure.

"And you'll be fine before your important chat tonight?"

I felt my stomach clench tight again. This time it had nothing to do with external chemicals. My body seemed to create its own waves of anxiety. I would finally meet Josh's parents face-to-face (or at least face-to-video) tonight.

· · ·

I had changed my clothes three times, leaving a pile of clothing rejections on my comforter, but still hadn't decided on the right combination. While I turned this way and that, looking at my reflection in the full-length mirror, Marshmallow sauntered in. "No matter how much you camouflage yourself, you'll still be fur-challenged."

Smoothing the wrinkles on my silk blouse, I said, "I need to make a good impression with Josh's parents."

"If you really want them to see how great you are, let me pop up on the video feed."

"How would that impress them?"

"Because someone who owns such an amazing cat can't be half bad."

I took my pile of discarded clothes and started placing them back on hangers. "You'd only be a distraction, Marshmallow."

"I know. People can't tear their eyes away from my handsome face."

Stifling the urge to throw a rumpled skirt at him, I said, "Go and watch over Nimbus, will you?"

Though I'd opted for a magenta silk blouse, I also wore my comfy jeans for the video call. They wouldn't see my pants since I'd be sitting down, and I figured wearing them might ease my nerves.

I went over to Unit 1 for the video conference. Josh opened the door to his apartment and greeted me with a sweet hug. "Ready?"

"Or not. But here I come."

"They'll adore you," Josh said, taking my hand in his and guiding me to the fish-shaped dining table, where the laptop sat open and waiting. I hoped he didn't mind my sweaty palms. Well, at least he hadn't dropped my hand in disgust yet.

"How come you don't look nervous?" I asked.

"Should I be?" he said, as his comforting scent of pine and woods washed over me.

I noticed he wore his usual work clothes: an Oxford shirt and belted slacks. The polished look made me go weak in my knees. Straight from the office, and he still appeared handsome—and unruffled about the looming parental call.

Then I noticed the telltale crumb lodged in the cuff of his sleeve. I snatched it up and said, "Gotcha! This is part of a fortune cookie." He ate them whenever he got nervous.

"Okay," he said, "maybe I am a little anxious. This is my first serious relationship in a long time." He flipped his bangs to the other side, mussing up his hair.

I smoothed the strands down and squeezed his hand. "We'll be doing this together."

Josh nodded and opened the chat app. "My parents promised it'll be low-key and casual," he said as he clicked on their profile image, an aerial shot of Hawaii, to start the video conference. While waiting for the call to go through, he squeezed my hand a few times, and I took several deep breaths to prepare.

Suddenly, his parents appeared onscreen. I found myself staring at a regal-looking couple. Josh's dad looked like an older version of Josh, but with more distinguished salt-and-pepper hair cut in a clean conservative way. No floppy bangs for him.

His mom looked breathtaking, with her striking cheekbones and doe eyes. She'd draped a shimmering golden scarf over her shoulders. This was her casual look?

Josh's father, though, wore a loose linen shirt. They introduced themselves by their first names, Kekoa and Lani, but I insisted on calling them Mr. and Mrs. Akana.

"About time Josh found a nice young woman to settle down with," Mr. Akana said.

The tips of Josh's ears turned pink.

His dad continued, "He's always busy studying. You can't date a textbook, I've told him so many times." I think Mr. Akana and Ma would get along very well.

Mrs. Akana spoke up in a velvety voice. "What my charming husband is saying is that we're pleased to meet you, Mimi."

"Thank you for carving out the time to talk. I know you must be swamped with running your own business," I said.

Mr. Akana gave me two thumbs up. "We own the best gas station chain in all of Oahu. I oversee the workers while Lani does the books."

Giving me a warm smile, Mrs. Akana said, "Josh tells us that you're also a businesswoman."

"That's right." I proceeded to give them a short summary of my experience with animals and how I'd transferred my love for them into opening up Hollywoof.

They both congratulated me on my success while Josh snuck a peek at me and grinned. His parents seemed to be accepting of me so far.

"Smart and beautiful," Mr. Akana said. "Sounds like a sure thing. When will we hear wedding bells, you two?"

Josh and I looked at each other in alarm. We'd agreed not to rush things.

Mr. Akana wagged his finger at Josh. "Don't wait too long, keiki. The best times of my life have been married to this lovely lady beside me."

"We've been together for almost thirty years now," Mrs. Akana said as she wiggled the fourth finger of her left hand at me. I noticed that her gorgeous wedding band and engagement ring set featured a giant diamond.

"And each year is better than the last," Mr. Akana said.

They turned to face each other and lost themselves in a long gaze.

Josh cleared his throat. "Cut it out, Mom and Dad. I think it's time for us to go."

His parents startled out of their trance, turned to the video screen, and wished us well.

We said goodbye, and Josh turned the computer off. "That wasn't so bad, was it? I'm just glad I stopped them before they started making out or something." He grimaced.

"They seem like a really sweet couple," I said.

"Yeah, you can get diabetes by watching them. Oh, sorry about Mom flashing her ring at you. She shows it off any chance she gets."

"I would, too, if I had a whopping diamond like that."

Josh scratched the back of his neck. "I don't know. Shouldn't she be over her ring by now? And less lovesick after all these years?"

"You're just saying that because she's your mom."

He laughed. "Maybe."

"I think it's super romantic." I could picture Mrs. Akana getting engaged and being infatuated with the shine and bling of her ring. I bet the heavy stone symbolized the weight of Mr. Akana's commitment to her.

Of course, any girl would be over the moon after being proposed to. She wouldn't be able to take her eyes off the new sparkle riding on her ring finger . . . Except I knew someone who hadn't been.

Josh waved his hand in front of my face. "Everything okay, Mimi?"

"Sorry, I got lost in my thoughts."

Checking the time, I gave him a quick kiss and hug. I knew he had to go in to work early tomorrow.

Plus, now I had predawn plans as well. To talk to a certain fiancé and see why his beloved hadn't been wearing her ring after getting engaged. Instead, she'd kept it hidden away in a box inside a closet in her apartment.

CHAPTER

thirty-one

BRANDON HAD MENTIONED before that he surfed before dawn Mondays to Fridays. True to his word, I found him alone on the beach near All Tide Up. He'd already donned his wetsuit and carried his board to the shoreline when I managed to catch up to him and call out his name.

He pivoted and faced me in the predawn light. "Mimi? What are you doing here?"

"I wanted to speak with you before you hit the waves."

His gaze traveled to the calm sea. "This early in the day, the water isn't choppy yet. It's the perfect time to go."

I studied the vast expanse of sand around me, free from the typical beachgoers. "No crowds to fight, either."

He propped his board up in the sand. "So, what can I do for you?"

"It's about the ring."

He looked puzzled.

"The one you gave to Helen." I noticed him shifting his tanned feet on the sand. "Marina still has the engagement ring. I thought you might want it back."

He stared out at the open water. "Marina can keep it. Too many memories that could haunt me."

Gee, he seemed so down. I thought I could cheer him up by asking, "What was your story? I love hearing about cute proposals."

He buried his toes in the sand. "It was a simple ask. Helen hated drama."

I still needed to figure out why she'd kept it locked up. Maybe it hadn't fit her. "Was the ring the correct size?"

His eyes pierced me. "Why would you ask that?"

"Because Helen, uh, wasn't wearing it the day she died."

He snorted. "Figures. Helen was hot and cold about our relationship. She had major issues with physical touch. Sometimes she'd let me hold her hand. Other times, she pushed me away. Daddy trauma."

I remembered the photo of Helen and Brandon from the townhouse. Despite the big smiles on their faces, I recalled that there had been a noticeable gap between their bodies. "Care to elaborate?"

He smoothed a hand over his wetsuit. "Dear Dad practically abandoned her at a boarding school while she was growing up."

I clucked my tongue, wondering how old Helen had been when she'd been sent away. Hearing the venom that had infused Brandon's words, I said, "You and Helen's father did seem rather frosty to each other at the memorial service."

"That tightwad had the money to make her life extra comfy as an adult, but he didn't. Heartless guy."

After he spit his last words out, Brandon unstuck his board and rushed toward the sea without saying goodbye. He'd had his eye on the ocean during our conversation, but I got the sense he was trying to find escape in the sea for himself, and perhaps from my anger-inducing questions.

· · ·

When I opened up Hollywoof, we already had a line of waiting customers. It felt like Nicola and I kept handling loads of clients without any end in sight. I even cut into my lunch break and barely managed to eat half a sandwich before returning to work. Things finally started slowing down in the late afternoon.

Around three, an owner and his mutt arrived. I smelled them even before they took their first steps into the shop. Nimbus hid her delicate nose behind her paws while Marshmallow glared at the newcomers. "Someone needs deodorant," he said.

The man handed his dog's leash over to me. "Sorry about the noxious odor. We had a run-in with a wild creature."

"Yes, I can tell by the eau de skunk," I said, trying not to scrunch my face in disgust.

"Can I drop my dog off and pick him up later? I'll leave my number for you," the man said.

"Yes, we'll call you when he's ready."

The man almost skipped out the door, and from behind the cash register, Nicola said, "It's your turn, right?" She gave me a hopeful smile.

I sighed. "This might take a while."

In the back, I prepped the solution of hydrogen peroxide, baking soda, and dishwashing soap. I'd need to scrub every inch of the dog with painstaking care.

Thank goodness his eyes didn't seem watery or red. The skunk must have missed his face when it sprayed.

I made sure to put on some thick rubber gloves for the job. After all, I didn't want to become a human version of Pepé Le Pew.

Using a soft washcloth, I concentrated on placing the mixture all over his body. I'd need to toss away the stinky cloth after this special bath. I let the solution soak in for about twenty minutes before I rinsed him off. Then I did the usual shampoo and dry.

After all the treatments, I sniffed the dog. He seemed much better, but maybe my nose had gotten acclimated. To be on the safe side, I spritzed him with a pet-safe vanilla perfume. There. Now he smelled like a furry cupcake.

We returned to the front, where I asked Nicola to contact the owner. Around the same time, a woman happened to walk into the store with her bulldog. She turned straight around. "We'll come back tomorrow," she said over her shoulder as she hurried away.

"Does it smell that bad?" I asked.

Nicola had her nose covered with a handkerchief and appeared on the point of fainting. If only she would unleash the same amount of drama during her auditions.

From his spot, Marshmallow began gagging. "Mimi, I can't hold my breath much longer. Need. Fresh. Air."

"Let's get some circulation in here." I propped the front door open.

Nimbus had started crawling toward the entrance when the mutt's owner, thankfully, arrived to pick up his dog. He flashed us a huge smile as he paid the bill.

The man almost tripped over the two cats as he left. They'd huddled near the doorway to stick their noses out and breathe in the fresh air.

"We should close early today," I said. "The cats don't feel too well. And if that lady customer was any indication, no one will be clamoring to enter the shop anyway."

Nicola agreed to stay an extra fifteen minutes to air out the place and spray Febreze everywhere. "But then I'm outta here," she said. "Gonna try to catch Thai Elvis during his return performance."

I gave her a puzzled look, and Marshmallow turned to me with wide blue eyes. "'Thai Elvis'? The fumes must be getting to Nicola."

Nicola kept on gushing. "You do know Thai Elvis, right? He's legendary. A superb performer at one of Thai Town's restaurants in East Hollywood."

Still no clue.

"He's here this week only," Nicola said. "I must catch him before he flies out again."

"Okay, then. Have fun," I told her. Nicola's words reminded me of someone I needed to track down before *he* left. As I led the sluggish cats out to the palm tree–lined plaza, it looked like they both needed naps to recover from their recent stinky encounter. Besides, it'd be easier to leave them at home when I met up with Scott Reed.

CHAPTER

thirty-two

SINCE I HAD left Hollywoof early because of the skunk situation, I managed to snag a meeting at four thirty with Helen's father at his hotel. We'd agreed to meet in the poolside area.

When I arrived, I realized that Scott didn't have a casual dress mode. He sat at one of those glass tables shaded with a giant umbrella and wore dark sunglasses, but he had still suited up. He wore dark formal business attire and was probably roasting in the bright sun. At least he'd left his scarf in his hotel room.

As he saw me approach, Scott pulled out the patio chair for me. When he wasn't railing at Principal Lewis, he could be a gentleman.

"Thank you, Mr. Reed." I sat down on the striped cushion seat and faced him. "I wanted to take time to say goodbye before you left—"

"Actually, looks like I'll need to prolong my stay in the States." He steepled his hands on the frosted glass tabletop.

"For pleasure?" He didn't look like a Mickey man, but maybe even he couldn't pass up time in The Happiest Place on Earth. Disneyland was a hop, skip, and a jump away after all.

"I wouldn't call contesting a will 'fun,'" he said, cracking his knuckles.

"I'm sorry to hear that. But why would there be a legal issue? Aren't you Helen's only relative?"

"Yes," he said, "but my daughter wanted to hand over her assets to a complete stranger."

Could it be—"Brandon?" The couple had been engaged so it'd be a natural wish on Helen's part.

"That surfer bum?" He banged his fist on the table. "He didn't deserve a speck of Helen's affections."

I chose my words with care. "Their relationship did seem . . . interesting."

He snatched off his sunglasses and stared me in the face. "What do you mean?"

"Oh." I waved my hand airily. "Just up and down at times. They got engaged, but she put the ring away. Stuff like that." But I wasn't about to mention Brandon's theory that Scott himself had caused the emotional roller coaster.

Scott tapped the sunglasses against the palm of his hand. "Maybe she did see through him. Atta girl."

"You really don't like Brandon, do you?"

He glanced around the empty pool area. "Let me show you one of his e-mails." Taking out his phone, he swiped at it a few times before showing the message to me:

Scott:

I plan on proposing to Helen at this epic restaurant called Perch.
Don't you think my little surfer girl deserves the best? A few
thousand to my account will do. Help a future son-in-law out.

After his signature, Brandon had added a postscript with his bank
account routing information. Perch, huh? The French-style rooftop bis-
tro in downtown L.A. boasted a breathtaking view of the skyline. It was
definitely a great spot to propose.

"Did you give him the money?" I asked.

"Absolutely not. If he wanted to court Helen, he should impress her
with his own resources." He ran a hand through his hair. "Why she
didn't pick someone more qualified is beyond me."

I wondered if "qualified" equaled "moneyed" in Scott's eyes. "I
heard that Helen went to a stellar school," I said.

"You bet she did—all on my dime. Sure, I was busy at the time with
work and travel. I didn't have it in me to be a great single dad—her
mother died giving birth to her—but I made sure to provide her with
the best education. My girl grew up surrounded by high-class families
from the Los Angeles area: the Perezes, the Chius, and the St. Jameses."

A list of prominent local families. I employed the parroting tech-
nique I'd been taught in college to show him empathy. I said, "Sounds
like you tried to give her a top-notch education surrounded by high-
class peers."

"That's right, but little good that did. She still ended up with greedy
quote-unquote friends. And pursued teaching, of all things."

I raised my eyebrows.

"You know what they say. 'Those who can't do, teach.'" He slipped on his sunglasses. "I'm a doer myself."

"Well, it's too bad you have to extend your stay and change your original plans," I said. "But at least you can enjoy the good weather out here."

After I'd said goodbye, he leaned back in his patio chair, but his shoulders remained stiff. He didn't seem like one who would be into R&R. And neither was I—not when I had my sister's reputation on the line.

· · ·

I knew who to turn to for legal advice, so I asked Josh to meet up for dinner. Even though he had to work late, he agreed that he could take a quick break with me.

It took me about an hour to drive there, which didn't include securing metered parking. At Josh's workplace, I waited for him in the freezing lobby of his office building. He worked in a staid brick complex, a far cry from the glass and chrome skyscrapers of the neighboring edifices.

I rubbed my arms and sat down in the nook near the staircase. The Charlie Chaplin statue on the bench revived a fond memory of my chatting with Josh in this very spot while we were defining our relationship. I patted the top of Chaplin's hat with fondness.

Soon, I saw Josh's sleek frame coming down the staircase with hurried steps. Aw, he didn't want to keep me waiting.

His brow furrowed as he searched for me in the open lobby.

"Over here, handsome," I said from the bench.

His brown eyes glittered when he spotted me. "Mimi. I could get spoiled by these spontaneous meet-ups."

He offered his arm to me, and I looped mine around his. I seemed to float out of the building.

We walked a few blocks before reaching Grand Central Market. Despite being a downtown landmark, the outside looked like an unassuming tan building, particularly with its multilayered windows from the apartments located above the ground level.

On the first floor, though, we found a cafeteria filled with glowing neon signs and bustling customers. Tantalizing smells sizzled in the air and made my mouth water.

I dropped Josh's arm to point at a few restaurant signs with names that sounded interesting: Eggslut, PBJ.LA, and Sarita's Pupuseria. As we passed by other vendors, I pointed at more stalls I wanted to explore.

He chuckled. "First time?"

"I rarely go downtown"—my eyes flicked toward him—"except to visit a special someone."

We strolled hand in hand (my favorite kind of walking) to inspect every single eatery. After making a circle, we'd narrowed down our selections. We soon nabbed a small metal table.

Josh insisted on paying for our meal. He ordered a stack of fancy PB&J sandwiches, including an espresso-inspired one, while I opted for the filled flatbreads of Salvadorian pupusas. Using the cutlery, we shared bites of each other's food. There was something titillating about trading the morsels as our forks bumped into each other in passing.

Finally, we took a pause to chat.

"Sorry again for the short notice," I said.

"This beats eating cold pizza with the other guys in the office. Only by a little, though." Josh shot me a roguish grin, and I flicked a piece of bread at him.

He twirled his fork in the air. "Too bad I only get a quick dinner break. I still have a lot of work to finish this evening."

I cut up a piece of pupusa, making the cheese inside ooze out. "I don't want to add to your load, but when you get a chance, could you look something up for me?"

His brows drew together. "Is this concerning the murder investigation?"

I pushed the piece of flatbread around my plate. "Yeah. I spoke with Scott Reed, and he mentioned staying in town longer—to contest Helen's will."

"Really?" Josh put his fork down.

"It might have to do with Brandon. You saw how the two of them butted heads at the service."

"So, you think she left something to her boyfriend—"

"Fiancé. And I don't think Daddy Moneybags approves."

"But she's an adult," Josh said, "and legally capable of making her own decisions."

"He seems like the kind of father with very strong opinions." I relayed Scott's perception of Brandon, and the way the surfer had attempted to extract money.

"I can check whether the will's been filed," Josh said.

"Thanks." I took a bite of my pupusa with its hearty mix of cheese and pork filling.

Josh placed his hand on top of mine for a brief moment. I loved the extra warmth and feeling of being protected that came over me. "Speaking of parents, what about yours? That Ultimate Date Night must be coming up."

My appetite fled at his words. I pushed my plate to the side. "Alice already ordered the food in advance and made sure Ma will be home that evening."

"Sounds like an excellent plan." He reached out and tucked a loose strand of hair behind my ear.

I tingled at his touch. But a negative thought still wormed its way in my mind. Would it still be like this for us a few years down the road? In psych class, I'd read about the honeymoon stage in a relationship called limerence. It typically lasted only two years.

I must have started scowling because Josh spoke up and said, "I made something to cheer you up."

He'd created a jagged heart out of his sandwich for me by carving the bread with his fork and knife. Dorky, but at least he was my very own dork.

Dinner ended too soon, and Josh had to return to work. After, I'd left downtown using the 110, a smile playing across my lips. He'd given me his heart, albeit a PB&J one.

I didn't even mind the slow crawl on the freeway and spending my time staring at taillights colored a romantic red. On the side of the highway, I noticed the downtown buildings twinkling with warm light.

My hope even spilled over to my parents' meeting tomorrow night. Ma and Dad definitely loved each other—they just needed to spend time again in the same room together. And the Lee sisters could make that happen.

My thoughts switched to another couple. If Helen had lived, how would her marriage to Brandon have fared? Would they have made it? Their desired Vegas wedding didn't inspire any confidence. Plus, the fact that she'd left the ring behind in its velvet box. Oh, I'd forgotten to pass on the message.

I waited until I'd reached my apartment to tell Marina. In the carport of my complex, I pulled out my cell phone and texted her.

Me: Hi. Spoke with Brandon. He said to keep the ring.

Marina: No kidding?

Me: He didn't want to be haunted by her memories.

Only after I sent the text did I realize his oddly negative choice of words.

CHAPTER

thirty-three

AT HOLLYWOOF THE next morning, Nicola and I encountered an unusual request. A short man proudly wearing a mustachio came in with his Scottish terrier. "Do something stellar with his facial fur," the owner said before dropping his dog off.

Nicola and I stared at each other for several moments.

"What a request," I said. "Where would I even start?"

She snapped her fingers and said, "I've got it. I'll make a list of the best-mustached actors ever to inspire you."

Within five minutes, she'd narrowed down her picks to three contenders and showed me their accompanying photos. "Here goes . . . Burt Reynolds for a fun PI look, Hugh Jackman as Wolverine, and Groucho Marx for a comical effect."

"Thanks for the visuals," I said. "Now it's time to create a mustache masterpiece."

I took the dog to the back room and started clipping away. As I snipped, I realized that the ratio of fur to body on an animal was quite different than its human counterpart. I decided to use the electric razor to make quick work of his massive amount of fluff.

Then I fine-tuned through trimming with scissors around his sensitive face. Using careful motions, I clipped away subtle centimeters at a time. As a finishing touch, I curled the mustache by applying sculpting gel to the ends.

When I brought the terrier to the front, Nicola whistled. "That's some impressive cutting."

Nimbus napped through the commotion, but Marshmallow opened one eye to assess my handiwork. "Is he *supposed* to look like the Lorax?"

I wagged my finger in warning at Marshmallow.

The owner took that moment to return. Checking out his styled dog, he said, "Marvelous. I love it."

He paid the bill and gave his terrier a big smooch.

I shuddered. Blech. I couldn't imagine being kissed by a bristly face. I definitely preferred Josh clean-shaven. Mmm. I had started reliving one of our recent kisses when my phone rang with his caller ID.

"I was just thinking about you," I said when I picked up.

"Really?" His voice dipped low and intimate.

I craved a kiss from Josh, but I'd settle for his intoxicating voice instead.

"Mimi, are you there?" he asked.

"Sorry, I was daydreaming."

Marshmallow sniffed from his corner. "Fantasizing, more like."

Josh cleared his throat. "Unfortunately, I'm calling about business. I managed to see a copy of Helen's will."

My mind snapped back with sharp focus. "What did you find out?"

He made a clicking noise with his tongue. "Helen's liquid assets are to be divided between Roosevelt Elementary, Elite Nobility Academy, and a local cat shelter. But the townhouse is deeded to Marina."

"Her roommate?"

"Yes. She's also the executor of the will."

"That's interesting." I thanked Josh for his help and blew him several kisses over the phone. (Marshmallow hacked in the background.)

At lunch, Nicola left on her break. She wanted to try out the new fruitarian restaurant, a fad diet among certain celebrities. I also took a break with Marshmallow, opening up my brown bag lunch at Hollywoof. We sat in the waiting area while I ate my tuna salad sandwich.

In between bites, I filled him in on my conversation with Josh. Then I asked, "What's your verdict, Sherlock?"

He twitched his nose. "Something smells fishy here, and it's not your lunch. When exactly did Marina know she would inherit a luxury townhouse?"

I crumpled my brown paper bag. "Tell me what you're thinking, Marshmallow."

"Could she have been plotting Helen's death all along?"

"But she was grieving," I said. "Don't you remember all those hours she spent at Déjà Vu trying to distract herself from her sorrow?"

Marshmallow let out a short yowl. "Or was that to distract *you and others* from thinking of her as a possible suspect?"

"I guess you do have a point."

"Remember, Marina reduced her hours at the antique store recently," Marshmallow said. "Why? Because she knows she doesn't need to worry about rent."

Had it all been an act? I needed to find out when exactly Marina had learned about the will and its contents.

Thinking about the legal document reminded me of another beneficiary from Helen's estate: the Elite Nobility Academy, where she'd gone to get her fancy-pants education. When Scott had given me a list of the other families, the St. James surname had stuck out to me. I was pretty sure he'd been speaking of Pixie or one of her relatives. If I wanted to learn more about Helen's background, I knew who I could turn to.

Besides, at the country club, Pixie had mentioned wanting to meet up again. Why not cash in on the opportunity? I texted Pixie to make sure she was free, and we settled on a time to connect later in the evening.

• • •

As I drove up the twisting turns near Hollywood Hills, Marshmallow purred. He couldn't wait to visit Pixie again—and he'd insisted on having Nimbus come along to show her how the "rich and famous" live. This late at night I had a hard time spying the iconic "HOLLYWOOD" sign out of my window, but I marveled at the glow of the city lights as I wound higher up the incline. Los Angeles looked like it was made from jewels at this height.

There was no way I could miss Pixie's distinctive house, which clung to a hilltop. Constructed in an oval shape, it differed from the surrounding houses made in sharp geometric shapes; rectangular edges seemed to be the most popular choice.

When Marshmallow, Nimbus, and I showed up on her doorstep and rang the bell, Pixie hurried to open the door. She flung her arms around me. "Mimi, I love it when you visit. Working from home all the time"—she telecommuted a lot—"makes me appreciate face-to-face connections even more."

She cuddled Marshmallow. "Hello, handsome."

And she extended her hand to Nimbus for the kitten to sniff. "And who's this sweetheart?"

I explained about the stray kitten I'd found near my sister's school. "I'm going to keep her until I find a suitable owner."

"Too bad I've got my hands full with Gelato. Otherwise, I'd definitely want this cutie around."

Maybe he'd heard his name because the shih tzu soon came tumbling through the doorway. "Hold your horses," she said, scooping up the energetic little dog.

She led the way into her beautiful home. No matter how many times I visited, I still held my breath whenever I saw the gleaming travertine floors and sparkling floor-to-ceiling glass windows.

We finally ended up in the kitchen, where Pixie placed an excited Gelato down. He ran in circles around the cats, his tail wagging double time.

"Do you want an iced tea, Mimi? Or something more celebratory this evening?" Pixie asked.

"Nothing with alcohol, please. I won't be able to handle those winding roads buzzed."

She lifted her shoulder in a gentle shrug and whipped up some beverages. I received a bright blue concoction while she ended up with a frothy green drink garnished with a wedge of lime. She gave Marshmallow, Nimbus, and Gelato separate bowls of purified volcanic water.

"Do you want to go outside to the patio?" Pixie asked. "I just got new furniture for the space."

"Sure." I glanced back at Marshmallow, but he'd already claimed the massage mat, a device he'd enjoyed the last time he'd come. As he vibrated on the soft pad, he said, "Ah, I've missed this. I'll stay here while you two kids go and play outside."

Both Nimbus and Gelato decided to remain near the water bowls, using almost synchronized licks to drink their water. Seeing that all the pets were settled, Pixie and I went to her backyard. However, we left the patio door open a crack just in case.

Under a fabric awning, two long couches faced each other. In between the furniture sat the pièce de résistance, a fire pit filled with rocks that sparkled like emeralds and sapphires. At least I hoped they were made from glass, but who knew? Maybe Pixie really did have money to burn.

"Have a seat," Pixie said as she sank into one of the couches.

I settled across from her, placing my drink in the cup holder anchored in the armrest.

"There's also a button there to make your seat recline," she said.

I pressed the silver button near me, and my legs shot up. With an embarrassed smile, I readjusted the seat.

"How is everything at Hollywoof by the way?" she asked.

"Busy, but please drop by anytime. Remember, Gelato gets grooming services for free *fur-ever.*"

She gave a tinkle of a laugh. "Wasn't that smart of me to invest in Hollywoof?"

"And I can never be thankful enough for your help."

She waved my comment away. "What are friends for?"

"Speaking of friends, I heard your last name mentioned the other day." I eyed my glass of electric blue with a twinge of suspicion. "Do you know the Reed family?"

She sipped her lime drink. "Maybe. What are their first names?"

"Scott is the father, and his daughter is named Helen." I tasted my own vivid blue drink. It reminded me of a few floral Asian teas, like jasmine and osthmanthus.

Pixie placed her drink in her cup holder and tapped a finger against her chin. "Helen Reed . . . Why does that name sound familiar?"

"She attended Elite Nobility Academy, if that helps."

"Ah, right. Helen was quite a few years younger than me. She was schoolmates with my youngest sister."

I put my footrest down and leaned forward to hear her better. "Do you know anything about her background?"

"It's sad, really. Helen practically grew up at the school. Her father almost never visited, and families would take turns hosting her on holidays. But I think Helen and my sister lost touch over the years. I can't remember the last time she's mentioned her." She paused. "How do you know the Reeds?"

"She was a colleague at my sister's elementary school."

"It figures that Helen would go into education. She often said her teachers felt more like her real parents than her biological ones." She crossed and then uncrossed her elegant legs. "Did you say 'was' a colleague? Did she move away?"

I bit my lip. "Helen died recently."

"Dear me." Pixie fidgeted on her cushion. "What happened?"

"It's unclear even now. The police are involved . . . and Alice is on their suspect list."

She shuddered, and I didn't think it was because of the cool temperature. Still, she said, "Let's turn on the fire. Help bring some brightness and warmth to this night." Hopefully in more ways than one.

Pixie turned on the fire pit while I said, "She left all her money to a few great organizations: two schools and a cat shelter."

"Generous," Pixie said. "And I bet the abundant funding will help those in need."

"Why would you think it's a lot of money?"

She licked her lips. "Helen wasn't a flashy sort of person, not like some other trust babies. She wore her clothes until they became threadbare. Saved up."

"What's a 'trust baby'?"

Pixie blinked at me. "It's when someone gets a chunk of money after they achieve certain milestones. She was a double trust kid, got a windfall at eighteen and then was promised more after she tied the knot. Was she married?"

"Engaged," I said, drinking some more of my bright blue drink. The floral taste had grown on me.

"What a shock for the groom-to-be."

Especially if he'd expected extra funding to come his way, I thought.

"I'm glad she found someone special." Pixie stared into the flickering flames of the fire pit. "For a while, my sister told me Helen kept falling for the wrong type of man."

"The arrogant kind?" I asked, remembering Brandon's swagger.

She ran her finger over the rim of her glass. "Money-hungry ones. I heard she used to ask prospective suitors if they'd date someone just for their money."

I snorted. "Of course, all of them said no."

"Naturally, but then they'd assume she was rich if she used that question to weed out boyfriends. Plus, she did go to a fancy boarding school."

I chewed on my fingernail. "Nowadays, people can just search online to confirm their is-she-rich theories."

"One reason why I'm still single." Pixie took another sip of her drink. "But at least life doesn't get complicated this way."

Yeah, and you get to stay alive.

From inside the house, I heard a whimper and sprang to my feet. "That must be Nimbus. She hasn't been feeling too well."

We reentered the house to find Nimbus lying down, her head on her paws, looking dejected. Pixie crouched to her level and checked on the kitten. "Poor soul. But I have something that might help. Mimi, why don't you hold Nimbus and check out my new splurge?"

I scooped the kitten up, with Marshmallow tagging along behind, and followed Pixie. She walked over to what looked like a linen closet. However, the door opened to reveal a giant glass cylinder on the inside.

"Put the kitten in the machine," Pixie said.

"What is that thing?"

"It's an oxygen chamber. All the rage in Japan."

Nimbus stared up at me with wide eyes, while Marshmallow started purring at her. I hope he was encouraging her. After a while, she relaxed in my arms.

Pixie opened the door to the chamber, and I placed Nimbus inside.

"This will pump pure oxygen directly to her and give her an energy boost." Pixie closed the door and pressed some buttons on the control panel. She let the machine run for several minutes.

At the end of the oxygen therapy, Nimbus did seem perkier. She even licked Pixie's palm.

"Wow," I said.

"All animals need oxygen," Pixie said, shutting the closet door. "So make sure to take off any extra covers and keep the windows open at night while she sleeps."

I'd try out Pixie's advice for sure. I thanked her for the oxygen chamber and her time. "Again, feel free to drop by Hollywoof," I said. "Or I can schedule you in."

"Yes, do that. Whenever you're available, Mimi. No rush," she said.

I left with a bounce in my step. I'd learned a lot from tonight, not only how to help Nimbus but what would aid me in my investigation.

CHAPTER

thirty-four

NIMBUS SEEMED TO feel better the next day. She even woke me up by jumping into the bed at seven in the morning. Gee, that oxygen infusion must have really done the trick.

I wondered how much the fancy machine cost. Probably way beyond my pet groomer's salary. On the other hand, I could use Pixie's other snippet of advice for free: Keep the windows open. The fresh air blowing in last night must also have helped.

A few minutes later, Marshmallow also climbed onto the bed. "You had a slumber party and didn't invite me?" He swished his tail in my face, and I sneezed.

"There is a cause for celebration," I said. "Nimbus has more energy. Must be from the oxygen chamber."

"Speaking of last night . . ." Marshmallow sprawled next to my head and peered at me with his intense blue eyes. "You and Pixie had quite the discussion about Helen."

"Yeah, they both attended that fancy boarding school."

Marshmallow wiggled his ears. "I heard through the open patio door. Helen's a trust baby, which means she had a huge estate. You know, one of the prime reasons to kill someone is for their money."

I sat up with a start. "You're right. And who doesn't care about money? My sister. That by itself should clear her name."

Marshmallow licked his paw. "Give it a try, but you know Detective Brown—and my apologies to swine—but he can be pigheaded."

Since the cats had woken me up early anyway, I had time to see the detective before opening shop. I figured it'd be better to plead in person.

After a phone call to the station, though, I had to change my route. Detective Brown wasn't at his desk like usual. Instead, he'd been called upon to do a Coffee with a Cop activity. These regularly scheduled events brought the police and the public together in order to ensure an atmosphere of collaboration in the community.

Detective Brown had been delegated to enjoying coffee and conversations at Cup O' Joe. I knew of the location since I'd met up with Nicola there before, prior to her becoming my second hand around the store.

When I parked near the coffeeshop, I immediately spotted a long table, with a giant carafe and plenty of papers, set up outside. The various pamphlets probably offered tips about neighborhood safety and instructions on how to join the citizens' police program. A few uniformed police officers greeted passersby and smiled at them.

Detective Brown, on the other hand, sat at a tiny table apart from the informational brochures. He wore his signature gray sport coat and had his arms crossed over his chest. Although he had a foam cup on the table, like he was open to a conversation, his eyes were focused on the pavement.

Thank goodness they'd held Coffee with a Cop outdoors, a perfect location for pets. I took the cats and approached the detective.

He didn't notice until I'd taken a seat at his table. I laid Nimbus across my lap while Marshmallow sat near my feet.

Finally, Detective Brown looked up. A scowl crossed his face. "Miss Lee, please wait your turn. This event is to establish connections between the police department and local residents."

I glanced around. "Seems like nobody's clamoring to see you. Besides, I *am* a concerned citizen."

"Oh, come—" On hearing the accidental command, Nimbus leaped off my lap and rushed over to the detective. She placed a paw on his shoe and gave a gentle meow.

The detective's scowl fled, replaced by a general softening of his features. "Hey, little furball." He scratched the top of her head.

She responded by jumping onto his lap and lying down like she'd found the coziest bed ever.

"Okay, Miss Lee," Detective Brown said. "Maybe I do have time for a brief chat. And at the very least, it'll make the time at this community event go quicker."

I launched into my practiced speech. This time I decided to use a compliment sandwich (using layered positive-negative-positive comments) to help my attempt. "You're such an important investigator handling a lot of big cases. It must have been easy to miss noticing that Alice doesn't have the MOM to commit a murder. Since you're such an effective detective, I know you want to see justice served."

Marshmallow gave a soft hiss. "I think you meant to say 'defective detective.'"

Meanwhile, Detective Brown goggled at me. Had my talk been a revelation to him? He rubbed his nose. "What do you mean by 'MOM'?"

Oh. I'd shortened the key points to an acronym to better remember them. "You know. Motive, opportunity, and means. My sister doesn't even have the first 'M.' She loves working at Roosevelt Elementary and was a friend of Helen's. And money isn't a factor because if you look at Helen's will—"

He put a hand up to stop me. "I see your boyfriend Josh has been getting the legal scoop for you."

"Yes, but that's not the point." Splaying my hands on the table, I leaned toward the detective. "Alice has no stake in Helen's assets."

"Are you so sure about that?" Detective Brown took a leisurely sip from his foam cup. "Because she's affected by that will."

I blew out a puff of air. Now he'd started making things up. "Where do you get that?"

"By reading the fine print. Why, didn't your legal expert tell you?" He smirked. "Helen left a lot to the elementary school—earmarked for the kindergarten playground renovation that your sister's in charge of."

My jaw dropped. I remembered her finishing up a petition on February thirteenth when I'd first visited the school. But she was always raising money for the kindergarteners' needs.

"Guess Alice had motive and opportunity then." Detective Brown put up two fingers and wiggled a third. "All I need to do is figure out the means."

"What about the principal?" I said. "Or the other staff at school?"

"I'm still crossing my *t*'s, but it seems like the principal was in his office all day long, fielding calls and doing paperwork. And I'll double-check my notes from the staff interviews, but I'm about ready to close this case."

I shoved my chair back. Plucking Nimbus off his lap, I left without saying another word.

• • •

At Hollywoof, I opened the store in a dour mood. Even Nicola sensed my poor attitude and didn't bother with her usual superficial chatter. In fact, I kept asking her to take over for the simpler grooming duties. And when no customers were around, I requested that she keep to the back room, wiping down the tables and reorganizing the styling accessories.

I myself sat near the cash register, slouched, with my head propped against my elbow.

Marshmallow sauntered over and brushed his body against my legs. "Who stole your catnip, Mimi?"

I pinched the bridge of my nose. "I'm back to square one in the case. Detective Brown thinks Alice killed Helen . . . for money, of all the ridiculous reasons."

Marshmallow shook his fur out. "You've been in a tight spot before. And we all know that Detective Brown has no sense. You can never trust a man without pets."

"I appreciate you trying to cheer me up, Marshmallow, but I'm stuck." I patted his head. "I can't find the source of mercury, and the number of suspects is dwindling. Principal Lewis is in the clear. He was in his office all day long according to the detective."

Marshmallow put his nose in the air. "What about the other teachers? Or the janitor?"

"Maybe, but I still can't figure out how they would have access to the poison, particularly since I didn't find anything unusual in the science lab."

"You know what I like to do when my mind is swimming in circles?"

"No. What?"

"Take a nap." Marshmallow plopped down near my feet and closed his eyes.

"Um..."

"What I mean is, give your mind a break. Don't you humans have that saying about getting ideas in the weirdest places, like the shower?" He opened one eye. "Not that being drenched in water sounds very inspiring."

My phone chimed with a text from Alice. It read: See you tonight. Fingers crossed.

I groaned. "At least I'll have a distraction soon."

Both eyes now open, Marshmallow cocked his head at me.

"It's time for Alice and me to work our matchmaking talent—on our parents."

• • •

A few hours later, the cats and I arrived at my parents' home. From the porch, I could see the light on in the kitchen, which probably meant Alice was hard at work organizing the catered food. I myself had brought only a roll of streamers from the dollar store as a last-minute attempt at decorating.

When I rang the bell, Alice opened the door. I peeked over her shoulder. "Where's Ma and Dad?"

"I told Ma to stay in the bedroom because I was 'cooking' a special dinner. And Dad's not back from golfing yet."

I pointed at the purpling sky. "He's really using the last of the sunlight today, huh?"

"Come inside, and tell me what you think about the setup."

The cats and I went through the door. Upon seeing the dining table, I marveled at the food on display. An elegant porcelain platter with gold filigree held a mountain of roti. Tiny bowls surrounded the flat-breads like a Stonehenge of sauces and curries.

"How much food did you order?" I asked her.

Alice flushed red and gestured to a nearby kitchen counter, where I saw even more edible delights.

I spied satay sticks, a salad of exotic fruits, and even a container of spicy soup. "Um, aren't we supposed to leave them alone for a romantic evening together? This is enough food for the whole neighborhood to feast on."

Alice's hands fidgeted. "I had a hard time deciding. The restaurant had so many good options."

While I hung up a few streamers, twisting them for extra flair, Marshmallow crept toward the dining table. "If you need another stomach to fill, I'd be happy to volunteer my services."

The fresh bread and spiced curry smelled intoxicating, and I licked my lips. There'd be plenty of leftovers for me to indulge in later.

Maybe the deliciousness had started wafting over to the rest of the house because Ma's voice called out, "I want eat now. Can mah?"

My sister applied in the affirmative. "Can lah."

Ma emerged from the hallway with a gleam in her eye. "*Walao.* Cook so much. Spoil me rotten."

Alice blushed. "I can't take any credit. It's all from Roti Palace."

Ma surveyed the food. "Dis like Chinese New Year feast. Special happen?" She peered into my sister's face. "Find boyfriend?"

"Uh, no."

Ma turned to me and pointed at my stomach. "Make me grandma?"

"What?" I gestured to the cats around me. "These are the only little ones I have."

Marshmallow puffed out his fur. "Excuse me, I'm an *adult* cat, thank you very much."

"This meal is for you and Dad. An early celebration dinner for your anniversary," Alice said. "And I didn't do all of the work. Mimi put up the decorations."

Ma's gaze landed on my haphazardly placed streamers, and she arched an eyebrow. At least she hadn't laughed outright at my efforts.

"Why don't we all sit down and wait for Dad?" Alice said.

"Won't he be pleasantly surprised?" I said.

Ma let out a schoolgirl giggle, and we all settled around the table and waited. And waited.

Darkness set in. Soon, the gloom we felt wasn't just due to the lack of light.

"Is he okay?" Alice asked.

"I don't understand. Dad never misses dinner," I said.

Ma stayed silent, but her eyes started glossing over, and she grew distant.

"I'm calling him," I said. I dialed his number and put the call on speakerphone. When he picked up, my worry fled and morphed into frustration. He was okay, but . . . "Dad, where are you?"

"Princess One, what's wrong?"

I ground my teeth. "We're at home, waiting for you to show up for dinner."

"I didn't realize we had scheduled a family meal for tonight."

"Not technically, but you're always around for dinner."

"Oh, I didn't realize it was so late already. I'll grab some food here at the country club. Do you want me to bring back anything?"

I huffed. "Alice already ordered tons of food."

"I'm really sorry, but I had to take care of something." Or was it *someone*? I still remembered that secret note he'd been writing before.

Ma took a deep breath to center herself but whispered "Greg" in a very disappointed tone.

Dad coughed and said, "Be home later."

Instead of leaving like we'd originally planned, we tried to salvage the evening by turning it into a Girls' Night In. But I really didn't have the desire to eat more than a few bites of roti. Ma and Alice seemed to have the same lackluster appetite.

After finishing our "meal," Alice suggested painting our nails, but Ma and I weren't in the mood for a beauty ritual. We packed the food away into containers and placed them in the fridge. Disgruntled, Ma said she'd give them away at her next mah jong meeting.

Alice promised she'd stay overnight with Ma for emotional support. And when I started taking down the messy streamers, I couldn't help feeling that some part of my secure childhood innocence was also being dismantled.

CHAPTER
thirty-five

IN THE MORNING, I was grateful that the weekend had rolled around again so I could sleep in. Knowing Dad had stood us up for the Ultimate Date Night didn't leave me in a good mood. Even after the sun shone high through the window, I tried to pull the covers back over my head.

Marshmallow clawed them off. "You'd better have something tasty for me to eat after we skipped out on that feast last night. Why didn't you take the leftovers home with you?"

"I wasn't really thinking about food, Marshmallow."

Nimbus crept into my room and jumped on my bed. "Fish?" she said.

My tummy grumbled in response to her request. "Not a bad idea," I said, stroking the kitten's head.

Alice and I often boosted our mood through food therapy. Besides sweet desserts, like egg tarts and cheesecake, we often indulged in sushi as a pick-me-up.

I secured the cats in their respective carriers and drove along the 405 to the appropriate freeway exit. The neighborhood where I liked to find the choicest seafood was in Little Osaka. This restaurant row near Olympic and Sawtelle always seemed full of customers at all hours of the day. Parking usually involved a mad dash for an open spot, particularly since there weren't many attached lots, and the street meters filled up fast.

As I'd predicted, I couldn't score any parking spaces. Instead, I ended up on a residential street a few blocks away from the restaurants off the main road. Walking down the sidewalk and dodging other hungry customers, I decided to try out the new sushi restaurant I'd noticed advertised on Yelp. What I particularly liked about the establishment upon seeing it was the outside eating area, which would be perfect for my furry friends and me.

I leashed both Marshmallow and Nimbus to the legs of the table, but my cat gave me a sour look. "What's up with the chains?"

"It makes me seem like a conscientious owner."

"Yeah, right. You want my mug shot while you're at it?" Marshmallow groused.

"I'll be back in a few minutes," I said, bustling inside to place my order. Everything on the menu looked delicious, especially since I could see a glass display of the freshest catch on ice. The chef behind the counter flashed his knife at me as he sliced with quick strokes. I ended up choosing an assorted array of sushi, minus the throat-burning wasabi.

When I came back out, Marshmallow seemed to be studying the restaurant sign out of sheer boredom. "What's 'wild-caught' mean?" he asked.

"That the fish they serve isn't farmed. They're found in nature."

Pretty soon, a waiter brought out my order.

"Can I request an extra plate?" I asked.

"Certainly." He disappeared back inside the restaurant.

I poured some soy sauce into the dipping dish. After I ate a salmon roll, my stomach smiled. "Excellent."

Soon, I saw the chef coming out of the restaurant. His tall white hat almost brushed the top of the doorframe. He placed a plate decorated with cherry blossoms on the table and said, "I want to personally assure you that our seafood comes from waters tested for contaminants, especially heavy metals like lead and mercury. But we also make sure to catch the fish while they're young just in case."

I blinked at him. "Why does the timing matter?"

"Because contaminants can stay in a body for a long time, so the older the fish, the more dangerous the accumulation of chemicals."

I cut my eyes to Marshmallow and Nimbus under the shadow of the table. "My cats and I thank you very much for your assurance."

"Oh." He blanched. "You probably didn't know, but too much raw fish may upset their tummies. And, by the way, we only allow dogs on our patio."

Marshmallow stuck his nose in the air, affronted.

"But please make sure to tell your friends about us and our grand opening special," the chef said as he offered a slight bow and retreated back inside the restaurant.

"Did you hear that, Marshmallow?" I said.

"Yeah, he's cat-ist."

"I meant his talk about contaminants. Mercury can stay in a fish's system for a long time," I said. "Perhaps it can last for more than one afternoon . . . which means our list of suspects has now expanded beyond the people at school that day."

I placed two morsels of sushi onto the new plate and deposited them before the cats. "A tiny treat, and regular cat food for you later."

"Remember, I used to scrounge on the streets. Nimbus might be delicate, but I have a steel stomach." Marshmallow devoured both pieces. "I guess fish really is brain food because I just had an insight."

"Which is?"

"If we expand our list, then my original suspect, Marina, rises to the top."

I clicked my tongue. "Maybe. She was Helen's roommate, so plenty of opportunity there."

"And motive, too."

I pointed my chopsticks at Marshmallow. "How so?"

"Why, because she's mentioned in the will."

Marshmallow was right. Even though she hadn't inherited money outright (except perhaps a small executor's fee), she'd gotten the luxury townhouse free and clear.

"Don't forget that she has access to mercury at Déjà Vu," Marshmallow said. "We should check out that lead soon."

I finished up the sushi and pushed my plate away. "But for now, we've got another pressing mystery to solve. The one involving my dad."

• • •

Thank goodness I didn't find my dad golfing when I stopped by the country club. He was already in the doghouse with Ma, and he'd better be making it up to her big-time.

I strode up to the reception desk with confidence, squaring my shoulders and adding a slight swagger to my steps.

The man at the front widened his eyes. "Are you all right, miss? Did you pull a leg muscle recently? It's not advisable to go golfing with an injury . . ."

I scowled at him and restored my usual gait. "Actually, I won't be playing today. I'm here because my dad, Greg Lee, left his club here by accident. He came in yesterday. Could you check for his name on the roster?"

The man made no motion to search using the computer or look at any of the papers around him. "I'm sorry, miss. I can't provide access to information about our members."

I see. What happens in country club stays in country club. "Maybe you can just tell me if you noticed him around yesterday?" I described my dad to the man, from my father's height down to the cleft in his chin.

"If the gentleman left something on the grounds, we have an excellent lost and found system. He can retrieve it himself the next time he comes to play. We promise to keep his equipment safe."

I stared out the nearby large glass window, as though visually tracing my dad's footsteps from the other day. If he'd been here at all.

But would he have lied right to my face—or rather, to the phone? As I gazed upon the rolling green hills, I noticed some workers setting up a large canopy tent.

The man followed my focused stare. His eyes darted left and right. "Now if that's all, miss—"

Why was he being so cagey? A dark suspicion surfaced in my mind. "Is there a special event happening today?"

"Uh, no. That's for something scheduled for Friday evening."

I stared at the man, who'd started avoiding my gaze. "Who made the reservation?"

He mumbled, "That's confidential."

I crossed my arms to wait him out, but the unnerving trick didn't work. In fact, I ended up waiting so long that another member showed up. With a look of relief, the man pivoted his attention to the newcomer.

I gave up and started walking back to my car. On the way there, I decided to contact my dad's golfing buddy, Walt.

The call didn't go through. Instead, I got a message saying that I couldn't reach the subscriber. Was his phone busted, or had my number somehow gotten blocked? Weird.

Fine. I would find someone else with the pull to get confidential information from the country club. I needed a person with connections, and I knew just who to ask.

My fingers flew over the phone as I texted Pixie: Have an opening for Gelato's spa treatment. Ten-thirty tomorrow. Will that work?

Sounds divine, she replied. Thanks. XOXO.

CHAPTER
thirty-six

WHEN MONDAY MORNING rolled around, I made sure to wake up early. Thank goodness I didn't open the shop until ten. There would be plenty of time to drop by Déjà Vu and get some intel on Marina. We'd already crossed off motive and opportunity. Now we needed to see if she had the means to have committed murder.

On the way over, I also updated Marshmallow on the shenanigans with my dad and Pixie's upcoming grooming appointment at Hollywoof.

I parked in the lot before the antique store. Despite the cool morning air, I made sure to roll down the windows for Nimbus and Marshmallow.

"I'll only be asking a few questions," I said. "It should be quick."

But as I scrambled out of the driver's side, Merlin exited the store and approached me. Peeking through the windshield, he must have spotted the cats because he said, "Don't leave your pets outside. They're more than welcome in my store."

I got in the back seat and opened their carriers. "Marshmallow will be fine indoors," I said. "He's slow and lazy—"

My cat gave a hiss.

"But Nimbus will need to be held," I said.

"I'll volunteer." Merlin's eyes glittered like magic itself.

I handed over Nimbus, who tapped at Merlin's goatee, and then we bustled into the store.

"What brings you in this fine morning?" Merlin asked.

I spit out the lie I'd been rehearsing all weekend long. "My sister's school doesn't have enough science equipment. I thought I could bulk order some mercury thermometers for her."

I watched as Merlin strolled down a cluttered aisle with Nimbus in his arms.

His muffled voice came floating back to me. "We seem to only have a couple in stock. I swear we had more in our inventory before."

My heart hammered. Had Marina taken some from work to poison her roommate?

"Oh, what system do you have for keeping track of the goods?"

Merlin returned to the front and muttered under his breath. "I really need to do a massive cleanup around here."

"Do you use spreadsheets?" I asked.

He sat down behind the counter with Nimbus in his lap and brought out a few shoe boxes filled with papers. "Well, I make sure to reconcile the invoices with the sales receipts."

I bit the inside of my cheek. The messy stacks of bills definitely reflected haphazard accounting methods. "How often do you balance them?"

"About every month," he said with a lopsided smile.

"Um, could you let me know when you reconcile the numbers?"

"Certainly." He pushed up the spectacles sliding down his nose. "I'll tell Marina what I find when she comes in next, and she can pass the info on to you."

"She's so busy. Please don't trouble her." I placed my business card on the counter. "You can call me directly with the results."

Merlin seemed to stare past me for a minute. He took a deep breath before speaking again. "Has Marina seemed preoccupied to you lately? Is she involved with a gentleman caller?"

I fidgeted under his probing. What could I tell him? I didn't know a thing about Marina's love life.

"I don't mean to pry . . ." He pulled at his goatee. "Only I think her boyfriend's trying to trick her."

Noticing the puzzled look on my face, Merlin reached into the front display case with its jewelry and pulled out a diamond ring. He then searched the shelf behind him and found a loupe.

Handing me the tool, he said, "Examine this diamond through the magnifying lens."

I did so and saw an immediate brilliant glow from the stone. What does this have to do with Marina?

"Sparkly, right?" Merlin said. "A pure shine. CZ—cubic zirconia, that is—has more of a rainbow glitter."

"Oh-kay." I wondered if my jewelry lesson was done for the day and put down the loupe.

But he held up a gnarled finger. "Look again. At the edges."

I reexamined the diamond. "Um, they're sharp?"

"That's right. CZ has rounded edges, and it's not as durable as diamond. The ring Marina brought to me the other day had signs of wear, including cloudiness and chipping."

I sucked in my breath. "She showed you a ring?" Could it be? I glanced at Marshmallow, who gave me a subtle nod.

"What are the chances?" Marshmallow said. "It has to be Helen's."

Merlin held out his lined palm for the loupe. "She wanted me to examine the stone. It weighed about a carat, but I didn't have the heart to tell her it was a fake. I gave her a low estimate for its value, and she seemed disappointed."

Huh. Marina must have tried determining its worth once I'd confirmed that Brandon didn't want the ring back.

Merlin shook his head. "Maybe you can convince Marina he's the wrong guy for her. It may be old-fashioned of me, but if he can't even afford a real diamond . . ."

"Thank you, sir," I said. "I'll try."

Of course, I wouldn't breathe a word to Marina.

But I did dissect the conversation with Marshmallow back in the car when I placed him into his carrier. "It was cubic zirconia."

"Uh-huh." Marshmallow licked his fur. "And how did we get to this point? Because Marina got greedy and tried to assess the ring's value. That shows you where her heart truly is—not with her friend, but on the money."

"True, but . . ." I secured Nimbus in the back seat. "What bothers me is why Brandon would give Helen a fake ring in the first place."

"He's a classic cheapskate," Marshmallow said.

But I thought there might be more to the story than that. I mulled it over as I drove to Hollywoof in time for Gelato's grooming appointment.

• • •

Nicola had stepped out for a coffee run when Pixie showed up with her shih tzu. Her face glowed with delight as she surveyed Hollywoof. She'd seen the blueprints and visited prior to Hollywoof's grand opening, but she still seemed enthralled by the Hollywood-themed décor. She particularly liked the spotlight that shone down on the cash register and the shop's motto: "Where we treat your pets like stars."

Gelato couldn't stop barking inside the shop. He circled around in one spot, excited at seeing his new furry friends, Nimbus and Marshmallow, again.

"Can someone lower the volume on the shih tzu?" Marshmallow said.

Nimbus purred like a well-oiled motor.

Pixie gave me a sweet hug and said, "This place is amazing. You're an inspiration, Mimi."

"None of it would've happened without your help."

"Nonsense," she said, shaking her head. "It's your hard work that makes this business thrive."

I felt myself flushing with pride. "Thanks. And I have a special treat for Gelato today—an aromatherapy bath."

"Sounds delightful," Pixie said. "I'll just sit on the bench here and do some work while I wait."

She often telecommuted for her job, so I hoped my Internet connection was strong enough for her tasks. "By the way," I said. "The other staff member, Nicola, might return while I'm in the back room."

"I'll be sure and say hello," Pixie said.

I waved to her and escorted Gelato to where the grooming magic happened. For the special occasion, I'd bought a nontoxic bottle of pumpkin spice essential oil. I figured the fragrance would match the signature cloves-and-cinnamon perfume Pixie often wore.

After mixing the essential oil with the dog shampoo, I started the washing process. The smell of Thanksgiving rose into the air.

"And for you, Gelato, I'm adding in some extra pampering." I'd picked up a few Swedish massage techniques on YouTube and copied them to soothe Gelato's aches. I knew active dogs could really develop tight muscles, and I made sure to pay extra attention to any kinks I found.

When I finally rinsed Gelato off, he thanked me by shaking his body out. I squealed as water drops flew everywhere.

I blow-dried and fluffed out his fur until he looked more like walking cotton candy than a dog. When I brought him to the front, I spied Pixie and Nicola deep in conversation. Or rather, Nicola was regaling my friend with her near celebrity sightings: the back of Brad Pitt's head, Morgan Freeman's voice from down a hallway, and Rihanna's luxe car. How long had Pixie been listening to her monologue?

In a loud voice, I said, "Ta-dah." I presented the new-and-improved Gelato.

"Hey there, handsome," Pixie said, standing up and taking Gelato in her arms. "You smell enchanting. Is that . . ."

"Yup, pumpkin spice."

Pixie sniffed deeply. "Mmm."

Nicola joined in on the conversation. "Speaking of 'spice,' I think I saw Posh Spice at Pink's Hot Dogs the other day."

I wanted to speak with Pixie alone, so I said, "That's fascinating, Nicola, but Pixie doesn't know any movie folks except for . . ." I paused as though wracking my brain, but I knew Pixie would fill in the blank.

Pixie gave a brilliant smile. "I'm in touch with that famous producer, Dalton. Well, I know his wife, Lauren."

Nicola paled upon hearing her ex-boss's name. Besides letting her go, the woman had given her little love and had worked her to the bone.

I jumped in with a suggestion. "You know, Gelato was so excited by the bath, he flung water all over the floor."

Pixie wagged a finger at her pooch. "Always a little ball of energy."

Nicola took my hint and volunteered to clean up the grooming area. "I better dry up the puddles." She said goodbye to Pixie and scurried away.

"Hard worker," Pixie said.

"I admit, it's nice having an extra pair of hands." *But not ears*, I thought. "I have a favor to ask of you, Pixie."

"Sure. Is everything okay?" A worry line creased her forehead.

"You know folks at the country club, right? I remember running into you in your golf cart."

"Yes, I have clients who are long-standing members."

I bit my lip. "I saw an extravagant canopy set up there the other day. Do you think you could find out more details about it?"

"Probably, but it might take some time to locate my clients and gain access to the info." She placed a hand on my shoulder. "What is this about, Mimi?"

I replied with a quavering voice. "It might have something worrying to do with my family. But then again, maybe it's nothing. That's what I need to figure out."

"I'll ring you as soon as I find out anything," she said.

While I waited for Pixie to locate some answers, I knew how I could distract myself. I'd do my own questioning—of a certain suspect against the lulling backdrop of the ocean.

CHAPTER
thirty-seven

WOKE UP BEFORE dawn the next day for a surfing lesson with Brandon. He'd been booked the previous afternoon and evening, but this morning's dawn slot was available. And I knew why as I yawned in the near darkness. I had to pass by the sound-asleep cats on my way out the door.

At All Tide Up, I read and signed the waiver form, gulping at the terms and conditions. Then Brandon gave me a hang loose sign. "Ready to ride the waves, Mimi?"

Uh, no. But I still managed to change into the rental wetsuit. It smelled like seaweed and clung to me in an unflattering way. I felt like a human version of a sushi hand roll when I finally left the dressing room.

Brandon selected two boards. "We're on dawn patrol today."

I didn't manage to ask him any questions while walking down the beach, what with the early morning hour and trying to trudge through the sand without falling flat on my face. Thank goodness not many people were around to witness my wobbly gait. But Brandon himself seemed to be a chatterbox today.

"This is the best time to go out," he said. "Look at the precious water."

We'd reached the edge of where damp met dry sand. "The ocean seems gentle this morning," I said.

"It's called, 'glassy,'" he said. "Smooth water and great to learn on. Here's your official funboard for today."

"My *what*?" I asked. "Will it guarantee my fun?"

"Surfing is always a refreshing experience," he said. "And we call any medium-length surfboard a 'funboard.'"

So he wasn't making me any promises then.

Brandon wasn't a bad trainer. After chalking a line on the middle of the board, he advised me to balance on its center. He even had me practice sliding from tummy to standing, with the board positioned on the sand first.

However, I was a horrible student when actually in the water. After wiping out for the fifth time, I licked the salt off my lips and said, "Let's take a breather."

On the shore, Brandon gazed out to the sea, but he put down his board. My own funboard already lay in the sand, and I longed to sprawl next to it but refrained. Brandon wouldn't take me seriously if I questioned him while prone.

I wrung out my waterlogged hair. "You know, I couldn't help but admire Helen's engagement ring."

His back stiffened. "You've seen it?"

"It's beautiful. In fact, I've been meaning to take the next steps

with *my* boyfriend." A slight white lie. I wasn't anywhere close to getting hitched. "Where's it from?"

"Er, probably the Jewelry Square," he mumbled.

"Huh?"

"That downtown area with all the stores." He pointed south. I guess
he wasn't very good with directions because the heart of Los Angeles
lay northeast of us.

"Do you mean the Jewelry District?" The section, near Hill Street in
downtown, was filled with merchants who peddled gold, silver, and
precious gemstones at wholesale prices.

"Right, that's it." He started tapping his fingers against his thigh.

"The diamond was huge. How many carats again?"

He held up three fingers, furrowed his brow, and then said, "Maybe
two?"

Hmm. Merlin had mentioned the stone weighing about a carat.

To continue my ruse, I said, "I know you mentioned a Vegas wedding. Any venues you'd recommend there?"

A genuine smile lit up his face. "I did discover this *far-out* place in
Vegas. It's a surfing-themed chapel. You can get married there with the
roar of the ocean piped in through subwoofers.

"And get this," he continued, "a large screen on the wall simulates
being in a green room."

"That sitting area before you go on a show?" I'd heard the term
mentioned by Nicola before.

"Nah, it's that secret spot when you're in the barrel of a wave. The
entire world around you turns green."

"Gee," I said, "that chapel sounds like a great fit since you two met
surfing."

His smile faltered, and his voice grew flat. "Helen didn't go for it. She wanted, er, a different sort of ceremony."

"Oh, too bad." I started shivering in the breeze that whipped at me, even through my wetsuit. Or maybe it was from the ice that had crept into his tone.

"You're cold," he said. "Do you want to go back into the water?"

"No, I'm done with the lesson." I lifted my board and wiped away the sand.

We traveled in awkward silence back to All Tide Up. I wanted to change the chilly atmosphere as we walked along and thought of an excellent way to break the tension. "So, Brandon, I never did get the full story. How did you pop the question?"

His board slipped from his fingers, but he managed to snag it before it fell all the way down. "I didn't."

We'd arrived at the storefront, but I stopped and turned to face him. "What's that?"

He blinked at me. "Helen proposed to *me*."

Huh? Then I remembered our previous conversation about how the proposal had been "a simple ask" and that Helen had hated drama. I hurried into the store to cover up my surprise, mumbling about needing to change.

In the dressing room, I reevaluated my entire conversation with Brandon on the beach. No wonder he hadn't known much about the ring. Helen had purchased it herself.

I took a while mulling over my thoughts, as well as getting the sand (that had somehow managed to seep through the suit) off my body. So long, in fact, that Brandon had to leave for his next appointment by the time I'd finished changing. I gave him a quick thank-you right before he stepped out the door.

Then I returned the wetsuit to the employee at the front.

"How did you like your lesson?" the woman with tousled pink locks asked me.

"I think I'm a natural . . . landlubber," I said.

The woman shook her head, making her colored hair fly. "I'm sorry," she said. "Did something go wrong during your session? Would you like to file a complaint?"

I held my hands up. "Nothing like that. Brandon's a great teacher. I think it's my fault I couldn't follow his instructions."

"Well, practice makes perfect." She painted a broad smile on her face. "We do offer a discount if you buy a package of lessons."

"I think—"

She'd already turned to the computer and started clicking on the mouse. "Except Brandon's unavailable in early March."

"That's fine. This one lesson is enough for me," I said.

She continued staring at the screen, fascinated. "He's blocked out time for a trip to Fiji. I so have FOMO."

I'd also have fear of missing out on a great vacay to the South Pacific. "Wait a minute. Fiji?" How could he pay for such an extravagant trip? "That's a nice vacation."

"I know, right?" She ran her fingers through her messy hair. "But whatever. He said he'd be coming into big money soon, so he can afford it."

Come again? I must have turned pale because the woman suggested that I sit down.

"Maybe the roiling waves got to you," she said.

No, it was her statement that had rocked me. I exited All Tide Up, determined to go back home and relay the latest discovery to Marshmallow.

CHAPTER

thirty-eight

WHEN I RETURNED home from the illuminating surf lesson, I told Marshmallow everything. Then I paced back and forth before him in the living room. "What does it mean that she initiated the proposal?"

Marshmallow held a paw up and waved it toward the kitchen. "Food first, discussion later."

Oh, that's right. I needed to feed the cats. After Marshmallow started eating, I continued thinking out loud. "So, Helen made the first move. And he accepted her proposal. Does that make him more trustworthy because she asked him first?"

"As much as anyone who goes into water for fun can be trusted," Marshmallow said, nudging his empty bowl toward me.

On autopilot, I refilled it with kibble and set out another dish for Nimbus, who'd arrived with a mewling cry. "But he'd already planned on proposing to her even though she beat him to the punch. And what's all this about getting some money? From where?"

Marshmallow shook his head. "I don't know, but I still think it's Marina. She had the motive and the opportunity. We just need to hear back from the shopkeeper about the thermometer inventory."

"Maybe . . ."

I cleaned up the kitchen and got ready for work. When I walked out of my unit, I saw the door to Josh's apartment fly open. He hurried out. His hair stuck up, and he carried a briefcase with the edges of a few documents caught in its clasp.

"Late start?" I asked when he jogged by my door.

"Overslept," he said, pausing before me with a sheepish grin. "Too many long nights."

"Wait a minute," I said, reaching up. I tamed his locks. "There, much better."

"Thanks, Mimi." He took a deep breath. "It's a heavy workload, but I'm glad I finally finished some important tasks. Will you be free later tonight?"

"Definitely. What time?"

"I'll be back around ten. I promised to get some drinks with my Trojan buddies right after work."

I made a mock angry face.

"Aw, you look cute when you pout," he said.

Wait a minute. USC colleagues . . . they must be law school friends. "Actually, there is a way you can make up for your betrayal. Can you go over Helen's will again?"

He swung his briefcase in the air. "Sure. Why?"

"Just wondering if Brandon, Helen's ex, got some sort of small settlement."

"That should be easy enough to find out." He launched into the first few lines of the USC fight song.

I shook my head at him but smiled. In return, he gave me a quick peck on the cheek.

"See you tonight, warrior," I said.

He said goodbye and left with a livelier spring to his step.

• • •

Hollywoof had gone to the birds. Right after we opened shop, we had a line of avian enthusiasts show up at the door. Marshmallow spotted the telltale wire cages first.

He corralled Nimbus, and they both hid behind the counter. Marshmallow said, "I don't want to hear their annoying chirps." *And probably better this way*, I thought. I didn't want the cats to scare off the birds.

The customers came in and asked for me by name. Apparently, Pavarotti's owner really had recommended my services to her bird-owning friends.

It took a while to get through each wing clipping appointment, but I made sure to take my time as I trimmed their feathers. When the last parakeet departed, the absence of the flapping of wings and twitters left the shop oddly silent.

Marshmallow and Nimbus crept out from their hiding spot, and Nicola tapped her manicured hands against the counter. "To tell you the truth, I kind of miss the singing."

Marshmallow flattened his ears. "If you could call it that."

He and Nimbus reclaimed their usual napping spot. They sprawled across their territory.

"Maybe I should get a pet bird," Nicola said. "Some famous celebrities own them." She counted them off on her sparkling fingertips. "Paris Hilton, Hilary Swank, Angelina Jolie . . ."

I darted a glance at Marshmallow, all splayed out on the floor. "Cats are much better."

He meowed in agreement.

"Maybe there's a special famous bird club I can be a part of. I could make connections that way. Oh"—Nicola gasped—"I just remembered. Steven Spielberg has a bird, too. We could bond over moulting."

"Um . . ."

That was all the encouragement Nicola needed to outline her new networking plan for creating six degrees of separation from getting cast in a feature film by way of bird ownership.

She was still burbling about the possible pet connection when my phone rang. I saw Pixie's name on the caller ID and answered right away.

"What did you find out?" I asked as I moved toward the waiting area.

She clucked her tongue. "I'm not sure you want to hear this, but . . . After using my client's clout, I found out that the canopy was reserved by Greg Lee."

I felt my knees about to give way, and I dropped onto the pleather bench. "My suspicions were right." In my heart, I'd known what she would discover. I bit the inside of my cheek to keep from crying.

She sighed. "That's not all. It sounds like it might be for a wedding."

"Are you sure about that?"

"Well, there's an officiant involved."

In a faint voice, I managed to whisper goodbye before ending the call.

My blood began to boil under my skin. I wanted to confront my dad right away, but calling him wouldn't be a good idea. I knew I'd hang up at the sound of his two-timing voice.

My fingers flew over my phone's keyboard as I texted: I know what you're planning at the country club.

The next moment seemed to last an eternity before he typed back. I hated keeping it a secret from you girls.

That's all he had to say? I wanted to hurl my phone at the floor and watch it break into a million pieces. To splinter apart. Like my shattered heart.

CHAPTER

thirty-nine

S OMEHOW I GOT through the day after the earth-shattering news that Dad had rented the wedding tent. I went through the motions of grooming in a zombie-like state. They say that misery loves company, but I didn't want to pass my sadness on to Alice.

I wrestled with whether I should tell my sister. In the end, I decided to delay the horrible news. People say, "Knowledge is power," but I subscribed more to the "Ignorance is bliss" school.

At home, I managed to pass away the time by eating an actual TV dinner in front of the screen, with a double serving of Coolhaus ice cream afterward. The UCLA alumna–created frozen treat boosted my spirits a little.

I totally forgot I had any evening plans when the doorbell rang. After shoveling another spoonful into my mouth, I plunked down my spoon and went to the door and found Josh standing out front.

My hand flew to my sticky mouth in astonishment. I also tried to discreetly wipe away any ice cream trails.

Josh's eyes darted to the TV tray with the tissue box and the bowl of melting ice cream. "What's wrong, Mimi?"

I sniffled, and he came through the doorway and embraced me. There was something extremely comforting about being in his arms. It also unleashed a floodgate of tears from me.

In between sobbing and drenching his dress shirt, I managed to share the story of my dad's betrayal. I couldn't look Josh in the eye as I talked, but spoke right into his shoulder.

He made reassuring noises, and eventually the bass hum of his voice, along with the circles he traced on my back, soothed me. I cried myself out.

After a few more moments of him holding me, I pulled away and wiped my eyes with the back of my hand.

"I'm sorry," I said. "You had something nice planned for the two of us this evening."

His mouth quirked. "Nothing fancy. Just a bit of stargazing in the courtyard."

That I could handle. And maybe the cool breeze would dry away any new tears. I glanced back at the cats. Would they also want to enjoy the fresh air?

Marshmallow shook his head. "No way am I voluntarily going to freeze my tail off. And don't involve Nimbus, either. I'm not letting her catch your strange human habit of staring at balls of gas in the sky."

"Let's go," I said, slipping my hand into Josh's.

We stepped outside. Josh had laid out a bamboo mat along with a thick blanket. We lay down next to each other, pulled the blanket over us, and gazed at the night sky. He took out a wrapped fortune cookie from his shirt pocket. "Want one?"

"Sure." As I slipped it out from the cellophane, I couldn't help but think of his collection of fortune cookies in the glass jar on his work desk. He said the positive sayings helped him feel better through stressful times.

He turned his head toward me, and his warm breath caressed my cheek as he spoke. "I wanted to surprise you," he said. "Like you did that time you gave me dinner alfresco in this very courtyard."

I'd brought him greasy Chinese takeout, so it wasn't the best of impressions, but somehow I'd drawn him in. (Maybe it had to do with the free fortune cookies.) He'd forgiven me for my meet-oops when I'd blundered during our initial introduction.

"What's your fortune say?" he asked.

I cracked open the cookie, pulled out the slip of paper, and read, "'That special someone loves to see the light in your eyes.'"

"So true." He held hands with me under the blanket.

Then we focused on the glittering stars above us. Okay, so I didn't see that many stars because of the light pollution in L.A., but I spotted some shimmers here and there. I let the cookie dissolve in my mouth and reveled in its vanilla flavor.

As I relaxed under the stars, my situation felt somewhat bearable. Maybe because I was forced to think about the enormous expanse of the universe. My problem didn't seem so big in comparison to the galaxy.

Josh squeezed my hand. "I'm not sure if this is any consolation, but I did have success in finding the info. Remember you asked me to learn more about Helen's will?"

I stopped focusing on the stars and looked at Josh's profile.

He kept staring at the velvet sky as he said, "Her fiancé doesn't get any kind of settlement from her estate."

Oh. I'd thought for sure—

"But there was a previous version of the will where Brandon had been entitled to a serious amount of money."

I squeezed Josh's hand tight in my excitement. Brandon had reserved his vacation in advance because, according to his coworker, he was in line for some money. Had he been plotting Helen's murder ever since he'd found out he was written into her will? Only he hadn't realized she'd changed it . . .

"Hope this helps," Josh said.

In all my deep thinking, I'd forgotten to thank him. "Definitely. I really do appreciate you getting these details, Josh."

He mumbled, "I wish I could somehow help you with your dad's situation."

"It's enough that you're right beside me as I go through it."

We turned our attention back to the stars. And even though I hadn't wished on a shooting star for Josh, I knew how lucky I was to have him in my life.

• • •

As I drove to work the next morning, Marshmallow and I discussed the case in the car. The conversation grew heated as we each provided evidence on our theories about who the culprit could be. Perhaps I even rushed through a few yellow lights because we were at Hollywoof a good fifteen minutes before opening time. However, I soon discovered we weren't the only ones to show up so early.

"Speak of the devil," Marshmallow said as we neared the shop's entrance.

Marina sat on one of the wooden benches scattered across the palm tree–lined plaza. She waved at us, not that I could miss her since she wore a bright construction orange top.

"She's probably not sitting around here to take in the beach air," I whispered to Marshmallow.

I jingled my keys and said in a louder voice, "Let me put the cats indoors, and I'll be right back."

After settling Marshmallow and Nimbus inside Hollywoof, I made sure to open the store window facing the street. "So you can hear better," I said to Marshmallow.

He nodded and perched on the windowsill.

When I returned outside, I noticed Marina trying to pat down her hair. It did seem particularly unruly today.

"Hi, Marina. What brings you to the area?" I asked as I sat down next to her.

"I found something," she said, cradling her purse.

"Go on. Show me," I said, giving her an encouraging smile.

She snapped open her bag, and her hand hovered above it. "You do know someone in the police department, right? I think you mentioned you had a contact."

I vaguely remembered telling her that I could use my connections in case Helen's father ever showed up uninvited and angry on her doorstep again. "Yes, I do know somebody."

"Great." She reached into her purse and pulled out a glossy brochure. "I found this among Helen's things."

The picture of a chapel and a smiling bride on the cover made the blood drain from my face.

"Are you all right?" Marina asked.

"Fine." I gripped the brochure tightly.

"Well," Marina said, "this could be of vital importance to figure out what really happened to Helen. You see, it's all a sham . . ."

I tuned her out as my mind fixated on the stock image of the generic bride. Who was the mystery woman Dad had fallen for? Might I even know her?

"Do you believe me, Mimi?" Marina asked.

I refocused on her.

She patted my arm. "Just read the brochure, Mimi. The evidence is all in there."

I promised her I'd do so on my lunch break. She walked away with a satisfied smile playing across her lips.

CHAPTER

forty

L IKE I HAD promised Marina, I looked over the brochure during my lunch hour. I needed the break, too. Nicola found me not as zombied out as before, but bad enough that she took over the simple grooming duties in the morning. She put me in charge of the register—and even then, Marshmallow sometimes had to whisper the right change amount to me.

At noon, I took Marshmallow out to sit in the sunshine with me in the plaza. I found it somehow fitting that we sat on the same bench Marina had vacated hours before. After I'd finished my peanut butter and banana sandwich (I found the combo comforting), I put on my earbuds and plugged them into my phone.

This way I could talk to Marshmallow without getting any odd stares. I waited until the lunch crowd of people flaunting impressive tanned bodies disappeared into the local beach restaurants before starting up our conversation.

"Let's take a look at this brochure then." I flipped open the trifold pamphlet.

"Yawn," Marshmallow said. "Who cares about these packages? Bouquet or corsage? Elvis serenade or not?"

"Can't help fah-lling in love," I crooned, using jazz hands.

He placed a paw on the brochure. "Oh, look. This paragraph is circled, Mimi."

"I know you're just trying to derail my singing career."

"No, really. It has an asterisk beside it." His paw tapped the paper.

I read the fine print out loud. "Ceremonies are not legally valid. No marriage licenses will be provided."

Marshmallow withdrew his paw. "Is it saying that people don't actually get married at this chapel?"

I read the brochure from cover to cover before folding it neatly. "Yes, this chapel specializes in pretend weddings. So that's why Marina was talking about it being a sham."

Marshmallow hissed. "Uh-huh. And she pinned the blame square on Brandon."

"She did what?"

He wiggled his ears. "Weren't you listening, Mimi?"

I blushed. "To be honest, I sort of tuned out."

"She said Brandon was responsible for Helen's death."

"But how?" I asked.

"Apparently, he blew his top after Helen figured out his plan to 'fake marry' her."

I snapped my fingers. "That does make sense. Marina's on to something. Brandon could be the guy."

Marshmallow bristled his fur. "You're just saying that because it supports your hunch that Brandon's at fault. Besides, wasn't he talking about getting married for real, like on a surfboard? Why would he want her dead before they tied the knot?"

I adjusted my earbuds as a pedestrian passed by. "What if he lost it because Helen got cold feet? Remember, he'd wanted a surfer's wedding. She changed it to a fake wedding instead. A lovers' quarrel turned deadly."

"Maybe." Marshmallow licked his fur. "Or perhaps Marina's trying to pull the wool over your eyes and throw Brandon under the bus."

"Why would she do that?"

"So you don't latch on to her as the culprit. Besides"—he swished his tail—"humans are natural-born liars."

My phone pinged. "I don't think so. Here's somebody who always tells the truth. Josh."

"Please. Even his name means 'to joke.'"

I rolled my eyes at Marshmallow and focused on texting.

Josh: Figured out a way to understand what's going on with your parents.

Me: There's really no use.

Josh: I searched for recent divorce filings and . . . nada.

Me: What do you mean?

Josh: Nothing's been served.

But there was an officiant. What was going on?

I thanked Josh but wondered about the strange situation. My dad had reserved the space for sure.

I'd better talk things over with my sister. In fact, maybe she'd have deeper insight into everything. In fact, hadn't she stayed overnight with them after the disastrous Ultimate Date Night? My parents might have let something slip to her then.

Marshmallow meowed at me and read over my shoulder.

As he twitched his nose, I said, "Nothing filed. Strange, right? I'm going to close up shop a bit early and head over to Alice's."

"Can you make a pit stop first?" he asked. "Déjà Vu is en route to your sister's place."

"What? Why?"

Marshmallow studied me with his intense blue eyes. "Merlin was supposed to contact you about the mercury, remember?"

I blew out my breath. "I have other things on my mind right now."

In a flash, Marshmallow had pounced on my phone and snatched it up with his mouth. The earbuds jerked away from me. "This is important," he said. "It's for Alice, so we can clear her name."

"Blackmailer," I said. With my phone as hostage, though, I agreed to his demands.

"All's well that ends well," he said, returning it to me.

"You know what, Marshmallow?" I said. "You're plain *clawful*."

He groaned, but from my pun, he knew I'd forgiven him.

CHAPTER

≡ *forty-one* ≡

AFTER WE ENTERED Déjà Vu, I noticed that the store looked different. The boxes piled near the register had disappeared.

Merlin smiled at us. Both Nimbus and Marshmallow pooled around his legs, and his grin grew wider. "Nice to see you, too, kitties."

I stood before Merlin. "Did you end up reconciling your books? Your place looks much more organized."

He adjusted the spectacles on his nose. "Finished all the paperwork this morning. Sorry I didn't get a chance to call you about the inventory and receipts."

My fingers danced across the glass counter with its embedded coins. "What did you find out?"

"Actually, we didn't have that many old thermometers in stock. And we accounted for all the ones that got sold."

I wrinkled my nose. "Who's 'we'?"

"Marina and I. She was indispensable in figuring out the numbers." He knocked himself on the head. "I'm not very talented at math."

Marshmallow let out a moan, and Merlin asked, "Is your cat all right?"

"I'm fine, but your shop might not be doing so well," my cat said.

Marshmallow had a point. If Merlin had relied on Marina to evaluate the stock, could I trust the results he'd gotten?

"Thanks for your time," I said to Merlin.

Oblivious, he gave me well-wishes for Marshmallow's improved health as I led the cats out the door.

"She cooked the books," Marshmallow said when we got back in the car.

"You don't know that."

"It's a strong possibility."

Merlin had relied on Marina to check on the inventory earlier in the morning. The timing was oddly coincidental. "I do admit it's suspicious that Marina came to visit us at Hollywoof—"

"To 'prove' her innocence. She even diverted your attention and used Brandon as a scapegoat by giving you that wedding brochure."

My hands gripped the steering wheel. The word "wedding" reminded me of the upcoming bound-to-be-awkward talk with my baby sis.

"Let's get this over with," I said as I revved the engine.

• • •

Alice greeted us with a warm welcome when we showed up at her place. I was about to spring some horrible news on her, and I couldn't stomach destroying her joy right away. Even after she invited us inside, I remained standing before her in the entryway, hopping from one foot to the other.

"Mimi, what's wrong?" My sister guided me to the dining table, a place where I could typically let go of my anxieties through food, but I continued standing near it. Marshmallow, though, led Nimbus over to lie down under the table, maybe to await future crumbs.

"Let me brew a pot of tea," Alice said. "Dragonwell, extra strong."

Dragonwell was the supreme selection of tea. "Emperor tea," Ma called it. She served it to us as a panacea for all kinds of pains, even heartaches.

I watched as Alice placed a kettle on the burner. Then she opened a tin canister, letting a whiff of herbs float in the air.

Only after the water had boiled and she'd transferred it to a teapot with a bamboo design to steep the leaves did I begin speaking. Both she and I could deal with this better over a nice cup of tea.

"It's about Dad," I said, spitting out his name like a licorice-flavored watermelon seed.

She poured out the tea into dainty matching porcelain cups. After setting them at the dining table, she gestured for me to sit down next to her. "Yeah, I got the e-mail a few minutes before you arrived."

At the table, I said, "Excuse me? He *e-mailed* you the news?"

She gave me a quick nod. "Actually, it was an Evite."

I almost fell out of the chair. "He gave you an electronic invitation to the ceremony?"

"Uh-huh. Who knew he was so modern?" Alice was handling the news well. Maybe she'd already been prepared for it since she'd spent time with Ma and Dad after the Ultimate Date Fail.

Josh had told me he couldn't find any divorce filings, though. "I don't understand. How can Dad get remarried?"

Alice gave me a strange look. "I wouldn't quite call it remarriage . . . By the way, you're on the guest list, too."

I pulled out my phone and checked my e-mail. "Nothing," I said.

"Try your spam folder."

There. An electronic invitation sent from my dad. My eyes misted as I lingered upon our last name. "Family is *satu*," or "number one," was our Lee motto. How could he have gone so astray?

Marshmallow purred from under the table and climbed onto my lap. "Mimi," he said, "read the heading."

I blinked back my tears and focused on the words. It read, *You're invited to a recommitment ceremony.*

"What?" I dropped my phone on the table with a clatter. "They're doing a vow renewal."

"Right." Alice smiled at me, and it seemed like the sun peeping out behind my rainfall of tears. "In the details, it says it's meant to be a surprise for Ma. That's why she doesn't have a clue about it."

"No wonder he's been so distant." I double-checked the ceremony date. Two days later. Exactly on time for this year's Leap Day. "He'd been planning a big anniversary celebration for Ma. I've had it all backwards." Dad said he'd hated keeping a secret from us—the organization of this important event.

Alice held up her teacup and clinked it against mine. "To our parents."

CHAPTER

≈ forty-two ≈

I HUMMED TO MYSELF as I dragged the suitcase that housed my special ethnic attire out of my closet. I'd tucked away my special ethnic attire. After all, I rarely had a chance to wear the colorful, distinctive clothes.

Placing the hand-me-down suitcase on the floor of my bedroom, I opened it to find the clothes protected under layers of tissue. I reached under the papers to pull out each item and examine it for moth damage. Thankfully there was none.

I started sorting the clothes by color and style. There were the casual short-sleeve tops, which I ruled out as too informal. Then I continued organizing and piling up the discards until I had narrowed the choices down to three outfits by the time Nimbus and Marshmallow wandered into my bedroom.

"Whatcha doin'?" Marshmallow asked.

I pointed to the selections laid out on my bed. "*Kebaya*, *sari*, or *qipao*. I need to pick one for Ma and Dad's special event."

Marshmallow jumped on the bed and tapped at the sari. "Isn't red the color of love?"

"You reminded me. Brides usually wear the lucky hue," I said, "so maybe that one's out of the running."

"Good. One down. A fifty-fifty choice, Mimi."

I was tempted to play eeny-meeny-miny-moe to help me pick. The curve-hugging qipao reflected my Chinese side, but I hated its high collar and was afraid the buttons would pop off and leave me exposed.

"This one's more comfortable," I said, touching the kebaya, a loose blouse coupled with a sarong.

"You know, if humans had better birthday suits, you wouldn't need fancy clothes to hide your boring skin." He strutted. "Look at my excellent fur coat, always available."

I folded up the qipao and repositioned the tissues in the suitcase. At the sound of the crinkling, Nimbus sprang up and launched herself at the papers.

She settled herself in the suitcase and started shredding the tissues with glee. A few moments passed in this frenzy before she began sneezing.

Shaking her head, Nimbus jumped out of the suitcase and backed away from it. She hissed.

"What's the matter?" I looked to Marshmallow for an explanation of her behavior.

After a brief discussion, Marshmallow told me that Nimbus had smelled something pungent in the suitcase. I peeled back the layers of tissue but didn't discover anything. Then I saw a camouflaged inner compartment. Unzipping it, I found a bag of old moth balls. Although expired, they'd probably kept my clothes from getting holes in them.

Guess Ma had placed them in the case before she passed it along to me. She'd used this very suitcase to hold her own collection of "off-season clothes" before.

"Sorry," I said to Nimbus as I threw out the offending packet. "I couldn't smell it at all."

Nimbus sneezed again.

"That little kitty's got a sensitive nose," Marshmallow said. "Better attuned than even mine."

"Must be your age," I said. "Just look at all your white hair."

Marshmallow covered his ears with his paws. "Keep your day job because stand-up comedy's not gonna work out for you."

Then Marshmallow meowed to Nimbus, and they left my bedroom. I watched the kitten go with rising curiosity.

She'd smelled the mothballs and had a really sensitive nose. Maybe Nimbus hadn't been the greatest eyewitness the day of the murder, but what if she made a superb nose-witness?

• • •

I'd ignored a vital olfactory clue. Nimbus had smelled something strange on Helen's skin the day she'd died.

I had a sinking suspicion of where that scent had come from. I dialed up Marina from the privacy of my bedroom to ask her for details.

She picked up after a few rings.

"Hi, it's Mimi." I didn't know if she had my name already entered into her phone's contacts or not.

"Yes? What's going on?"

"I think I figured something out," I said. "Can you do me a favor and take a peek at Helen's perfume bottle?"

"Sure. Let me get it from the closet." I heard some static over the line as she walked around the townhouse. "Okay, I've got it."

"Can you take a quick whiff?" I asked.

"Smells like strawberries . . . and something earthy?"

Or perhaps metallic. "Tell me what you see on the bottle."

"Uh, the name of the perfume is called Be Mine," she said.

"Anything else?"

"It's heart-shaped."

I paced around my room. "Can you send me a pic?"

My phone dinged after thirty seconds, and I zoomed in on the image, peering at the curved sides and the bottom with its stylized markings.

I tucked my hair behind my ear. "When did Helen get this perfume?"

"It's new." Marina clucked her tongue. "She got it a few days before Valentine's. Brandon left it on the doorstep with a tag addressed to 'My little surfer girl.'"

"I see," I said. "Now I have a giant ask of you. I'd like to set up a meeting at your townhouse . . . and get some justice for Helen."

Marina's voice steeled. "There's nothing I want more. Just tell me what your plan is, Mimi."

"Thanks. That's what I was hoping to hear."

CHAPTER

forty-three

ARRIVED WITH THE cats before the requisite time at Marina's townhouse. Using gloves, I retrieved the perfume bottle from the chest, opened it, and let Nimbus sniff. She arched her back in response.

"It's definitely the source of the funny smell on Helen—the poison," Marshmallow said.

I placed the bottle of perfume behind me and removed my gloves. Marshmallow and Nimbus stationed themselves beside me on each side, like guardian foo statues.

Marshmallow unsheathed his claws. "I'm ready for the showdown."

The doorbell rang right on time. I made him sweat it out, fiddling with my phone and clicking the mute button, before calling out, "It's open."

Scott Reed marched in with confident steps. He wore his usual suit, accessorized with a diamond-patterned scarf loosely knotted around his neck.

I gave my head a sad shake. "So, it was you all along."

He checked his watch. "How long will Helen's roommate be gone?"

I shrugged. "Marina told me before where she keeps the spare key, and she usually works mornings at the antique shop, so we've got time."

He looped the scarf around his neck. "Where did you put the evidence, Mimi?"

"All in due course."

His eyes swiveled around the room, but he wouldn't know where to even begin. "How did you figure it out anyway?" he said. "Know it was me?"`

"By the bottom of the bottle."

He nodded. "The foreign script stamped on by the manufacturing company."

I pointed to Nimbus. "Plus, this little kitty sniffed it out. She'd smelled something fishy on Helen and also acted odd when I draped her with that shawl you gave me from the memorial service. The one that's vibrant red from mercury—"

"Actually, it's cinnabar. Makes the bright color." His mouth twitched. "But mercury can be extracted from the ore. The manufacturer I own also added an extra catalyst to boost the poison and speed up its effects."

My voice came out scratchy. "How could you kill your own flesh and blood? You even tried to frame Helen's fiancé as the murderer. Left a package at the door supposedly from him. It was addressed to 'My little surfer girl.'"

"Such an easy trick. I mean, he mentioned his cutesy nickname for Helen all the time in his whiny e-mails to me begging for money."

"I really don't get it." My throat seemed to close up.

He ran a hand through his light brown hair but didn't say a word.

"Quid pro quo," I said, using a term I'd heard Josh toss around. "Tell me why, and I'll let you know where I put the bottle."

His lips flattened into a thin line, but he said, "Deal."

"Spill it."

"Helen forced me to do this. I did right by her, raised her up as a single father even though her mother had been *killed* by her being born." A vein throbbed in his forehead. "I provided Helen with an amazing education."

Her time with Pixie. "The boarding school," I murmured.

"Helen was an ungrateful little girl. But I figured she'd grow out of her adolescent moodiness, especially when she turned eighteen. I'd really hoped she'd buckle down and focus on the family business after her first trust fund kicked in."

I tugged my earlobe. "That's right. She was a 'double trust kid.'" Pixie had nicknamed Helen that.

"Yes, the second trust would follow whenever she got married." He looked at me without flinching. "I needed the money I'd trapped under her name. My business would've collapsed without the extra financial boost."

I raised my eyebrows. "You're not doing well financially? I thought you ran a lucrative international business."

He made a gurgling noise in the back of his throat. "I can see the writing on the wall. No one wants to buy the merchandise I sell anymore."

"But I saw customers at your booth during the crafts bazaar . . ." Which was an annual event. The pet toy vendor there had said Scott attended every year. How long had Helen's father been plotting her murder?

Scott didn't notice my internal dread. He said, "The customers at the bazaar wanted to know if I offered any dye-free materials. Everyone wants eco-friendly accessories with dull, ugly colors."

Huh. Isn't that what Indira had told me when she'd given me her latest versions of the doggie pouches? And the hues on those carriers *had* been more muted than her typical designs. "Couldn't you just have borrowed the money from Helen?"

"I practically groveled for it, but she wouldn't budge, even though I bailed her out last year with the school." His voice came out as a snarl. "And I couldn't alter the irrevocable trusts. She would get even more of my hard-earned money once she married."

Marshmallow growled from beside me as I said, "So you killed her before that could happen."

Scott started loosening the knot on his scarf. "I thought I'd thwarted the proposal by not lending Brandon any money, but they still got engaged. Helen even bragged about how she'd be married in Vegas. I had to act quickly."

Too bad Scott hadn't known the marriage would be phony, a fake ceremony planned by Helen to push his buttons.

"They'd even booked some vacation plans to a cozy Fiji resort," Scott said. "No doubt for their honeymoon."

Guess Brandon hadn't wanted to cancel their post pretend wedding plan even after Helen's demise. Must have been the siren call of stellar surfing that his coworker had mentioned.

"I didn't kill my daughter," Scott said. "She did it to herself."

I shivered. Is that how he could sleep at night—by changing the facts? "You gave her the poisoned perfume. Even primed her to wear it for Valentine's Day by the label on the bottle. Be Mine and a heart shape?" That was subliminal messaging at its most devious.

He shrugged. "The police don't suspect a thing. They never even checked the date of my plane ticket." The officials had taken his word that he'd arrived *after* Helen's death—just like I had. I'd bought his whole grieving father act with Principal Lewis at the Family and Friends Day hook, line, and sinker.

"I'd flown in earlier," he said.

I gulped. "At the beginning of the month. I remember the owner of Angelic Suites telling me you'd gotten the discounted hotel rate for booking your room for the whole month."

"Businessman to businesswoman," Scott said, "let's make a deal. If you don't tell a soul"—he reached into his suit pocket and waved a rectangular paper in the air—"you'll be able to cash this."

"I'm listening."

"I bet you could use an infusion into your banking account. Get even more clients with the latest grooming equipment." He slipped me the check.

I gasped at the large amount of money written on it.

"Deal?" he repeated.

I mumbled something unintelligible.

"Mimi, I'll be needing an answer." His tone was light but held a hint of warning.

My eyes flickered upward before I answered. "Fine, I won't say a word to the police."

"I knew you'd see the light." He played with the scarf loosely draped over his shoulders and smiled. "Now where's the perfume?"

I stepped to the side and revealed the bottle sitting on the floor.

His eyes lit up in recognition. But he didn't just grab the bottle like I'd anticipated.

Instead he lunged forward and whipped his scarf up at the same time. "Too bad you tied your scarf on so tight, Mimi."

Before I could scream or even react, he'd looped the scarf around my neck and started tightening it.

I heard Marshmallow hiss with fury. Pinpricks of light appeared at the edges of my vision.

CHAPTER

forty-four

SCOTT'S VOICE SEEMED to come from far away. "I run a business, not a charity. Sorry, Mimi. I can't be giving away my hard-won money."

An angry snarl erupted from beside me. Then came a scampering of paws.

The pressure on my neck eased as Scott began bellowing. His face distorted and grew red.

I sank to the floor, clutching at the tight fabric around my neck. Somehow I managed to place my finger between the scarf and my throat. I gulped in a few breaths.

I saw Marshmallow running away from Helen's father at full tilt. In my cat's mouth, I spied the heart-shaped bottle of perfume.

Marshmallow dodged Scott and hurried into the kitchen. Nimbus followed close behind, trying to run interference between the two, but Scott didn't pay the little kitten any attention.

"Here, kitty," Scott said to Marshmallow. "Give me the perfume."

Marshmallow let the bottle drop out of his mouth and gave a sharp meow.

Scott didn't hear Nimbus's responding mewl as he said, "Good kitty."

Nimbus darted around Scott's legs, grabbed the bottle, and leaped like an acrobat on top of the refrigerator. She perched there like a regal princess, peering down on the common peasants below her.

While Scott tried yanking on the fridge to topple it, I managed to loosen the scarf even more so that it didn't strain against my neck.

Scott grunted as he continued to push and pull against the refrigerator. In the meantime, the blessed sound of nearby sirens could be heard.

He was still battling with the fridge when the police barged in. I saw Detective Brown and caught his eye. He looked relieved to see me.

"Thought you'd be quicker," I said, my voice strained, as police officers surrounded Scott and detained him.

"You know L.A.," he said. "Traffic." A pause. "Are you all right, Mimi?"

I nodded, rubbing my neck gingerly.

Scott struggled against the police holding him. "How did they find out?" He glared at me. "You said you wouldn't tell."

I showed him my phone, which I'd used to contact Detective Brown earlier. "You said it all yourself. I didn't breathe a word to the cops."

He deflated in the arms of his captors.

Even with the detailed recording, the police took my statement. They also checked my breathing and examined my throat. No damage beyond a red ring around my neck that would fade away in time.

After they'd finished with the documentation, Detective Brown frowned at me. "I got a clear recording of the incriminating conversation, Mimi, but that was a dangerous game you were playing."

"I had to clear Alice's name." I intertwined my index and middle fingers together. "We're close sisters after all."

"Still, you risked your life."

I wandered over to the back door, pulled it open, and let out a sharp whistle. A flurry of pounding steps later, and Marina appeared on the threshold.

"Everything work out?" she said. "I made sure he didn't run out the back or anything."

I jerked my thumb over my shoulder.

Marina followed the movement and smiled as she located Scott being held by the cops.

I nodded at Detective Brown. "See, Marina would've come running if I'd called."

"It's hard to make any noise when you're being choked," he said.

Marina's hand flew to her own throat. "Mimi, did he try to strangle you?"

I then remembered the dangling scarf on my neck and yanked it off. "Here's his lousy souvenir."

Detective Brown took it with gloved hands and placed it in an evidence bag. "How did you manage to stop him by the way?"

"My cat got him off me," I said.

Marshmallow preened himself.

Detective Brown scrunched his forehead. "Does your cat always do that? It's almost as if he understood your comment."

"He has impeccable timing," I said. "In fact, he snagged the perfume bottle so Scott had to chase him and leave me alone."

"Ah," Detective Brown said, but then he stepped over to the refrigerator, where Nimbus lay curled up. "But if so, how did this little one end up with the perfume?"

"Marshmallow dropped the bottle, and Nimbus pounced on it. Then she leaped on top of the fridge."

"And Scott couldn't reach the incriminating evidence up there." The detective smiled up at Nimbus. "Smart kitty. Seems like she's the star for today."

"Excuse me?" Marshmallow made his eyes appear more slitted. "I hatched this spectacular plan."

"Come on down, Nimbus," Detective Brown said, pointing to the floor.

The kitten followed his command and placed the bottle at the cop's feet.

"You'd sure make a great detective cat," the cop said as he stored away the perfume in another evidence bag.

"She *is* available for adoption," I said.

Detective Brown put away his gloves and stroked Nimbus. She purred up a storm. "I might just take you up on that offer."

"I knew you'd eventually see the power of pets," I said with a grin.

Marshmallow rubbed against my leg. "Wow, Detective Brown, an animal lover? Will wonders never cease?"

I nodded and whispered, "And they say cats aren't magical."

CHAPTER

forty-five

WITH SCOTT IN custody, things had started to settle down by Friday and I was looking forward to a brighter occasion. I'd taken the day off to prepare myself for Ma and Dad's recommitment ceremony. Good thing, too, because I got an emergency text from my sister at seven that morning.

Fashion disaster, she'd texted, adding multiple exclamation points. Turns out that she'd just discovered tiny holes in the dress she'd been planning to wear.

I spirited away to Roosevelt Elementary with a collection of potential outfits for Alice. Even the traffic seemed to cooperate with my mission, and I arrived at the school in record time.

On campus, I spotted Richard raising the flags on their poles. I passed by the lawn, and he said, "Miss, visitors need to check in with the front office."

He hadn't mistaken me for my sister this time around.

"Mimi Lee," I said, extending my hand.

He shook it with a firm grip. "Oh, that's right. I met you at the science lab."

I scrutinized him from head to toe. He'd gotten rid of his puffy down jacket and wore a short-sleeve shirt with jeans. "You look different," I said.

"I feel great, younger even." Under the brim of his Dodgers cap, he stared at me with deep intensity. His eyes looked as clear as water, not cloudy blue like before. "I got my cataracts taken care of," he said.

"I'm so glad you can see better," I said, my voice pitching higher out of genuine enthusiasm.

He tilted his head at me. "Has anyone ever told you that you and Alice have similar voices?"

"Well, she is my baby sis."

"And a great teacher," he said. "Everyone loves her at the school."

"That's so nice to hear," I said. "I'll let you get back to work then. And don't worry, I'll make sure to sign in at the front office."

I practically danced over there. Based on the janitor's remarks, Alice had gotten back into everyone's good graces.

As I stepped through the door, I could smell the aroma of cooked bacon wafting in the air. The receptionist chewed and swallowed before speaking to me. "Sorry," she said. "Trying to fit in breakfast before the parents stampede inside. I'm so glad the microwave is working."

A text pinged on my phone. Alice said she was running late to meet up with me.

Before I could sit down, Principal Lewis came out of the staff room with a huge grin on his face. He held a steaming mug in his hands, and the fragrance of fresh coffee drifted my way.

Both the microwave and the coffeemaker seemed to be working

well. The cataract surgery must have gone splendidly for Richard since he seemed to have started fixing things around the campus.

The principal came over and set his mug on the counter. He stood in front of me and said, "Mimi, are you here to visit your sister?"

I swung the bag in my hands. "Dropping off something."

"Well, it's great to see you." He cleared his throat and said his next words in a halting manner. "So, uh, would you like me to greet you with a wave? A handshake? Or a verbal hello?"

"I'm okay with a hug."

He proceeded to give me a gentle grandfatherly hug. Stepping back, he said, "It's always good to ask for permission."

"A wise rule," I said.

He puffed his chest out. "Let it be known that Roosevelt Elementary is an excellent place to get educated—even for the principal."

"And everything is fine at the school, now that the investigation's all wrapped up?"

The principal retrieved his mug and sipped his coffee. "Right as rain, Mimi. All the hullabaloo is gone, and our reputation has been restored. Plus, the sub is going to become a permanent teacher, so we'll be fully staffed again."

"That's excellent," I said.

Principal Lewis nodded to me and shuffled off to his office. Soon after, Alice arrived on the scene.

"Sorry," she said, her cheeks flushed from speeding down the school hallway to meet me. "I got caught up with some of the other teachers. We're trying to plan a Happy Hour for next week."

"Okay, Miss Popular," I said. "Ready to try on some clothes?"

She wrinkled her nose. "Thanks for bailing me out."

I think she meant it in more ways than one. Handing Alice the bag,

I said, "I'll always be here for you." Whether that meant rescuing her from the fashion—or the regular—police.

• • •

All of us guests faced the latticed gazebo in anticipation. I smoothed down my flower-embroidered shirt for the umpteenth time since my arrival. Thank goodness the kebaya had sheer sleeves, which kept me cool. My nervousness had ratcheted up my body heat. Josh, sitting beside me and wearing a sleek suit, squeezed my hand.

From my other side, Marshmallow clawed at a cat collar with an affixed bow tie. Pixie had pulled some strings to allow a pet on the illustrious country club grounds. But she could snag an invite for only one cat—although Nimbus seemed pretty busy anyway, what with adjusting to and getting pampered by her new owner, Detective Brown.

Marshmallow grumbled. "When does fashionably late turn into unforgivably tardy? And why did humans invent clocks in the first place if they never bother to check them?"

I stroked Marshmallow's back to calm him (and me) down. Then as the sky was clothing itself in majestic purple, Ma and Dad arrived on the grounds. They came strolling in from the direction of the parking lot, arm in arm. Ma didn't notice our group because she only had eyes for Dad, who'd spruced up for the occasion by wearing a black-and-white penguin tuxedo. Ma also wore an elegant ensemble, a silver blouse and black skirt combo.

Besides us family, Dad had invited a group of Ma's friends, including the mah jong ladies and those in the general Malaysian Chinese community. He'd also asked his accounting buddies and golfing friends to come. As Ma and Dad approached, we erupted in a cacophony of applause, cheers, and even a few wolf whistles. Ma finally noticed every-one seated in rows on the lawn, and her mouth dropped open.

She unhooked her arm from Dad and swatted him. "You say lunch, not a *pai dui*."

"Yes, it is a kind of party. And we'll still eat some food, Winnie," he said, gesturing at the nearby canopy tent.

Then Dad beckoned to someone in the crowd. An older gentleman stood up. The paper in his hands shook as he took slow steps toward the gazebo.

Ma squinted at the old man. "Is that—"

Dad grinned. "Yes, it's the very same driver from the Malaysia tour bus. But today he'll serve as an informal celebrant for our vow renewal."

After he and Ma stood near the gazebo and faced each other, the officiant began the ceremony. Their old bus driver issued the standard vows for Ma to repeat, which she complied with, her eyes misting up.

When it came to Dad's turn, he turned his head toward us and said, "I'm amending the first line of the usual vow, but the rest will be standard."

Dad cleared his throat. "Winnie"—he looked deep into Ma's eyes—"I take you to be my lawful wedded wife, to have *piping hot rotis together* and to hold *anniversary celebrations . . .*"

The ceremony then proceeded along, the officiant saying the rest of the lines and my dad parroting back the words. At the end of the vow renewal, my parents gave each other a tender kiss.

I caught Alice's eye from two seats over. She wiped away a tear. Even Marshmallow gave an approving purr.

Josh touched my shoulder, and I turned to him. "All these years and still in love," he said, his eyes glittering like promises of a sparkling future.

Up in front, Ma clapped her hands. "*Sihk fan lah*," she said. "Time to eat. Smells *shiok*!"

We all headed for the food tent. My parents had first dibs on the dishes, but I'd made it pretty quickly to the buffet, too. Rows of roti and sauces lined the table, and I stood a few people away from Ma and Dad.

Dad's golf buddy, Walt, stood behind him in line. He leaned into Dad and said, "Thanks for helping me compose that note. I sure wish my marriage was as rock solid as yours."

I suppressed a groan. All that stress I'd suffered from the scribbled note. It'd all been because Dad had been ghostwriting for Walt.

Walt mumbled, "My soon-to-be ex is getting paranoid. She's now inventing calls from new women—even blocked one of my 'flings.'"

Ack. That must have been me she'd hung up on and blacklisted.

Dad clapped his friend on the back. "Too bad, Walt. But we can't all have *winners* like my Winnie."

Ma blushed at the compliment. Dad smiled and turned to place some roti on both of their plates.

I couldn't wait to dive into the food when it came my turn. My plate ended up with a mountain of roti and sauces. I kept on adding items as I moved down the table. At the very end, I noticed a stack of pamphlets advertising Roti Palace. They lay next to a gorgeous floral centerpiece made with red peonies.

We then returned to our seats to eat. But only moments after taking my first bite of roti, I saw Ma dash into the tent again. She came rushing back out with the floral centerpiece in her hands.

"Need toss flower," she announced.

Alice and I grimaced at each other. Ma managed to wrangle every single unmarried woman in sight. In the end, about half a dozen of us stood in a small circle near the gazebo.

"Ready?" Ma asked. She glanced over her shoulder to pinpoint my position. Then she turned her back to us and tossed the bouquet.

With ferocious force, the bundle of red flowers looked like they would smash into my face. I ducked. At the same instant, Alice's hand flew out—probably to protect me—and caught the bunch.

Ma turned around. Seeing the results, she said, "Alice ah?"

She marched over with determined steps to my sister and grabbed her arm. "Many friends here. Lots single adult sons."

Ma has her mojo back, I thought.

Alice gave me a helpless look as she got dragged away, while I returned to Josh and Marshmallow.

"Too bad you didn't catch the prize," Josh said in a teasing tone.

"Well, I still feel like a winner being here with my two valentines." As Marshmallow climbed onto my lap and started purring, I leaned my head on Josh's shoulder and basked in the joyous moment.

ACKNOWLEDGMENTS

To those enjoying a second round of adventures with Mimi and Marshmallow, I owe you my heartfelt gratitude. For new readers, thank you for taking a chance on a sassy cat. I'm indebted to multiple bloggers, bookstagrammers, librarians, and booksellers for recommending my novel. Special thanks to local bookstores who've given me support, including Bel Canto Books, Book Carnival, Mysterious Galaxy, and The Ripped Bodice.

If you're interested in learning about my behind-the-scenes writing life, sign up for my newsletter at jenniferjchow.com. You can also connect with me on Facebook, Instagram, and Twitter under @JenJChow. Please feel free to leave a kind review for *Mimi Lee Reads Between the Lines* and suggest it to family, friends, enemies—really, anyone you can think of!

Props to my stellar lit agent, Jessica Faust; fellow chicken admirer James McGowan; and the entire amazing team at BookEnds.

I'm extremely grateful to Angela Kim for her sharp editorial eye. Of course, thanks also to my wonderful copy editor and proofreader. The revised version of my manuscript is so much smoother because of all your input. I'm very honored to be a Berkley author. Extra thanks to Carrie May and the art department for creating a purr-fect cover! Also, I really appreciate the excellent marketing and publicity team, including Brittanie Black, Stephanie Felty, Jessica Mangicaro, and Natalie Sellars.

Thanks to my fab writing community, including my local critique group (SBW). I also value my online friends from 2020 Debuts, Binders, and Charmed Writers. And I'm happy to be a part of some *awesome-sauce* mystery groups like Crime Writers of Color, International Thriller Writers, Sisters in Crime, and Mystery Writers of America.

Huge thanks to all my relatives who continue to encourage and support my writing. And, of course, my love overflows for my hubby, Steve, and my children, who put up with the *clickety-clack* and my general dreaminess whenever I'm writing a story.

© 2019 by Julie Daniels

JENNIFER J. CHOW is the author of the hiss-terical Sassy Cat Mysteries, the Winston Wong cozies, *Dragonfly Dreams*, and *The 228 Legacy*. She lives in Los Angeles, where she hunts for all things matcha. Connect with her online and sign up for her newsletter on her website.

CONNECT ONLINE

JenniferJChow.com

JenJChow